Match Me, I'm Falling

The School for Spinsters
Book Two

By Michelle Willingham

ARE YOU SIGNED UP FOR DRAGONBLADE'S BLOG?

You'll get the latest news and information on exclusive giveaways, exclusive excerpts, coming releases, sales, free books, cover reveals and more.

Check out our complete list of authors, too!

No spam, no junk. That's a promise!

Sign Up Here

www.dragonbladepublishing.com

Dearest Reader;

Thank you for your support of a small press. At Dragonblade Publishing, we strive to bring you the highest quality Historical Romance from some of the best authors in the business. Without your support, there is no 'us', so we sincerely hope you adore these stories and find some new favorite authors along the way.

Happy Reading!

CEO, Dragonblade Publishing

Additional Dragonblade books by Author Michelle Willingham

The School for Spinsters Series
A Match Made in London (Book 1)
Match Me, I'm Falling (Book 2)
Match Me If You Can (Book 3)

Chapter One

London, 1816

T HE SOUND OF the vase shattering broke through the stillness. Lady Ashleigh Pryor hurried toward the drawing room already afraid of what she would find. Her father's voice cut through the sound of her mother's tears. "I told you last week that we were invited to the Duke of Suffolk's ball tonight. Must I always repeat myself? Or is there a reason why you never listen to me?"

"You n-never spoke of it," her mother started to protest. "I didn't know."

"And somehow you accepted an invitation to Lady Shelby's ball instead?" he mocked. "A viscountess instead of a duchess? What were you thinking?"

Her mother said nothing, and Ashleigh felt the rise of apprehension in her own stomach. She knew she had to intervene, but if she said anything wrong, it might make matters worse for her mother. Sometimes it was better to remain silent and let his fury blow over, pretending as if nothing was wrong. But she wouldn't know the right course of action until she entered the room.

"Is something wrong, Father?" Ashleigh asked in a cheerful voice, feigning ignorance. She didn't look at her mother, who was weeping on a chair while the shards of a porcelain vase were scattered on the floor beside her. Cecil had thrown the vase at Georgina, meaning to intimidate her. It wasn't the first time the marquess had done such a thing, but Ashleigh's stomach knotted at the familiar behavior.

He let out a sigh of disgust. "Your mother accepted an invitation to Lady Shelby's ball instead of the Suffolk ball. I already told His Grace days ago that we would attend."

Ashleigh knew nothing about his plans. As far as she was aware, they'd accepted Lady Shelby's invitation last week. Her father often claimed he'd told them something when he hadn't. Sometimes she wondered whether he did it on purpose, just for an excuse to berate his wife. She took a breath and steeled her courage.

"What if I attend Lady Shelby's ball on the family's behalf, Father? Then the two of you can attend the Suffolk ball," she suggested. "I can go with Persephone, since I know her family is planning to go."

Her father's face tightened. "Don't be ridiculous. You are the one in need of a husband, Ashleigh. The gentlemen at the duke's ball will be of higher quality." He spoke of suitors as if he were choosing a bottle of wine. "I have a few possibilities in mind for you."

Ashleigh didn't delude herself into believing he would ever allow her to choose her own husband. This was about status and making the right connections among the gentry. As the Marquess of Rothburn, Cecil Pryor believed he was one step below God, and her future husband would need to reflect that position.

"You wouldn't want to offend His Grace," Ashleigh said. "And I can pass along your greetings to Lady Shelby. She may not even notice if you aren't there."

Before her father could answer, she turned to Georgina. "Will you help me choose my gown for tonight, Mother?"

"Your mother has other duties," Cecil snapped. "Your maid can help you choose."

She didn't miss the way her mother shrank back in the chair. Georgina's punishment was about to continue, and there was nothing Ashleigh could do to stop it. The ache in her stomach turned to acid, and she hesitated before asking, "Which ball am I attending?"

Her father sighed. "I suppose if Persephone's mother and father accepted the invitation to Lady Shelby's, there may yet be some strong suitors there."

It had nothing to do with her pleas, Ashleigh knew, and everything to do with the fact that Persephone's parents were the Duke and Duchess of Westerford. "Prepare yourself now, and I will summon another carriage to take you to Lady Persephone's residence," her father continued. "I will allow you to attend with Persephone. You will join her and attend the ball with her family. Your mother and I will attend the Suffolk ball instead." He spoke of it as if it had been his idea and not hers.

Ashleigh nodded and walked to the doorway. "All right. But really, I could use Mother's assistance."

"No," her father answered coldly. To his wife, he commanded, "Meet me upstairs. We have to discuss your inability to listen."

Ashleigh noticed her mother's hands shaking. Then Georgina clenched them together as if she could make them stop.

"My lord, please," Georgina begged. "I am sorry. Truly, I am."

But her father's face was cold and unyielding as he repeated, "Upstairs. Now."

Georgina stood slowly from the chair, wiping the tears from her cheeks. She sent a warning look toward Ashleigh as if pleading with her not to make Cecil angrier.

Both of them left the drawing room, and Ashleigh sat down in her mother's chair, reaching for one of the shattered pieces of porcelain. Her time was running out. Although she'd saved her pin money, pretending that she'd used it to buy new clothes, she knew better than to believe she had enough to escape this house.

She had to find a way to make money quickly—and a lot of it—if she intended to run away from home. There was a cousin who lived in the north who might give her a place to stay, even if it was only temporary.

Or if she married a man who lived far away from here, that would do as well. But after seeing the nightmare of her parents' marriage, she wasn't at all eager to wed. From what she'd witnessed in private, a husband could control every aspect of her life, giving her no freedom at all. She didn't want to exchange one prison for another.

Ashleigh gripped the edges of her skirts, feeling utterly lost and helpless. Although she might be able to manage her own escape, she didn't have enough funds to rescue her mother as well.

In her mind, she imagined a small cottage where they lived together in peace, with no one to belittle them. No one to bully them or chastise them for failing to anticipate his wishes. Ashleigh took a breath and steeled her resolution. Somehow, she would find a way to get her mother away from Cecil.

She simply had to.

Now that his business was concluded in London, Cameron MacNeill had made a list of requirements for his future wife. He'd heard a great deal about the mysterious Mrs. Rachel Harding, proprietress of Mrs. Harding's School for Young Ladies. Or the School for Spinsters as it was better known by the bachelors in London.

Rumor had it that young women who'd lost all hope of finding a husband were schooled by Mrs. Harding in how to become more beautiful and how to behave in polite society. Apparently, Mrs. Harding and her partner had enjoyed a great deal of success in matchmaking. He hoped they could find a wife for him who met his qualifications.

As for himself, he'd done a great deal to appear ordinary to the ladies of the *ton*. He'd grown his beard out until it nearly touched his chest, disguised his Scottish accent, changed his last name slightly, and he wore unremarkable clothing. Occasionally, he asked a lady to dance, and most appeared horrified by the prospect.

It didn't bother Cameron at all. He didn't want a flighty young rose who cared only for balls and diamonds. He wanted a woman with courage, one who would never shy away from adversity. She would need it to live in Scotland. He traveled a great deal, and she would be left alone to raise his son Logan.

And for his boy, he wanted to find someone kindhearted and gentle. Someone who would embrace her role as a mother and Lady of Kilmartin.

He'd never told anyone in London that he'd built his own fortune and owned a castle. To the *ton*, he was Cameron Neill, a pathetic excuse for a man—not Cameron MacNeill, Chief of Kilmartin. And given the dangers he'd faced during the Peninsular War, he preferred to remain unnoticed. The less anyone knew about him, the better. They didn't need to know his title, or that he had a great deal of wealth, or anything about his past. Unfortunately, he'd done such a fine job of disguising himself that even the ladies who might have suited him as a wife had looked the other way.

But if they could not see beyond physical appearances, he didn't want them. He needed a wife who could manage the day-to-day affairs of Kilmartin while he served the Crown. Time was running out, so he'd arranged a meeting with Mrs. Harding, in the hopes that she could find him that wife. Money was not a concern of his—only time. And so, he'd decided to seek her assistance. It might mean wedding a lady who was not a beauty. But that didn't matter to him at all—in fact, he preferred a marriage in name only.

After the footman showed him inside the modest townhouse, he found Mrs. Harding waiting for him in the study. The woman was surprisingly young—in her late twenties at most—and she wore a dark blue gown with her mahogany hair pinned up neatly. Although she dressed like a governess, he suspected that in the right clothing she might be quite attractive. For a moment, he considered it.

"Mr. Neill, do sit down. Would you care for tea?"

"I would, yes," he agreed. Although he kept his gaze neutral, he didn't miss the slight frown when she saw his beard and rumpled appearance.

She gave orders to the footman and then withdrew a pen and paper. "I understand you are seeking a wife, Mr. Neill. Is that correct?" She dipped her quill in the ink well to take notes, which pleased him.

"I am," he agreed. "And before I tell you my requirements, I must ask that this discussion remain confidential between us." He didn't want anyone to know that he had a son. Truthfully, he wasn't certain he should tell his bride beforehand, though he supposed that wasn't fair. But she might not agree to marry him if she knew.

"Of course," Mrs. Harding answered.

He passed her the list, and she took out her spectacles to read it. He'd chosen five primary qualities and had written only seven words on the paper to list them.

1. *Kindness*

   (Because he wanted his son to love her.)

2. *Of noble birth*

   (Because he needed a highborn lady who would not be intimidated by the size of his castle at Kilmartin or be looking to marry for money. In fact, it was better if she believed he didn't have any.)

3. *Confident*

   (She should be able to manage a small army of servants without being afraid.)

4. *Responsible*

   (She would need to manage his affairs during his absences

and would have to willingly accept motherhood.)

5. *Celibacy*

(He didn't want to share his bed with a woman again. He'd lost his first wife Rebecca when she'd given birth to Logan. The guilt of watching her die—and knowing it had been his fault—haunted him still. He wanted a woman who understood that they could be friends but nothing more.)

The footman returned with a tea tray and scones. Mrs. Harding offered cream and sugar, but he took his tea black. She poured him a cup and gave him a scone before she finished reading the list.

"So, five things," she noted. "These shouldn't be difficult, except for nobility. Women of noble birth with high dowries typically have their choice of gentlemen. Are you looking for a wealthy bride to rebuild your own finances?"

"Not exactly," he answered. "It does not matter to me whether she has a high dowry or not. My preference is not to wed a woman who is only interested in wealth."

Her expression softened. "Interesting. I will take these into consideration. But before we discuss this any further, I should like to know whether you are amenable to changing . . . certain aspects of yourself?"

He knew she was referring to his unkempt appearance. "No. I would prefer to find a wife who does not dwell upon physical appearances. She should be kind, softhearted, and willing to be a mother to my son. I have no need for an heir, and this marriage will not be a true one." He paused a moment and added, "And I do not wish for her to know about my son until after we are married since it may deter some women."

"It may," she agreed, "but is it wise to keep such a secret from her?"

Cameron avoided an answer by saying, "Surely there are

women who have come to you who would prefer a friend rather than a husband. Regardless of the obligation?"

She paused a moment. "It sounds as if you want a nursemaid instead of a wife. Is it possible that you do not need to be married at all?"

He didn't miss her delicate insinuation that he preferred male company. With a shrug, he said, "I would like my son to have a mother. And my home needs a lady's presence."

She gave a slight nod of acknowledgement. "Well, be that as it may, my young ladies work very hard at transforming themselves. They become confident women who deserve outstanding marriages. If you are not willing to make any concessions at improving yourself, then perhaps it would be best if you find your own wife without my assistance."

Her dismissal was obvious, but Cameron wasn't about to argue. He had reasons enough to disguise himself and had no intention of making a change. If that made him obstinate, so be it.

He stood from the chair. "If you do find a lady who might be interested in such an arrangement, let me know."

"I have my doubts, but we shall see. If you ever decide that you wish to avail yourself of my services—that is, if you wish to have your choice among women, do let me know. I should be glad to arrange lessons." She paused a moment and added, "Lady Shelby's ball is this evening. Do you plan to attend?"

He hadn't, but he seemed to recall receiving an invitation. "Perhaps."

"One of my potential students is attending. And there will be many eligible young ladies there. You should go." She tilted her head to the side as she studied him. "And you should shave beforehand."

He ignored her suggestion and simply gave a nod. "Thank you for your time, Mrs. Harding. Good afternoon."

As he left, he took his hat and coat from the footman. A ball wasn't quite what he had in mind, but he decided to remain in the shadows and gather information. Then he could decide on potential candidates.

As he walked down the steps toward his carriage, his gaze shifted from side to side. He took notice of the bystanders, the street conveyances, and in an instant, he weighed any potential dangers. It had become a habit as natural as breathing, and it had kept him alive on the battlefield more than once.

Tonight, he would enter an entirely new battle—and it was one he intended to win.

MRS. HARDING STOOD at the edge of the ballroom with her dearest friend and business partner Cedric Gregor. They were here to attend Lady Shelby's ball for two reasons—first, to observe the behavior of a prospective student, Violet Edwards. And second, to observe Cameron Neill. Rachel idly wondered whether Violet might suit Mr. Neill, but she needed to observe them when they didn't know she was watching.

"Has he arrived yet?" she asked Cedric.

"I haven't seen him," he answered. "But I do see your new pupil over there." He nodded in the opposite direction.

"How is Violet faring?"

"She's not speaking to anyone, likely because of her stutter. And she's making a list." His face softened with amusement. "She took your assignment very seriously, I must say."

"Unlike Mr. Neill." She let out a sigh of frustration. He had come to her, asking for her help in finding a wife but was unwilling to change anything about himself. And while she truly believed there was a happy match for everyone, she didn't think she could work with a stubborn client who deliberately dressed poorly and wore a long beard. Why he believed he could find a wife looking like a beggar was beyond her. "I don't think he'll come."

Cedric gave a noncommittal shrug. "If he arrives, I can try to learn more about him."

"I just don't understand. When he came to our school wearing that beard and those clothes . . ." Her voice drifted off. "He's nothing at all like the sort of gentleman a lady would want to marry. Even if he isn't handsome, he can obviously afford better clothes if he intends to hire us for assistance."

Cedric seemed to consider it a moment. "And you say he refused to shave or change his appearance?"

She nodded. At that, her friend started to laugh. "Don't you see, Rachel? He's doing it on purpose. Because he doesn't want to attract women like those." He glanced over at Lady Persephone and Lady Ashleigh. "He wants someone different."

Different indeed. She doubted if any woman would be interested in such a man, not only because of his appearance, but also because he truly didn't want a wife. He wanted a mother for his son, and she did understand his desire for secrecy. It would indeed discourage many young ladies from considering him as a match because they were not ready to become a mother. Perhaps he should consider a slightly older woman, or a young widow. Or even better, a woman who could not bear children of her own but longed for a child.

"I am going to look around," Cedric said. "Take inventory of our gentlemen and debutantes."

"Tell me if you see anyone who would suit either Miss Edwards or Mr. Neill," she advised.

He nodded and disappeared into the sea of guests. Rachel made her way closer to the lemonade, and it was then that she noticed Mr. Neill on the outskirts of the crowd. So, he had decided to attend. His gaze moved from one lady to the next, as if he were choosing one of them as a prospect. He even glanced over at Lady Persephone and Lady Ashleigh, his stare lingering for a moment. Persephone was now speaking to Miss Violet Edwards, whose stutter was apparently getting the best of her. The girl's cheeks were scarlet while Persephone taunted her. Ashleigh stood beside her, and the look on her face was one of dismay. It appeared that she wanted to say something but was afraid it would make matters worse.

Mr. Neill was watching Ashleigh, and when he saw Violet's humiliation, his face held pity. Even so, Rachel dismissed the idea of pairing them together. Violet didn't meet most of the conditions on his list beyond being kind and responsible. The young woman lacked confidence, and a young child might take advantage. Not to mention the fact that she suspected the young woman would eventually want children of her own, so his celibacy requirement wouldn't do.

Rachel turned back for a fleeting moment, and Mr. Neill had already disappeared again. Strange how he managed to be here one moment and gone the next. She had the sudden feeling that there was so much more to this man than anyone realized.

He didn't need a delicate flower for a bride. No, he needed someone to stand up to him, to ignore his list, and be a true match. But who among these women had that sort of courage and would not be put off by his appearance?

After a while longer, Cedric returned to her. His face appeared pensive. "I think I may have something—or someone at least—who can help us. She is in dire need of funds."

"If that is the case, then she doesn't meet Mr. Neill's requirement of indifference toward wealth." Rachel dismissed the idea.

"Oh, she comes from a wealthy family," he said. "But I overheard Lady Ashleigh speaking to a friend. She was offering to sell her jewels, but her friend wouldn't buy them. So, being the inquisitive sort of man I am, I asked her if I could be of service. I gave her our information and told her that if she is in need of funds, we may be able to use her assistance. Particularly in regard to Miss Violet Edwards."

The idea was startling, but Rachel was beginning to see possibilities. Miss Edwards was afraid of Lady Ashleigh, and in order to help the young woman overcome those fears, she needed to face a challenge. "You are a brilliant man."

"Just so." He bowed lightly and smiled. Then he added gently, "You know, Mrs. Harding, there are other men in the world who are also brilliant. You deserve your own happiness."

She wasn't at all ready to entertain such an idea. The thought of losing her independence and being subjected to a husband's whims was something she wanted no part of. "Not yet, Cedric." But she smiled and offered, "What of you? Will we ever find a match for you, my friend?"

His expression turned pensive. "Someday, perhaps. Though I cannot say I don't dream of finding a person who loves me for who I am."

She took his arm and gave it a gentle squeeze. In a low whisper, she added, "The right gentleman will find you one day. I have faith."

Chapter Two

Four days later

HER TIME WAS running out. Ashleigh didn't know how she was going to escape her household, but if she didn't, she would remain her father's pawn forever.

Strangely, a new possibility had arisen, one that had offered her a way out. She'd met a gentleman named Cedric Gregor at Lady Shelby's ball. He worked at Mrs. Harding's School for Young Ladies and had overheard her talking to Persephone. Ashleigh had hoped to sell some of her jewels for her escape fund, but Persephone had only laughed at the idea. As the daughter of a duke, Persephone had no need to buy anything. All she had to do was point her finger, and her papa would buy it for her. But Mr. Gregor had mentioned that there was a way he could help her earn money.

And Ashleigh needed funds desperately. For that reason, she'd agreed to come to Mrs. Harding's school early the next day. She had met with Mr. Gregor again, and he'd given her the instructions, along with ten pounds.

"What is it you need me to do?" she'd asked.

"Something unusual," he admitted. "And you will be paid another ten pounds if you are successful."

Unusual? Ashleigh was starting to wonder if she'd made a mistake by coming here alone. She'd sent her carriage and footman away, believing that she was meeting with Mrs.

Harding. Now, it seemed she'd been mistaken.

Mr. Gregor seemed to recognize her alarm and answered, "Oh it's nothing dangerous, and certainly nothing that would bring you harm. It's only that we have another new student who is trying to learn confidence. She is painfully shy with a terrible stutter. I believe you know Miss Violet Edwards?"

A sudden sinking feeling caught in Ashleigh's stomach. Mr. Gregor had been there that night at Lady Shelby's ball. She wondered if he'd seen the way Persephone had tried to humiliate Miss Edwards. Likely, he had.

Persephone had wanted to make a wager with Lord Scarsdale, suggesting that he should ask Miss Edwards to dance in order to embarrass her. Ashleigh had tried to talk Persephone out of it, but the duke's daughter had been particularly vicious.

The memory bothered Ashleigh even now. Miss Edwards had done nothing to deserve such nastiness. And once again, Ashleigh had been helpless to defend a victim against a bully. Did that make her a coward? Shame burned within her at the memory.

But what else could she have done? She'd quickly learned the futility of intervening after witnessing her father's behavior toward her mother. Bullies could not be stopped by arguing or trying to intervene.

On the one occasion she'd tried to stand up for her mother's sake, it had been like throwing oil on the fire of Cecil's fury. He'd raged even more at his wife, and Ashleigh had instantly regretted it. Better to say nothing and let the storm of anger die down than to kindle it with opposition.

"Lady Ashleigh?" Mr. Gregor prompted.

"Sorry." She shook away the memory of that night. "Yes, I know Miss Edwards."

"I want you to be rude to her. Cruel, even," Mr. Gregor said. "I want you to behave to Miss Edwards the same way your friend Lady Persephone did. Humiliate her, belittle her—whatever it takes. Make her cry if you must."

"No!" Ashleigh said, pushing the money aside. "I would never do such a thing. How can you even ask it of me?" Did he believe she'd been part of the mockery the other night? It certainly seemed so.

She started to rise from her chair, but Mr. Gregor motioned her down. "Hear me out. This is meant to help Miss Edwards."

"Asking me to be rude and humiliate her is not helping her."

"She needs to find her confidence," he said. "All her life, Miss Edwards has hidden in the shadows, unable to speak to anyone because of her stutter. If she does not find a way to control it, she will be sent away to her grandmother's. Her grandmother has suggested that daily beatings will rid her of that stutter. We are trying to help her avoid that."

Ashleigh felt the breath leave her. She knew well enough what it was to watch someone else be harmed, and a sick feeling caught her gut. "Why would—why would being rude help her?"

"Miss Edwards needs to become angry," he said. "Anger is the only thing that will save her and help her find her courage. She needs someone to ignite that rage, so she can face the worst of her stuttering. I believe that you are just the sort of trigger she needs, and we are willing to pay you to do it." He paused and slid the money back to her. "You did say you are in need of funds."

She stared down at the money, a sense of hopelessness cloaking her. This was only a portion of what she needed. But it was good money, and a way out from her father's house.

"This is not who I am," she said softly.

"Does it matter?" he asked. "Miss Edwards needs to be pushed to the edge. Whether or not you believe me, you would be helping her. Perhaps you owe her that since you didn't stand up for her."

Her face burned with embarrassment for he was right. She did owe Violet something. But behaving like Persephone was a horrifying thought. She didn't want to treat the young woman in that way.

And yet she understood why Mrs. Harding and Mr. Gregor were forcing Violet into this situation. Even though it was awful, it could help the young woman to grow angry. All Ashleigh had to do was set aside her conscience and pretend to be her father or Persephone for a short time.

She wanted so badly to refuse. But he was offering her good money that would help her escape with her mother. She couldn't simply turn away from that, even if she despised herself for what she was about to do.

"We want you to pretend that you are another one of our students," Mr. Gregor told her. "Miss Edwards believes it will be a dancing lesson. In fact, it will be a lesson in something entirely different—we want to see if she can defend herself at all."

"I don't want to be this cruel," she admitted. "But I know you're right. She does need to face her fears."

"Miss Edwards needs to confront her troubles in a place where no one else will see her," he continued. "You do need the money, yes?"

She nodded. "I don't like it. But I will do what is necessary." With reluctance, Ashleigh took the money and put it in her reticule. She would have to find a way to make Violet upset, to provoke her into anger.

"I am not passing judgment upon you," he said quietly, walking to the door with her. "It's playacting with a greater purpose."

"Violet is going to hate me even more than she already does." And she fully understood why. How could she not, when Persephone had made her life so miserable, and Ashleigh had done nothing to defend her?

"She might," Mr. Gregor agreed. "But if you do well in this, I might have a means of helping you escape your household."

She froze, her face whitening at his offer. "What are you— what are you talking about?"

"I am very thorough when it comes to hiring people," he said. "I know about your father's . . . temper. And of his plans to choose a husband for you."

She started to shake her head. "I don't—I can't—" Words utterly failed her as she tried to ascertain how he could possibly know about this.

"There is another gentleman looking for a wife," he said. "He wants an unusual marriage—one where he can take his bride to Scotland, far into the Highlands. And he wants a celibate arrangement."

Ashleigh went utterly still at the proposition. If she agreed to the match, she would live nowhere near London and would be far from her father's reach. If she brought her mother with her, even better. She would almost consider marrying any man at all if that were possible.

All men wanted heirs, didn't they? But she could see what Mr. Gregor was suggesting. If she challenged Miss Edwards in the way they needed her to, he might help her.

"And you would introduce me to this gentleman?" she ventured.

"Possibly," he said. "He has promised to provide a good settlement on a wife. He wants a marriage in name only. I believe that may be what you prefer."

It was something to think about, Ashleigh decided. "All right. After this . . . dancing lesson, you may set up a chance for us to meet. I will consider it."

"Very good. Now follow me—it's time for the lesson." He led her down the hallway to the music room. She found the dancing master waiting, and Cedric met her gaze. "Remember what we talked about." To the dancing master, he added, "You are not to intervene when the ladies speak to one another. Lady Ashleigh has specific instructions to follow that are related to Miss Edwards' lessons."

And then he departed. In less than a minute, she saw Violet entering the room with Mrs. Harding nearby. The young woman's eyes widened with horror. Ashleigh steeled herself and tried to imagine what Persephone would say. It was time to be the rudest, most despicable person she could think of.

"Hello, Miss Edwards." Ashleigh greeted her, forcing a knowing smirk on her face. "Or should I c-call you V-violet?"

Miss Edwards appeared horrified, and her face reddened. She remained silent, but her eyes revealed dismay.

Ashleigh was rather proud of the young woman for not responding, but there did seem to be a slight spark of anger in her eyes, which was what they'd wanted. A ripple of guilt caught her, and she despised herself for behaving like this. She'd sounded exactly like Persephone.

Mr. Brown said, "Good afternoon, Miss Edwards. I was just telling Lady Ashleigh that I will be teaching you both a country dance. Now face one another with your shoulders back. Chin up."

Ashleigh hadn't expected being rude to be so difficult. But she reminded herself that twenty pounds brought her a great deal closer toward her own goal of escaping her father's household. It might be a horrible way to earn the money, but this was all she had. She forced herself to continue.

"Do you even know how to dance?" Ashleigh taunted. "I've never seen you with a partner at the balls."

Violet straightened her shoulders and ignored her once again. Ashleigh found that her respect for the young woman was only increasing. If anyone had spoken to her like that, she'd have been furious.

"Now take each other's hands," the dancing master continued. Ashleigh seized Violet's hands, wondering if it would provoke her to pull away. Instead, Miss Edwards seemed to retreat inside herself even more.

After learning a few more steps, Mr. Brown began to play the pianoforte. Ashleigh began to dance, for she knew these patterns well. Violet stiffened, and even though she followed the steps, the woman's discomfort was evident.

In the corner, Ashleigh noticed that a door was cracked open. Mr. Gregor must be watching the lesson. And though she didn't like it, she reminded herself that this was a role to play. It wasn't real, and she couldn't think of it in that manner.

She pushed again, pretending it was her father speaking. "Ww-why are you here?" she taunted Violet. "I suppose you didn't have a choice, did you? No man would want to m-marry s-someone like y-you. You're the worst of all the s-s-s-spinsters."

Tears gathered in the woman's eyes, and Ashleigh's own stomach burned with guilt. But what other choice was there but to continue? "Go ahead and cry. I know you want to." She took Violet's hand and gripped it hard as they moved through the dance steps.

Silent tears flowed down the woman's cheeks. The sight of them made Ashleigh turn her own face away to hold back her own tears. She loathed herself for being so cruel. It seemed that she'd broken Violet instead of making her angry, which wasn't what she'd wanted to do at all. She had to find a way to provoke Violet's rage, for a furious woman could overcome any number of problems.

Ashleigh thought a moment and came up with one more thing she could do. When they reached the end of the line, she stuck out her foot at the last second. Violet couldn't stop herself in time, and she hit the floor hard.

I hate this, Ashleigh thought. *I'm no better than my father.*

"Oops," she said. "I guess I took the wrong step." She held out her hand, but Violet didn't take it. Instead, the young woman swiped at her tears and stood up. The dancing master made no mention of her fall, nor did he ask if Violet was all right. Instead, he continued with the lesson as if nothing had happened.

It seemed that all Ashleigh's efforts were for nothing. The young woman refused to stand up for herself, no matter what else she tried.

When the lesson was over, Ashleigh remarked, "I think you're wasting your time, Violet. And your money. This will never work."

Violet left without saying anything at all. Once she'd gone, Mr. Gregor emerged from the room on the opposite side. He paid the dancing master and waited for him to leave. The instructor glanced at Ashleigh with a frown but said nothing.

When Mr. Gregor approached her, Ashleigh's cheeks were burning with her own humiliation. "That was the worst thing I've ever done in my life. Don't ask me to do anything like that again. I hated every moment of it."

Mr. Gregor gave her the remaining ten pounds without saying anything. From his expression, she could tell that he didn't believe her. "You were quite good."

"I only did it because I need the money very badly."

"For your escape," he agreed. "And yet, your father is a marquess. Some would say that, even as controlling as he is, you've never wanted for anything. Are you certain you're not running away because you aren't getting what you want?"

All of a sudden, her own anger came rushing in. "My father's wealth and a title don't mean anything. You know nothing of my life or the prison I'm trapped in."

"Some would say your cage is made of gold."

Ashleigh reached for the music sitting on the piano and swept it onto the floor. "And is that gold worth it when I watch him hurt my mother? When I see her sobbing afterwards or watch the way she cowers from him?" She paced across the music room. "She's disappearing, day by day. And I can't do anything to save her. Under the law, she belongs to him."

His expression shifted slightly. "And you think twenty pounds will help you?"

"I barely have any pin money. Neither of us has anything at all, beyond jewels. And even those he keeps locked away. On the night of a ball, he chooses what we wear. If I ever lost a single ring or necklace . . ." She let her words drift off. Her rage was starting to dissipate, and she took a deep breath to calm her emotions.

"I must disappear from London and find a way to take my mother with me. It's the only way I can help her."

"What of your extended family?" he asked.

"I have a cousin I've never met who may or may not help. But my other relatives are loyal to my father. My mother's family are all dead. She didn't have brothers or sisters."

Mr. Gregor reached down to pick up the fallen music. Ashleigh bent over to help. "I'm sorry for making a mess. I just . . . lost my temper."

After the sheet music was neatly stacked, Mr. Gregor said, "I will try to arrange an introduction sometime this week to the gentleman I spoke of earlier."

She let out a breath she hadn't known she was holding. "Thank you. Who is he, might I ask?"

"I must discuss this with Mrs. Harding, so I cannot disclose his name as of yet. But if she agrees with me, I will send word."

"I would consider the marriage," she said slowly. "But only an elopement in Scotland. I could never gain my father's permission here. Could he make that happen?"

Mr. Gregor studied her for a long moment in silence. Then at last, he answered, "I will have to ask."

CAMERON REMOVED HIS hat when he entered Gunter's Tea Shop. Mrs. Harding was waiting for him at a table, and he greeted her as he took the seat across from her.

"I will admit, I did not expect you to agree to this meeting," the matron said. "I'll confess that it wasn't my idea, but my partner Mr. Gregor believes he may have found a possible match for you."

"I am glad to hear it." He rested his hat on his knee and added, "I attended a ball the other night and realized how many unsuitable women there are. I wouldn't trust half of them with a cat, much less my son." Then, too, he didn't want to spend a great deal of time in London. If Mrs. Harding could find the right candidate and allow him to return home sooner, so much the better.

"A nursemaid could still fulfill your requirements," she offered.

But he dismissed the idea. "My son deserves a mother, and that is what he shall have."

From the bemused expression on her face, he was wondering whether Mrs. Harding had truly found him a suitable wife. "If you find a bride for me, I can pay you handsomely."

"Which I find quite interesting," she remarked. "For someone without a title, you seem to be remarkably unconcerned about money."

"I've an inheritance," he said. That was all she needed to know.

"As it happens, we do have someone in mind who might suit your needs. The young woman's circumstances have changed somewhat. Mr. Gregor suggested her to me, and he has set up a meeting for you to meet her."

Now this was welcome news. "Who is she?"

"First, I must ask you to agree to my rules. If I introduce you to the lady, you must stay and speak with her for at least fifteen minutes. Anything less would be rude."

It wasn't an unreasonable request. If he met the lady and didn't like her, he couldn't exactly walk away immediately.

"Agreed," he answered. "Is she here now?"

Mrs. Harding didn't answer that question. "My second rule is that you may not cause a scene in public. If you do not approve of the match we have chosen, be kind. There is no need to damage her reputation or yours. After the fifteen minutes is over, one of us will ask if you wish to continue your conversation with the lady. If not, we will escort her from your table."

Once again, he considered the rule to be reasonable. "All right."

"And last, you must give her a fair chance. Quite often, men judge women before they get to know them. Just as she will likely judge you by your appearance. Let her get to know you, and you must do the same."

He nodded. At that moment, she rose from the table. "I will now bring you to meet her."

Cameron offered his arm, and Mrs. Harding took it. She guided him toward the back of Gunter's, and then he caught sight of her partner, Cedric Gregor. The man was facing him, while a young woman had her back to them. Her auburn hair was pulled up and intertwined with white ribbons. Her day dress was white with some sort of embroidery. She appeared to be slender, her posture poised.

From this vantage point, he imagined she would be horrified at the sight of him. He steeled himself for her response, and then Mr. Gregor rose from his seat.

"Lady Ashleigh, may I present Mr. Cameron Neill?"

Her initial smile faded as she glanced at Mr. Gregor. "You're not serious."

Cameron glanced at Mrs. Harding. "I don't think we'll need fifteen minutes." The lady had made her feelings clear enough. As for his own opinion, he recalled that her best friend had mocked a young woman with a stutter, and Lady Ashleigh had simply watched. He could never give his son into the care of someone like her.

Mrs. Harding wasn't listening to their protests, and instead gestured for him to sit down. "Keep your word, Mr. Neill. And you, too, Lady Ashleigh. No scenes. Behave yourselves."

And with that, they departed.

Lady Ashley's mouth tightened in a grim line. "Surely, this is a mistake."

"Oh, undoubtedly. I think we can both agree that we would not have chosen one another?"

"Not in a thousand years."

Her honesty eased the tension, and in a way, it made the meeting more bearable. At that moment, a young man came to take their orders. Lady Ashleigh hesitated, and Cameron said, "Since we are already in agreement, you might as well choose an ice." He'd already promised Mrs. Harding he would wait fifteen minutes.

She ordered a raspberry ice, and he chose lemon. After the

man departed, Cameron leaned back in his chair. "But I can't for the life of me imagine why a young woman such as yourself—the daughter of a peer—would seek help from Mrs. Harding's School for Spinsters."

"That's not what it's called," she muttered. "And I could ask the same of you."

"I plan to find a wife who wants a marriage in name only," he remarked. "Someone willing to run my household, since I am often away."

She frowned. "And they thought I would suit?"

"For some reason." He shrugged, and the waiter brought over their ices. He dug in with a spoon, while she did the same. "You're not at all the sort of woman I could ever imagine as my wife." Lady Ashleigh might be beautiful, but he could never tolerate a cruel person. He wouldn't dare put his son at risk.

"Nor could I marry a man like you," she answered. She tasted her ice, and her face transformed as she savored it, closing her eyes. It unsettled him, for there was no denying her beauty. It was her personality that he found abhorrent.

"I would like to know why you asked for Mrs. Harding's assistance. Aren't you a viscount's daughter?"

"My father is a marquess," she corrected. "And yes, I am an heiress. Finding a husband isn't the difficult part. It's gaining my father's consent."

Once again, her expression shifted. Cameron prided himself on reading people, and whatever was on her mind right now bothered her deeply. He sensed exactly what it was.

"Your father plans to choose your husband. Or he's already chosen him. Am I right?"

She gave a single nod. "My life is not my own to live. It's a prison."

"And you want to marry someone else without your father's knowledge or permission."

"Someone who would be willing to give me my freedom," she admitted. Then she quickly said, "Not you."

"Of course not. I've no wish to wed a woman who is entertained by the misfortune of others."

At that, her face turned scarlet. "You know nothing about me."

"I know that your friend tormented a young lady with a stutter. And you stood by and watched. That's not the sort of woman any man wants to marry."

"And was I supposed to humiliate Violet further?" Ashleigh demanded. There was a darker emotion coloring her words. Almost as if she were embarrassed. "I cannot stop Persephone. She's spoiled and the daughter of a duke. She does whatever she pleases. I asked her not to tease, but she ignored me."

He gave a nod. "You let her run all over you, just as your father does. I'm beginning to see why you need assistance from Mrs. Harding. But even though I now understand what they were thinking—you want your independence, and I want a wife who does not mind my travels—we are not suited."

Again, she nodded. For a few moments, they ate in silence. She set down her spoon and asked, "I don't understand why you even want to marry."

He had no intention of telling her about his son. Only his future wife would know about Logan, and even then, only after he'd brought her to Scotland. "I have my reasons."

She studied him for a moment. Then she frowned. "When was the last time you shaved?"

"Years ago." He'd let it grow because the disguise was necessary for his wartime assignment. And by the time he returned home, Rebecca had been heavy with child. She'd disliked the beard, but she'd understood why he'd kept it.

Now, it was more out of his own wish to disguise his face. He didn't want anyone to notice him—he wanted their glance of disgust before turning away. It was the best way to gain information. No one paid him any attention whatsoever.

"You aren't that bad looking beneath it," she offered. "If you were to shave, I imagine there's a young woman who would be glad to marry you. Violet Edwards, perhaps. Or Emma Bartholomew."

"Perhaps," he hedged, not recognizing the names. "But I require a woman with a backbone."

Ashleigh smiled at that. "It won't be mine. I've no interest in wedding a man with secrets, who doesn't want to be a true husband, or who fancies himself a wizard with his long beard."

He nearly choked on that. "A wizard, am I?"

"Or a warlock. I half expect you to cast a curse on me for not defending Violet. You know perfectly well that if I'd done anything to interfere, Persephone would have made it far worse. Sometimes it's better to remain silent and let it go."

He didn't believe her at all. Lady Ashleigh was nothing but a spoiled heiress who couldn't be bothered. "Anyone who stands aside and does nothing when someone is attacked is just as guilty." He finished his own ice, and her face turned crimson again.

"I don't think there's anything left to say, do you?"

He shook his head and tossed a handful of coins on the table to pay for the ices. "I wish you luck in finding a husband, Lady Ashleigh."

For it would never be him.

ASHLEIGH COUNTED HER savings four times, but there still was not enough. She had hollowed out the interior of a book and hidden her pouch of money within it. A moment after she'd returned the book to the shelf, she heard footsteps approaching. A knock sounded at her door, and she opened it.

Her maid greeted her and said, "Lord Rothburn has asked to speak to you in the drawing room, Lady Ashleigh. And he has a gentleman with him."

"Who is the gentleman?" she asked.

"I don't know, my lady. I've not seen him before."

Ashleigh wondered what her father was planning. But she smoothed out her dress and fixed her hair. A sudden feeling of uncertainty caught her stomach, and she had a feeling her father had chosen a suitor for her to marry.

"What is my father's demeanor?" she asked her maid. "Does he seem to be pleased?"

"Yes, my lady. He and the gentleman seem to be good friends."

The feelings of anxiety only heightened as Ashleigh left her room and descended the stairs. As she passed her mother's room, she saw the open door. Georgina was seated beside the hearth, staring into the flames. From her profile, she appeared carved out of ice. Misery lined every feature, and Ashleigh knew there was nothing she could say to make it better. Her mother was as trapped as she was.

Although she understood what Mrs. Harding had intended by introducing her to Mr. Neill, Ashleigh wasn't that desperate yet. Somehow, she would find another way to get them out. Would this suitor provide a way? If he was friends with her father, likely not. But she had another twenty pounds. Perhaps there was other work she could do for Mrs. Harding to help Violet.

When she entered the drawing room, her father greeted her with a warm smile and reached out for her hand. "My dear, thank you for joining us. I am most pleased to introduce you to Victor Colfax, Viscount Falkland."

Ashleigh offered her hand, and the viscount kissed it. She guessed he was similar in age to her father, possibly in his mid-fifties. He had lost most of his gray hair, save that around his ears. He was clean shaven, except for long sideburns that reached his chin.

"Lord Falkland is to be your new husband." Her father beamed at her, while sending her a simultaneous look of warning. "I have accepted his proposal on your behalf."

A wave of panic washed over her, and Ashleigh clenched her lips together to stop herself from blurting out a refusal. Instead, she took a deep breath and then asked, "I'm sorry, but what did you say?"

Had he already arranged the engagement without even asking her? That was a foolish question. Of course he had.

"We've been discussing the betrothal details," Cecil continued. "You will go to live with Falkland in Yorkshire. He has an estate there, and he is eager to wed. By next year, you could be holding his heir in your arms." Her father's smile deepened. "Now, aren't you pleased?"

Ashleigh was torn between wanting to tell the truth—that she was utterly horrified by the prospect—and the realization that her next move would dictate her father's mood and behavior tonight. If she refused the suitor or dared to defy Cecil, he would not only rage at her, but he would likely take it out on his wife as well.

Careful, she warned herself. Now was not the time to voice her true opinion.

"I am . . . overwhelmed." She let out a breath of air. Overwhelmed by the fact that her time was running out. She would have to leave even sooner than she'd imagined.

"That's to be expected," Lord Falkland said. "Rothburn, I never realized what a beauty your daughter is. I am very much looking forward to this marriage." His eyes slid over her body, and Ashleigh felt her own sense of disgust rising. The idea of enduring the touch of this man was like being covered with spiders. No—it could never happen.

"When?" she managed to ask at last. She needed to know how much time she had left to plan her escape.

"Oh, we'll want to have the banns read," her father said. "A month or so, I should think. Unless our bridegroom is eager and wants to procure a special license?"

Lord Falkland laughed. "I am eager indeed." He studied her again with a leer and added, "There is a masquerade ball Saturday next. Will you be attending?"

"Of course," her father answered. "Our family would not miss it. The Duke and Duchess of Westerford are hosting it."

So, she had at least a week—possibly a month before the wedding, if her father was to be believed. But she never knew whether he was telling the truth.

"Then I hope to claim a dance with you there," Lord Falkland said. He took her hand and raised it to his lips again, letting them linger this time. Ashleigh couldn't bring herself to give a false smile. But at least she didn't pull her hand away.

"We will meet again to discuss the dowry and the wedding arrangements," Lord Falkland said to her father. Then he released her hand and bowed.

Ashleigh waited until both men had left the room before she sank into a chair. Hot tears gathered in her eyes, but she held them in. Instead, she made plans, imagining where she would go. She could start with her cousin's house in the north and beg for help. After that, perhaps she could travel to Germany or Italy. Somewhere far away where her father could never find her.

Or Scotland, her brain suggested.

No, she could never consider marrying Mr. Neill. They had already agreed it wouldn't work. She told herself that it didn't matter he'd suggested a marriage in name only. She would only be exchanging one prison for another. And the man had no title, lands, or wealth. Money meant power, and her father had plenty of that. If she ran away with Mr. Neill, her father would have him arrested for kidnapping—or he would bribe someone to bring her home again. It was too dangerous.

If only there was another gentleman with whom she could elope, someone who would take her far away from here. And then they could send someone to fetch her mother and take Georgina away from Cecil.

Ashleigh let her mind fill up with images of a small cottage somewhere in the countryside. She would learn to cook and clean. If it meant leaving this life behind, she would do anything.

Perhaps Mrs. Harding had another gentleman who might suit her. Someone with enough money to offer the escape she so desperately needed who could not be intimidated by her father.

"I am proud of you, Ashleigh," her father said when he returned. She glanced over at the door, and he continued. "I know this came as a shock to you."

He didn't seem to care that she hadn't spoken but kept on. "But trust that I do know what is best. Falkland will make an excellent husband for you."

She waited several moments before she finally gathered her words. "How did you decide on the viscount?"

At that, her father laughed. "Funny you should ask. I lost a hand of cards. Falkland already has plenty of wealth, so he asked me for your hand in marriage instead. I thought it an excellent trade."

Ashleigh's hands clenched into fists. "You sold me?"

"Sold is such a vulgar word. He won you, my dear. And what a prize you are. He promised that there is no need for your dowry—he wants only a young, beautiful bride to give him a son."

She couldn't even bring herself to look at him. Her father appeared utterly delighted with himself. It took everything within her to maintain the cold façade that might convince him she didn't care. Quietly, she rose from her seat. "I must dress for dinner."

"Yes, yes, of course." Her father laughed softly. "This marriage will be quite a match. I promise you will be pleased."

But she left the room, knowing the marriage would never happen. She would never consent, no matter what Cecil said or did. And now, it was imperative that she finish her plans to escape.

It was her only way out.

Chapter Three

C AMERON RODE ALONG the banks of the Serpentine, enjoying the peaceful fog and clouded skies. Fewer people were strolling about, giving him the chance to think more clearly. He'd asked to meet with Cedric Gregor in the hopes of finding another match.

He understood why they'd suggested Lady Ashleigh, though he wasn't entirely certain about her circumstances. At first, he'd dismissed her as a spoiled heiress. But after talking to her, he had to admit that the conversation was far less stilted than the others he'd attempted. Ashleigh spoke her mind and was direct, a quality that he respected. Yet, it still didn't make sense why she would want to flee the life she had.

He'd made a few discreet inquiries, and there was gossip among the servants that the marquess was overly harsh and controlling toward his wife. Certainly on the rare occasion Cameron had seen Lady Rothburn in London, the marchioness had been shy and withdrawn.

If Lord Rothburn mistreated his wife, then it made sense why Ashleigh was afraid to stand up to Persephone's viciousness. Cameron had experienced his own share of cruelty as a child, and he'd learned how to be secretive, finding more elusive ways to fight back.

Though he'd already discarded the idea of marrying Lady Ashleigh, he still wondered about her family. He had an instinctive sense that something wasn't right.

He dismounted his gelding near the bridge, watching as the mists slid over the banks of the lake. A family walked together along the edge, a mother, father, and a young boy. The sight of the child caught him like a spear thrust into his chest. It had been over a month since he'd seen Logan. This boy had darker hair than his son but the same enchanted curiosity. He was picking up a fistful of gravel, flinging it into the lake before his mother stopped him.

The unbidden memory intruded, of Logan clinging to him, sobbing when Cameron told him he had to travel to London. "No, Da!" he'd shrieked. "You stay."

For a moment, the emotion inside him cracked as he remembered the feeling of his son's arms around his neck. Even though Logan was three, he still had baby soft cheeks and tangled hair that wouldn't lie flat, no matter how they combed it.

His son had cried himself to sleep that night. And Cameron had left before dawn without saying another goodbye. He couldn't do it.

Aye, his laddie had nursemaids to look after him. Certainly, Cook spoiled him fiercely. But the love of servants wasn't enough. Cameron had to remain focused on his task of finding his son a mother. Logan needed her to love him—someone who could be all the things he couldn't.

But the more he thought of the London heiresses, the more judgmental he became. Most couldn't think beyond the next waltz, much less walk the hallways all night with a sobbing baby who cried during a fever. Cameron had done the best he could to be a father, but what did he know of parenting? He'd never known anything, save the orphanage. He would never be a good influence.

His gaze shifted back to the young family walking along the Serpentine. The mother and father took their son by his hands, and they swung him up off his feet. The boy giggled and called out, "Again!" The parents smiled at one another and indulged the boy.

Cameron made an inward vow to return home soon. He missed his son, no matter that he'd tried to push away the unwanted emotions. It simply bothered him that he couldn't find the right woman.

Then, without warning, he saw Lady Ashleigh walking along the banks. It was surprising to see her on an outing this early. She wore a soft green gown the color of new leaves on a spring day while her hair was tucked under her bonnet. She had her arm linked with her mother's, and from the expression on her face, she was trying to coax her mother out of melancholy. The marchioness strolled beside her daughter, but her gaze was stony and bleak. Though he couldn't overhear their conversation, Lady Ashleigh seemed to be trying to keep up the matron's spirits.

Cameron noticed that they had a maid with them but no footman. Without hesitation, he moved from his position on the bridge to quietly shadow them as protection. He had a little time before his meeting with Mr. Gregor, so he saw no harm in watching over them. He kept enough distance so Ashleigh would not see him, but not so much that he could not be there swiftly. The pair walked along the water's edge and passed the parents with their son. Lady Ashleigh didn't look at the boy but continued walking. Her mother, on the other hand, froze in place.

Ashleigh spoke softly to the marchioness and guided her toward a bench where they sat down. They watched the young boy playing, and soon, the child approached Ashleigh with a fistful of mud. He spoke to her and showed her the mud.

Cameron expected her to pout or ignore the child. Instead, she removed her glove and walked to the water's edge. She scooped up a handful of wet sand and brought it to the boy, pouring it on top of his own mud. He laughed and then went to rejoin his parents.

But it was Ashleigh's smile that held him spellbound. She

didn't look at the child as if he were a dirty nuisance. Instead, she'd joined in with whatever game he was playing. He watched her wash her muddy hand in the water and dry it with her handkerchief before replacing the glove. It was a side to her that he'd never expected to see.

He prided himself on reading people well, but perhaps he'd misjudged her. He remained in place, and soon, Mr. Gregor joined him.

"Mr. Neill," the man greeted him. He glanced over at Lady Ashleigh and her mother, but his expression revealed nothing. "Shall we walk?"

Cameron forced his attention away from Ashleigh and her mother, inclining his head. "Indeed."

"You are attending the masquerade ball at the Duke of Westerford's, are you not?"

"I received an invitation, yes."

"Good. There are many young ladies who will attend the ball. I have another one in mind, and I plan to arrange an introduction if that will suit?"

"I would be glad of it." But even as he spoke the words, his gaze shifted back to Lady Ashleigh and her mother. They were returning back the way they had come, and he saw a small carriage waiting.

"Excellent." Mr. Gregor seemed well aware of Cameron's lack of attention, but he continued on. "The lady is rather shy, but I believe once she finds her confidence, she may indeed be what you're searching for."

"I look forward to it," he said.

"I suppose you should know that Lady Ashleigh is now betrothed to Viscount Falkland. Her father arranged it recently."

That forced his attention back to Mr. Gregor. "What did you say?"

"Lady Ashleigh is betrothed. So, you needn't worry about her as a potential match."

"She found someone, then?"

"No, her father did. I imagine they will be wedded within a fortnight. Her bridegroom seems eager enough."

A flare of uneasiness caught up with Cameron, but he reminded himself that Ashleigh wasn't the woman he intended to wed. They'd agreed upon it that day at Gunter's.

Why, then, did he feel like she was about to make a terrible mistake? And more, why did he feel responsible for stopping her?

HER BELONGINGS WERE packed, and her banknotes were tucked beneath her corset. Even so, Ashleigh felt no excitement whatsoever—only fear and a hollow emptiness. There wasn't enough money to take her mother away with her. The numbness caught her stomach, but there was no alternative. The only way to save Georgina was to save herself first. She would find a place for them to live and send for her later.

Ashleigh had never imagined her escape would be like this. But she had asked one of the footmen to pack her trunk inside one of the carriages. She intended to plead a headache and leave the masquerade early, with no one the wiser. Everything was ready.

She wore a gown of ice blue silk and held a black lacy mask. She'd worn as many jewels as her father would permit, for she intended to sell them later.

Georgina knew nothing about her plans. There was only a letter Ashleigh had hidden in the desk. But with any luck, she could disappear, and no one would be the wiser.

A knock sounded at the door, and when she called out for the person to enter, she saw her father at the doorway.

"I'm ready," she said.

Instead of offering his arm to escort her downstairs, Cecil entered her room and motioned for her maid to leave them alone to talk.

"Is everything all right?" she asked.

There was a slight pause as he closed the door behind him. The expression on his face made Ashleigh take a step backwards. She'd seen that look before when he'd chastised her mother.

"One of my footmen told me of your plans to run away this evening," he began.

The blood seemed to drain from her face, and panic roiled in her stomach. "What?" She tried to behave innocently, as if she knew nothing of any such plan, and added, "I don't understand."

She should have known better. The servants were all loyal to him because Cecil paid their wages. She'd been stupid in her attempt to bribe anyone. The only person who could help her escape was either Mrs. Harding, or herself.

Her father took a step closer and seized her wrist. "Don't ever lie to me." His voice was calm, as if he'd caught her at a minor infraction instead of trying to flee for her life. He kept her wrist tight in his grasp, in a not-so-subtle reminder of the command he held over her.

"Your trunk is downstairs," he continued, "and the servants have orders to unpack everything." Once again, his voice was chillingly neutral. "Now, we will attend the masquerade ball. Your mother is staying home tonight. She is . . . feeling unwell."

A sour feeling caught in her stomach, and she lowered her gaze. "Then I should not go to the ball, either."

"You will do whatever I tell you to do." He released her wrist, and added, "I can see that I've been too lenient on you. Lord Falkland will be attending tonight, and as his fiancée, you must be there. We will announce your betrothal, and you will behave like a lady."

"I . . . need my cloak," she said. He waited for her, and she opened the wardrobe. Though she had planned to take more of her jewels, the chest was gone.

"Where are my jewels?" she asked.

"You will wear the ones you already have on," he answered. "I've taken the rest, along with all your pin money. You won't be going anywhere, Ashleigh. And if you even try something foolish, you will be punished."

She reached for her cloak and said nothing. Inwardly, her mind raced, for she could no longer keep her original plan. Instead, she would have to improvise. Perhaps she could ask Persephone to let her stay for a few days. Surely her father would not refuse the duke's daughter. Or if she found Mrs. Harding, she might ask the widow for help, with the promise of future payment.

Ashleigh was trying to make a mental list of possibilities so she wouldn't start crying. Now, whatever option she chose, she would have to leave with the clothes on her back and sell whatever she could. Heaven help her if she got caught. And the last thing she wanted was to attend a masquerade ball tonight. If she could somehow convince her father to let her remain home, it was her best chance to escape.

"Father, please. I don't want to go—" she started to say.

His face turned grim, and his hand clenched into a fist. "You do not defy me, Ashleigh. Not ever."

CAMERON REMAINED ON the outskirts of the ballroom, studying each of the young ladies. Earlier today, Mr. Gregor had mentioned other possible candidates for a bride who would attend the ball. But the man had been elusive, not particularly willing to give names.

He saw Lady Persephone, the duke's daughter, dressed up as a swan in the masquerade. Lady Ashleigh remained close to her father, wearing ice blue silk that contrasted against her auburn hair. Around her throat she wore pearls, along with matching ear bobs and a bracelet. There was no mistaking her wealth.

But something caught his attention—the way her father was gripping her arm. Ashleigh's expression appeared anxious, and her posture reminded him of a woman in pain. Cedric Gregor had mentioned she was betrothed, but he didn't see another man nearby.

It didn't matter. She wasn't his responsibility or his concern. So her father had chosen a husband for her. Didn't most fathers do that? She would have a life of comfort, no matter which man she married. Cameron dismissed the thought, and then noticed another young lady arriving. She wore an emerald gown that appeared to be fashioned of leaves. In one hand, she carried an apple, and he recognized that she was meant to be Eve.

She wore a mask, but he was fairly certain it was the shy woman he'd seen a while back, the one whom the other young ladies had teased. Although no one else seemed to recognize her except the Earl of Scarsdale, Cameron was fairly confident he'd identified her. The lady had the same hair, the same coloring, and she even had the same shyness.

She might be a possibility. He considered it, but his gaze kept drifting back to Lady Ashleigh. He couldn't understand why he was drawn to her, except that he could sense danger of some kind. Her father released her hand briefly, but when he reached out to her again, Ashleigh flinched and turned her face aside.

The marquess had struck her. Cameron was convinced of it. All his life, he'd been able to sense when something was not right, as if there were a visible aura in the room. And he didn't doubt that the marquess had hurt Ashleigh in some way. But what was he supposed to do about it?

He began making his way through the crowd, stopping now and then so as to make his path less obvious. The shy woman dressed as Eve was now dancing with Lord Scarsdale, and from the sudden look of longing on her face, Cameron suspected she had already decided whom she wanted to wed.

He saw another wallflower standing apart from the others. She had black hair, and her mask was white. Her gown had rose-colored short sleeves and dipped to a green fitted waist and skirt. A mermaid, he realized. That was her costume.

"Emma!" someone called out to her. The young woman appeared startled and glanced around. For a moment, she stared in his direction, before she looked away. She took hesitant steps, nearly bumping into the doorway before she disappeared.

She couldn't see well, Cameron realized. Her stare had not been one of dismay or revulsion when she'd looked at him. It had been entirely empty. For a moment, he wondered if the young woman would be all right, but then he saw her with a middle-aged woman who appeared to be scolding her. Was she the one Mr. Gregor was thinking of?

Cameron stopped by the open doorway, pretending to look out over the gardens. He kept his face angled so he could see anyone approaching from his peripheral vision.

Then the next thing he knew, Cedric Gregor was bringing over the shy young woman who resembled Eve to meet him. "Good evening, Mr. Neill," he remarked. "I would like to introduce you to my niece."

Cameron pretended as if he hadn't seen them approaching and turned his head. "Forgive me, what did you say?"

"I said I wanted to introduce you to my niece." Cedric gestured toward the young woman, whom they both knew was decidedly not his niece.

Cameron glanced at the young woman, wondering if Mr. Gregor truly intended for her to be a possible candidate. "Is this about our earlier discussion?" In other words, was this the match they'd chosen for him?

He could see from the young lady's expression that she didn't like what she saw but was pretending it didn't matter. She ventured a smile that didn't meet her eyes.

"No, not at all," Cedric responded with a smile. "I thought the two of you might become acquainted."

Idly, Cameron wondered if she wasn't intended as a wife candidate, then what was the purpose of the meeting? Or perhaps Mr. Gregor wanted to ensure that she spoke to many people at the ball.

"Mr. Neill has been out of the country during the past few years," Mr. Gregor explained. "He has only recently returned."

He paused and added, "I see Mrs. Harding over there. I'll leave the two of you to get acquainted, but we will be just there on the other side of the terrace."

So they would chaperone the conversation from a distance. There was no mistaking the dismay on the young woman's face from the way her smile grew uncertain and then faded. She took a moment, steeled herself, and smiled again as she extended her hand.

Now what was that all about? Cameron paused, waiting to see what she wanted from him. Then he realized it was her way of greeting him. He hid his amusement and took her gloved hand, shaking it firmly. "A pleasure to meet you, Miss—er, I didn't catch your name."

"It's a masquerade," she answered. "You're n-not supposed to know who I am."

Cameron caught the stutter she was trying to hide, and then he understood Mr. Gregor's purpose. He wanted the young woman to practice speaking with more people. He offered an encouraging smile and answered, "Just so. Though I suppose you already know my name."

"Just so," she repeated.

He laughed, and for a moment, he saw genuine humor in her expression before it faded. She was studying him again, as if she might be truly considering him for a husband.

"Are you enjoying yourself this e-evening, Mr. Neill?"

"It's not quite what I thought it would be." It was as neutral an answer as he could muster since he had no idea whether he would find any other candidates for a wife. "I wasn't expecting so many people."

He waited for her to continue the conversation, but it fell flat, stretching into silence. In the distance, he spied Lady Ashleigh starting to walk toward them. He wasn't certain why, but his instincts flared again that something was wrong.

The shy young woman was apparently waiting for him to speak, so Cameron offered, "I hear that the Duke of Westerford has a magnificent library. Over a thousand books, I'm told. Have you seen it before?"

"No. This is the first time I've . . . been to a b-ball here," she confessed.

"I must admit, I am tempted to go and see the library for myself." It wasn't the truth, but he was simply making conversation. "Would you like to come along?" The words broke forth before he realized what he'd said. He'd essentially suggested that she meet him alone in a closed room. Which hadn't been his intention at all.

Her cheeks flushed at the idea, and she shook her head. "No, thank you, Mr. Neill. But I will wish you a good evening."

It wasn't surprising that she'd made a hasty departure. Ah well.

After she'd fled, Cameron moved back into the shadows, intending to quietly see if Lady Ashleigh was all right. To his surprise, he overheard her apologizing to the young woman. He finally caught the lady's name—Violet Edwards. It was the young woman Ashleigh had mentioned at Gunter's as a suggested match.

Then he overheard Ashleigh admitting that she'd done something terrible because she'd needed money. Why would an heiress need money? He supposed she was still intent on running away. Her demeanor held only remorse, and although Miss Edwards appeared reluctant to forgive her, Ashleigh had evidently humbled herself.

It was as if she were trying to make amends while she still had time. Which meant she likely intended to run away tonight. Cameron wasn't certain that was a good idea. It was dangerous for a woman to travel alone.

After Miss Edwards departed, Lady Ashleigh started to walk in his direction. Behind her, Cameron spied her father approaching with an older man. Ashleigh saw them too and quickened her pace to catch up to him.

"Are you—" he started to ask.

But she pleaded, "Dance with me, please. Quickly, before they catch up to me."

It seemed she wanted to use him for an escape. But Cameron offered his arm and led her to the dance floor where the musicians had begun a waltz. Though she smiled brightly, he saw beneath the false expression. There was fear there, of a woman afraid of her father. With a closer look, he spied a redness around her mask. His gaze sharpened, and he realized it was swelling.

"Who struck you?" he asked quietly.

"It's nothing." Ashleigh lifted her chin and stared back at him. "Just pretend you don't see it."

He was more certain than ever that her father had done it. And he suspected it had something to do with her suitor. Cameron's mood darkened for he despised any man who would strike his own daughter. There was no reason for it. Ashleigh appeared desperate to control her emotions, and her smile was forced. He sensed her fragile mood, as if the slightest kindness would shatter her.

"Why did he hurt you?" he asked. He saw her wince and realized that he'd tightened his grip on her waist. Immediately, he loosened his hold.

"Because he found out I meant to run away tonight and leave London," she told him. "My footman betrayed my plans."

Cameron glanced at her father as they danced past the two men. "I presume the man with him is your betrothed?"

"Unfortunately." Her expression turned frustrated, and her mouth tightened. "I've been trying to avoid Viscount Falkland ever since he arrived half an hour ago."

"He's rather old, isn't he?" Though he knew it was common for gentlemen to take younger wives, particularly if they did not have an heir, the viscount appeared old enough to be Ashleigh's father.

She nodded. Then she added, "I don't know how much longer I have. Tonight seemed to be my best chance to get away. But I fear that chance is gone." Her words drifted off, and he heard the hopelessness within them.

"Where will you go once you find a way to escape?"

"I . . . had plans. But now—" Her words broke off, filled with hopelessness.

"Then you need more time," he said. "You should write to a relative."

"I have a cousin, but if I go to him, I'm afraid my father would find me too easily," she admitted. Her mood dimmed, and her expression turned apprehensive. In her blue eyes, he saw her look of despair. Then he noticed the delicate curve of her cheek and the auburn hair that framed her face. She truly was a lovely young woman, though troubled.

She's not the bride for you, his conscience warned. Ashleigh came from a family of vast wealth, so she had never known hunger or suffering. She'd lived within a sheltered world, and he didn't know if she'd ever experienced real life.

"Thank you for rescuing me for a moment, Mr. Neill," she said. In a low voice, she added, "You really ought to consider courting Miss Edwards. Though she's terribly shy, she might be more of what you're looking for."

"Do you even know her?" he asked.

"No, but I've come to respect her," she admitted. "She's doing everything she can to change her life."

"Isn't her family looking for her? I thought Mr. Gregor mentioned something about it."

Ashleigh's smile faced, replaced with a flash of guilt. "They are, yes." With a pained look, she admitted, "And if they find her, it's probably my fault. Her sister threatened me if I didn't tell her where she was staying."

"Why would you say anything at all?" It bothered him that she couldn't keep a secret.

"I didn't intend to," Ashleigh said. "I told her that Violet was safe and not to worry. But Charity found out I was selling my jewels. She suspected I was planning to escape. She threatened to tell my father if I didn't tell her where her sister was." But in the end, that hadn't mattered since her own footman had told him. She let out a sigh. "I don't think Charity would do anything to hurt Violet. She only wanted to know whether her sister was all right."

Cameron studied Ashleigh's face, reading her emotions. She believed what she was saying, that she didn't think Charity would hurt Violet. But it made him wary of trusting her with any secrets at all.

"I hope you're right, for her sake."

Guilt flushed over her cheeks, and she lowered her gaze. A few moments later, Lady Persephone joined the dancing. As soon as the duke's daughter spied Cameron, her expression wrinkled. "Ashleigh, what on earth are you doing?"

He felt the instant the tension tightened within her. "Dancing with Mr. Neill." Though she kept her voice light, he sensed the defensive tone.

"You cannot possibly. I don't even believe he was invited. My father would never allow someone who looked like *that* to enter our doors." Persephone's face was aghast, but Cameron paid her insults no heed. He was more interested in how Lady Ashleigh would respond. Would she defend him? He waited a moment to see, but her face turned crimson, and she appeared at a loss for words.

"I—that is—" Her words broke off in dismay as the dance ended and Persephone pulled her away. He had no opportunity to bow or thank her for the dance.

He knew that the moment Ashleigh reached the other side of the room, he would become the subject of Persephone's ridicule. The mockery didn't bother him, for he knew this was only a disguise he wore to dissuade others from paying attention to him.

But Ashleigh had begged *him* to dance instead of any other man. She could have walked right past him and asked someone else. He wondered why she'd sought help from him, of all people.

Her friend was clearly gossiping, and Ashleigh appeared embarrassed by it. Given his clothing and long beard, it was no surprise that Lady Persephone would denigrate him. Cameron ignored them and began making his way around the perimeter of the room. He needed to concentrate on finding his own bride. His gaze turned back to Miss Edwards. Did she truly have an unyielding interest in Lord Scarsdale or would she consider someone like him instead? She might be very good with children. In his mind, he thought of the possibilities.

But once he reached the opposite side of the room, he over-heard the Marquess of Rothburn boasting to Lord Falkland. "I let her believe the wedding will be in almost a month, Falkland. But now that we have the special license, I think it can be managed within a day or two."

"Excellent," the viscount answered. "I look forward to the wedding." With a laugh, he added, "And the wedding night, of course. I *do* need an heir."

The marquess laughed, and Cameron realized he was clench-ing his fists. What kind of father would joke about something of that nature? It wasn't right at all. He was beginning to sympathize with Ashleigh and her fate, even as he warned himself not to get involved.

But as he started to walk toward Miss Edwards, he had a feeling that it would not be so easy to turn a blind eye to what was happening to Lady Ashleigh. He risked a glance at her and saw that the marquess had already brought Lord Falkland to greet her. She kept her gaze downcast, but her posture revealed fear and uncertainty.

He had no reason to help her. No reason to get involved. It would only complicate matters.

And yet, he knew if he stood by and did nothing, he would one day come to regret it.

Chapter Four

I T WAS TIME to make her escape. Ashleigh had played the role of dutiful daughter, and then she'd spoken discreetly to one of Persephone's footmen, asking him to hire a hansom cab. She had decided to spend the night at Mrs. Harding's residence and ask Mr. Gregor for his assistance in selling the jewels she was wearing and arranging her journey.

She could travel north and spend a day or two with her cousin before continuing her travels before her father could catch up with her. Terror clenched her stomach at the thought of all the things that could go wrong. She would have to hire someone to protect her—someone who couldn't be bribed. She'd have to sell her jewels and hope that the money would be enough for traveling. So many difficulties—and the more she thought of what lay ahead, the more her fear intensified. It would take a miracle to make an escape now.

Mr. Neill had left hours ago, and part of her wondered whether she'd made a mistake in not considering marriage to him.

He didn't want you, her brain reminded her. Though she didn't understand his reasons for seeking a wife instead of a housekeeper, she should have at least considered the match. He'd admitted that he traveled often, and he wanted a marriage in name only.

Isn't that what you wanted? her brain reminded her. *A marriage that isn't real?*

Her face burned as she thought of another reason for refusing—she'd always dreamed of marrying a handsome nobleman. And part of her *did* want children one day. She simply couldn't imagine being wedded to a man like Cameron Neill, who dressed like a pauper and looked as if he hadn't shaved in five years. He wasn't at all attractive on the surface.

But when she looked beneath all that, he *did* have nice eyes. Eyes that never seemed to miss anything. He was constantly alert, aware of everything happening around him. There was a mystery about him, something she didn't understand.

With a sigh, she took her cloak from one of the maids and turned to leave. Unfortunately, her father had anticipated her move and was now waiting for her.

"Are you ready to go home?" he asked.

Ashleigh nodded, hoping that she could escape amid the crowd of guests and quietly slip away. She simply had to reach the hired cab before anyone else did. Her heart was pounding hard, and her father took her arm as they went to say farewell to the duke and duchess. Ashleigh murmured her thanks to them and went to the door. Her father's grip had lightened since she'd pretended obedience. From the top of the stairs, she saw several carriages lined up, and near the back, she saw the hansom cab.

You'll never escape, the voice of reason warned. *It's not possible.*

Her breathing grew shallow as her fears tripled. She would have only one chance to run—and even then, she didn't know if this would work.

She walked slowly down the stairs. When her father turned to speak with the viscount, she felt his grip loosen even more. Just then, a large group of guests came down the stairs behind them, and Ashleigh saw her chance.

She jerked free of his grasp and hurried among the other men and women. For a moment, her father couldn't see her, and she darted through the darkness toward the hansom cab. She didn't stop to look behind her and never stopped running.

But the moment she tried to climb in the vehicle, her father seized her arm. He held it tightly, and when she dared to look at him, she saw fury in his eyes.

"You dare to think you can run from me, do you?" Her father's temper had brewed so hot, but she was shocked he would humiliate her like this in public. He clenched his fist and turned to begin dragging her inexorably back the way she'd run. She was losing her footing in the slick stones, but he was heedless to it. He gave her an arm-wrenching pull, and for a moment, the world seemed to tip upside down. She couldn't say what happened exactly, but one moment, she was standing there, and the next, she'd fallen hard to the ground, hitting her head.

"Come with me," she heard a familiar voice say. Someone helped her up and into the hansom cab. Ashleigh tasted blood on her lip, but she obeyed blindly. The gentleman got in with her and closed the door.

Her vision was blurred from hitting her head, and her face was on fire from the pain of scraping against the cobblestones. But dimly, she was aware that Mr. Neill was her rescuer. She didn't hear where he'd ordered the driver to take them, but frankly, she didn't care.

"I'm sorry for what he did to you," Mr. Neill said. "How badly are you hurt?"

"Do you have a handkerchief?" she asked. "My mouth is bleeding."

He gave her a linen cloth, and she removed her mask before pressing it to her lips. In the darkness, she let her tears fall, and the salt mingled with her blood. Though she was grateful he'd been there, she felt the enormity of this disaster crashing down over her. Her father would order his coach to follow hers, and the moment they stopped, Cecil would catch up to them.

"What happened to my father?" In the midst of her pain, she hadn't seen anything, but Mr. Neill must have done something to help her get away.

In the darkness, she couldn't see his expression. But after a few moments, he answered, "He won't bother you. There were a number of people there, and I saw a chance to help you leave."

He was being vague about his role, but she didn't question it. What did it matter now? She'd gotten her wish to escape. But because her father had seen her go, he would undoubtedly follow her—and the punishment for leaving would be severe. She touched her hand to her swollen face, trying to push back the fear.

"Why did he hurt you?" he asked gently. "Was it because you tried to run?"

"Yes." Her voice broke, and she couldn't stop herself from sobbing. "I was so stupid to imagine I could leave. He's never going to let me go."

In the darkness, he reached out and took her hand. She felt the warmth of his touch, and it brought her comfort. For a moment, she imagined he was taking her away from London, that somehow it was going to be all right.

"Where are we driving?" she asked. "To Mrs. Harding's?"

"Not yet," he hedged. "I'm taking you to my townhouse first, to have my housekeeper tend to your injuries."

"I can't go there," she insisted. "People will think you've compromised me."

He let out a slow breath and released her hand. "Not if we're careful. And it's less likely that your father will find you. I imagine your coachman knows that you visited Mrs. Harding's school?"

She let out a frustrated sigh. Her father would undoubtedly search for her there. "You're right."

"My housekeeper is quite good at healing. After she tends you, we'll make a plan of where you can go next."

"Thank you." She didn't know what had prompted him to rescue her, but she was more than grateful. At least now she had a real chance to flee the marriage. A terrible thought occurred to her, that if anyone *did* find out she'd gone to his home, no reputable man would want to wed her. But then again, the viscount didn't seem to be a reputable man. He likely wouldn't care what she'd done.

"I'm sorry I involved you in this," she said. "But I am grateful for your help."

"I wasn't about to stand aside and let him harm you again."

"Other men did." The bystanders had turned a blind eye, pretending as if they hadn't noticed.

Mr. Neill fell silent again, and soon enough, the hansom cab pulled in front of a nondescript townhouse. It was nothing grand or noticeable, and he helped her outside the carriage and paid the driver. She kept the handkerchief pressed to her face, and he led her through the front door.

"Will your servants talk?" she asked.

"They are discreet beyond measure because I pay them to remain quiet," he answered. Almost in response to his statement, a footman emerged in the hall and took Mr. Neill's hat.

The servant offered to take her cloak, but Ashleigh refused, saying, "I'll leave it on a little longer."

Mr. Neill gave orders for the housekeeper to meet them in the drawing room. "Lady Ashleigh was hurt, and I want Mrs. Cobb to tend her injuries."

He lowered his voice, and she overheard something else about food and drink. Truthfully, she couldn't imagine eating or drinking anything at all. Or perhaps it was for him.

Mr. Neill led her inside, and she realized that everything about the house was forgettable. There were hardly any colors or any decorations at all. There were no paintings, no art to speak of. It made her even more curious about him. It seemed that he did his best to blend in with his surroundings.

"Please, sit down," he offered.

She took a chair, and he lit several lamps, bringing them to a nearby table. She heard the clock chime half two, and after she sat down, the weight of her troubles sank into her shoulders. Now that the shock had worn off, she was beginning to feel the pain of her injuries.

Mrs. Cobb, the housekeeper, hurried inside with a basin, a basket hooked over one arm, a pitcher of water in the other. "My goodness. What happened to you, dear girl?" With a glance at Mr. Neill, she added, "You were right to send for me, sir. I'll have her fixed up in a wee bit."

"And have you brought—"

"The tea and whisky? Aye, of course. Samuel will be bringing it in."

Mr. Neill drew an end table closer, and Mrs. Cobb set her basin upon it, pouring water inside. Then she dipped a clean linen cloth into the water. Sympathetic brown eyes stared into hers, and Ashleigh had to resist the urge to look down. It felt as if the woman could see inside her. With her gray hair pulled back into a knot and her body shaped like a barrel, Mrs. Cobb seemed like a woman with a good shoulder for crying on.

Strangely, the housekeeper didn't ask a single question like most women would have. She didn't ask who had hurt her or where or why. She simply pressed a cold cloth to different parts of her swollen face. Ashleigh winced, but Mrs. Cobb said, "You're fortunate, my lady. It seems as if the bleeding has stopped. Did you hit your head at all? Are you dizzy?"

"I did, but . . . I'll be all right." Though she wanted to spill out her troubles, something made her stop.

"You'll have some bad bruises, but nothing too terrible," Mrs. Cobb said. Then she called out, "Samuel, I'll be needing that hot water now!"

A moment later, the footman brought in a tea tray with two kettles upon it. The housekeeper took out a bowl from her basket and poured hot water into it. Then she sprinkled some unfamiliar herbs and sliced up what smelled like ginger. Ashleigh watched her choose different things from her basket, an onion among them. Eventually it became clear that Mrs. Cobb was making a poultice.

"We'll wait until this has cooled down some," the older woman said. "Then, I want you to hold this to your face. It

51

should bring down the swelling."

While they waited for the water to cool, Mr. Neill gave her a cup of tea. Ashleigh took a sip and nearly choked when she realized it was laced with whisky.

"Oh, no. I don't drink spirits," she argued.

"Drink it anyway. You've been through enough tonight."

Though the first swallow burned her throat, the second went down easier. Then Mrs. Cobb gave her the poultice. "Hold this until it grows cold. It should make you feel better."

Ashleigh wrinkled her nose at the aroma but obeyed. Then the older woman packed away her supplies and exchanged a look with Mr. Neill. "Will that be all, sir?"

"Yes, thank you. See to it that Lady Ashleigh has a bed made up for her so she can rest. She'll need a maid to help her."

"Of course, sir."

"No," Ashleigh protested. "Absolutely not. I could never stay here unchaperoned at an unmarried man's house. I just—can't."

"No one is forcing you to do anything," he said. "Drink your tea, hold the poultice to your face, and we'll decide what's to be done. If you grow tired and wish to sleep, you can remain here."

He was starting to sound reasonable, which frightened her. The idea of a warm bed in a place where no one could find her was a wonderful idea. But she knew the consequences if she agreed to it.

"I have to return to Mrs. Harding's," she insisted. "Truly, I must."

"Then I will have my carriage take you there," he offered. "If that is what you wish."

She was exhausted, both physically and emotionally. The poultice smelled terrible, and the onion within it made her eyes water.

"Or you could travel to Scotland with me. And become my wife."

CAMERON SAW THE shock in her eyes, but instead of disgust, she lowered the poultice and stared at him. He expected her to outright refuse, but he also knew she was desperate with limited options. For a moment, she seemed to contemplate it.

Though he didn't know why, his instincts were telling him to wed Ashleigh. He couldn't say why or what had changed. Only a few weeks ago, he'd believed she was a spoiled brat who looked down on others. Now he was starting to see that she was trapped in a gilded cage and punished if she did anything her father disliked.

Her actions were guided by fear, not impassive behavior. She'd been trained to remain silent, so as not to make matters worse.

But she did have a conscience. He'd overheard her apologizing to Violet Edwards in secret. And when he'd watched her with that young boy near the Serpentine, she had seemed quite friendly to him, which boded well for her to become a mother.

Had he done the right thing by offering to wed her? He wasn't even certain Ashleigh would agree—or whether this was what he wanted. He'd fully intended to let her go her own path. And yet, for some impulsive reason, he'd blurted out an offer of marriage.

During the past four years, he'd lived each day by making swift decisions—and often, those decisions had saved his life. He'd learned to think on his feet and live with the consequences. And somehow, Lady Ashleigh *did* seem like the right woman to wed.

"Do you still want a marriage in name only?" Ashleigh ventured.

He nodded. "We would travel together to Scotland and live together for a time until I return to London. No one needs to know where you are. Or if you wish to tell your family, I could send word to your father to let him grow accustomed to the idea."

She lifted the poultice to her face again. Though she didn't agree, she also didn't refuse. "I need time to think about it. Will you grant me that?"

"I will. But your father will be searching for you." Though few people knew where he lived, it wasn't impossible to find out.

"If I were to agree," she said, "how would you get the marriage license?"

"It would be best if we married in Scotland," he offered. "You won't need your father's permission."

"I am of age," she said, "but you're right. It would be easier if we left London as soon as possible."

Then she *was* considering it. He poured himself a cup of tea, adding a little whisky while he sat across from her. "What do you know about running a household?"

She sent him a wry look. "I've been trained since childhood to be a marchioness." Then her expression shifted, and she admitted, "I took on my mother's duties sometimes." A pained look crossed her face, and she added, "If I marry you, I'll need help for my mother. My father . . . hurts her often. And since she is his wife, he can do it as often as he wishes."

Cameron said nothing, for it was one matter to marry Ashleigh in secret and protect her with his name. It was quite another to steal her mother away, for it would cause all manner of consequences.

"I can promise to keep *you* safe," he said. "But as for your mother—I don't know. I could try, but getting Lady Rothburn away from your father would be difficult. It might seem to the authorities as if I'm kidnapping her."

"Unless he's preoccupied with searching for me," she suggested. "If you sent someone to her now and offered to bring her to my cousin's house in the north, she might agree."

He gave a slight nod, for she was right. No doubt her father was scouring London for some sign of Ashleigh. And of course,

Rothburn knew Cameron had taken her. The only consolation was that the marquess didn't know where he lived. And even if he did find the house, Cameron's servants would never allow the man to trespass. Ashleigh was safe for now, but only for tonight.

"What do you want to do?" he asked. "Stay or leave?"

She raised her gaze to his, and in her blue eyes, he saw a fragile hope. "I suppose if I decide to marry you, there's no harm in staying. It's probably safer here."

"It is," he agreed. "But if you change your mind, no one will discover that you slept at my house. Rest assured, my servants would never speak." It had taken years to find the right staff, but all were impeccably discreet, and Cameron paid them better than anyone else. Thus far, if he made any request at all, it was granted swiftly.

"Mrs. Cobb can show you to your room," he offered. "In the meantime, sleep and decide what it is you want."

"We should set rules," Ashleigh suggested. "For both of us to follow."

He liked that idea a great deal. "We'll discuss it at breakfast." He rang for a footman and sent for Mrs. Cobb. When the housekeeper returned, he ordered, "Please ensure that Lady Ashleigh has everything she needs. She will want to rest after what happened."

"Of course, sir. Right away."

He stood and walked with Ashleigh to the door. "You needn't worry about anyone following you. You're safe now."

She nodded, studying him for a moment. "Thank you for giving me a means of escape. And for trying to help my mother. If you can do anything at all for her, I would be so grateful."

He could hear the emotion in her voice, the fear mingled with hope. He didn't want her to cast him in the role of hero, not when it was too soon to tell what he could accomplish.

"I can make no promises," he warned, "but I will try."

"It's more than anyone else would do for me." To his surprise, she reached out and took his hand in hers, squeezing it. The unexpected gesture took him aback, for he'd never expected her touch. "I will write a note to Mother and send it with your footman."

"I wouldn't," he cautioned. "Your father might find the note."

Her expression dimmed, but she murmured an agreement. "All right."

She started to pull her hand away, but he held it a moment longer. "You can sleep a little while, but we must leave in the morning as soon as possible. You can sleep again in the coach later, if the roads aren't too rough." Then he released her hand and bid her goodnight.

"Goodnight," she murmured. For a moment, her blue eyes stared into his, as if she were seeing him for the first time and taking his measure. Her skin was swollen and bruised by her eye, but despite her injury, her beauty was undeniable.

As she turned away, he noticed the slender dip of her waist, the curve of hips. Though he'd promised a celibate marriage, he couldn't quite suppress the instinctive flare of need. It had been so long since he'd been with a woman.

But Rebecca hadn't wanted him. She'd never felt anything during their marriage except duty. She'd been slender and delicate, and though she had shared his bed, nothing he'd ever done had roused a passion in her. It was as if her fear reigned over all else. After a time, he'd stopped visiting her. It didn't matter how gentle he'd tried to be, she hadn't liked lovemaking. It was yet another reason why he intended to have a celibate second marriage. Better to only be friends, because clearly, he didn't know how to bring his wife enjoyment.

Keeping his physical disguise was a good way of keeping distance between them. The last thing he wanted was a true wife. It was better if Ashleigh didn't know anything about his past, much less the secretive life he lived.

He hoped she would never find out.

ASHLEIGH AWAKENED A few hours later, frightened at first when she didn't remember where she was. Then she raised her fingertips to her face and felt the tenderness. Reality drove out the shadows of sleep, and for a moment, she felt the rush of fear.

Was she willing to trust in a stranger? She knew so little about Cameron Neill. Though she recognized that her choices were limited, marriage was a serious step. What if he had only said the things she wanted to hear?

She got out of bed and walked to the windows, pulling aside one of the drapes. The bright sunlight made her squint, but when her eyes adjusted, she noticed that they were in a part of London she'd not seen before. It seemed to be among the merchants, which made sense. Mr. Neill had no title, so he must make his fortune by another means.

He'd said nothing about her lack of a dowry—and there was no question that her father would refuse to provide it if she did marry Mr. Neill.

Doubts swelled within her like a rising tide. What if she was exchanging one prison for another? *He could be lying to you,* her heart warned. *It's not a good idea to trust him.*

She had slept in her chemise but remembered that the maid had helped her remove her stays. There was a bellpull nearby, so she rang for someone to help her dress. In the meantime, she donned her petticoats and began to tie them. Truthfully, she had no idea what to wear since all she had was the ballgown from last night. A few moments later, a soft knock sounded. "Who is it?" Ashleigh inquired.

"It's Sarah, my lady. I've come to help you dress."

She called out for the maid to enter, and when the young woman came inside, she had a dress over one arm and a small wooden bowl. "Will you be joining Mr. MacNeill for breakfast?"

"MacNeill?" Ashleigh echoed.

Sarah laughed. "Sorry. Mr. Neill is what I meant." Before Ashleigh could ponder the mistake, the maid added, "I could ring for a hot cup of chocolate, if you'd like something to drink, my lady? And Mrs. Cobb asked me to give you this for your face." The maid held out the bowl. Inside, Ashleigh found a cold piece of linen soaked in herbs.

"Thank you," she told the maid. "I would like to get dressed first, and then a cup of chocolate sounds wonderful."

Sarah helped her with her stays and then held out the morning gown she'd brought. "This belonged to Lady Kilmartin. I think it may fit you."

Ashleigh had no idea who that was, but she agreed with the maid. "It's much better than the ballgown." She turned around, raising her arms. The maid lifted the green morning gown over her chemise, corset, and petticoats. It fit perfectly, and she was grateful to have something more appropriate to wear.

Sarah was about to ring for the chocolate, but Ashleigh asked, "Is Mr. Neill already at breakfast?"

"He is, my lady."

"Then, it might be best if I join him, and you can have someone bring the chocolate to me in the dining room instead." They had plans to make, and she didn't want to keep him waiting. Ashleigh took the cool cloth and pressed it to her face. The scent of herbs was light, but the cold water eased her discomfort.

The maid walked to the door and opened it, likely intending to lead her downstairs to the dining room. But Ashleigh caught a glimpse of her reflection in the looking glass, and she couldn't help but stare. The injury around her temple had caused her eye to swell, and it was already beginning to turn darker. Her lip was no longer bleeding, but it was tender to the touch. All in all, she looked awful.

Sarah asked no questions but simply waited in silence. Ashleigh followed her, but deep inside, her terror had reawakened. Her mother had likely borne the brunt of the marquess's temper in Ashleigh's absence.

But if she *did* accept Mr. Neill's offer to wed, was it an impetuous decision that would come back to haunt her? She didn't know.

The maid led her into a small dining room. The table was hardly large enough to seat four—nothing at all like the large mahogany table at her father's house. Cecil had hosted many supper parties there, and Ashleigh had entertained the guests, as had her mother. It was obvious that Mr. Neill had never hosted anyone at this house.

Everything would change if she accepted him as her husband. No longer would she live the life of a noblewoman—she would have to embrace the life of a commoner's wife. She had no idea what he did to earn money or even how he'd gained invitations to some of the more exclusive balls in London. It was strange, really.

But she had asked Mr. Neill to give her time, so she would simply avoid going through with the marriage until she knew whether she'd made the right decision.

The moment he saw her, he stood from his chair. There was a flash of surprise on his face when he saw her gown, but he masked it immediately.

"Good morning," he greeted her. He wore a dark blue coat, buff trousers, and his shirt and cravat were both wrinkled. His blond beard was long enough to touch his chest, and she wished again that he would shave it. For when she looked past the barriers, she saw someone else entirely. Why would he hide himself like this?

Unless he had a reason to hide. She was starting to wonder if it was something else besides shyness.

Ashleigh answered his greeting and took a seat beside him at the table. A footman she'd seen last night silently came to offer her eggs and sausage. There was also toasted bread and jam, but she still found it difficult to eat. Her worries only seemed to magnify with every passing moment.

She spread jam upon the toast, but she didn't know how to

begin this conversation. What was she supposed to do now that she'd spent the night at his house?

"Did you sleep well?" he inquired.

She decided to be honest. "Not really. I think I may have made a mistake in choosing to stay here last night. I should have gone to Mrs. Harding's house instead."

He tilted his head slightly and then nodded. "I imagine you're afraid of rushing into a decision based on fear."

"And I don't know you," she confessed. "You've offered to wed me, but I can't agree to that when we've only encountered one another a few times. We've barely spoken at all."

"Agreed." He slid a piece of paper toward her, and she read it, not really understanding what it was. There were three words written upon the note. "But you really don't have anything to fear. I will make no demands of you, nor will we share a bedchamber."

Ashleigh glanced up at him, still not really understanding what she was reading. "But we would live together. What a man says he will do and what he actually does are often different."

His gaze turned to her face, and he studied her injuries. "You've witnessed this in your father's behavior."

She nodded. "His moods are as capricious as the weather. My mother and I learned to be careful before speaking to him. I worry about what happened to her last night. I wish . . ." Her words drifted off, and she studied the paper he'd given her. At the top, he'd written *Rules of Marriage*. And then he'd written the three words she'd glanced over before.

Freedom
Respect
Kindness

All in all, they were quite reasonable. The first one, freedom, meant the most to her for it was something she'd never had. But his definition of freedom and hers might be quite different.

"What does this mean?" she asked.

"They are my rules of marriage," he said quietly. "You will have the freedom to live your life as you choose within my household. I ask the same of you—that you do not question what I do or where I go. Allow me the same freedom I grant to you."

Once again, it sounded as if he was holding back secrets she wasn't supposed to know about. She desperately wanted to ask, but she held her silence.

"And the second rule? I am to respect your wishes in all things?" she predicted.

"We will disagree from time to time," he admitted. "We will respect each other's opinions and listen to one another. I will travel often, so you will receive the respect of my staff, who must obey you. And last, I will respect your boundaries, just as you respect mine. We will not share a bed."

Though she ought to be grateful for his reassurance, she found it difficult to believe. "What about years from now? Don't you want children?"

"There will be no children from our union," he said. "However, if you desire a child of your own . . . other arrangements will have to be made."

Shock suffused her as she suddenly realized what he was saying. Was he saying that . . . they would not have a true marriage because he was incapable of consummating it? Understanding dawned upon her, and some of her fear dissipated. He would have a great deal of trouble finding someone to wed if he could not give her children.

But was he implying that she would take a lover? That wasn't at all what she wanted. Perhaps he meant she would have to adopt a child. That, at least, was a possibility.

"And the last rule?" she asked. "Kindness?"

"I would ask that you be kind to me, and I will be kind to you. We will endeavor to make our marriage congenial."

His so-called rules were far more reasonable than she'd expected. She was starting to truly consider it.

"And what of your rules?" he asked.

She raised her eyes to his and said, "I have my own conditions before agreeing to wed you. I want time to know you better before I agree to marry you."

He hesitated for a moment. Before he could answer, she added, "I don't know you, Mr. Neill. I know nothing at all about the man you are—only what you say you are. And I know you've disguised yourself on purpose. You've said as much already."

"And do you consider me to be a man like your father?" His voice held a coolness to it.

"Probably not," she acceded. "But I would rather get to know you before I agree to becoming your wife. This marriage is very rushed—I'm not certain it's a good idea to marry a man when what I truly want is to escape my father's house. It's not fair to you."

She truly meant that. He wanted a wife in name only, but what if he could find a woman who truly loved him? He didn't deserve to bind himself to someone like her, not when there were other choices.

His expression held surprise, as if he'd not expected her to consider his own needs. Then he asked, "What is your second condition?"

"I want you to rescue my mother and bring her to your home."

His expression turned grim, and she knew it was because this was nearly an impossible request. "She must be willing to come of her own accord. If she refuses to leave with my footman, then I can do nothing." He rested his hands on the breakfast table and regarded her with all seriousness. "I will not kidnap a marchioness."

She nodded, understanding. "I truly believe she will want to come."

"And if I cannot do this? Will you refuse to wed me?"

She didn't know how to answer that. "I'm afraid of what will happen if I don't do something to get her out. Her spirit is slowly dying already."

"She must be willing," he repeated. "Beyond that . . ." He left his sentence unfinished.

It occurred to her that he might be concerned about adding a mother-in-law to his household. "I am not asking for her to live *with* us," she explained. "I only want her to be safe." She reached out to his hand and rested hers upon it. "Surely you know what it is to protect someone you love."

From the moment she touched him, his demeanor shifted. Touch wasn't casual to this man, she realized.

"Those are my only two conditions," she finished. "If I feel that we are a good match, then we will have our wedding in Scotland."

"Our journey to my home will take more than a week," he said. "After living together for that long, your reputation will be in ruins. At least consider the possibility of wedding me sooner."

She thought about it and finally said, "We will spend our journey getting to know one another during that week. If we do not suit, then I will find somewhere else to go."

Cameron paused and then nodded. "All right. One week it is." He poured a cup of tea and slid it towards her. "If you want any of your belongings from your house, I need to know now. We leave in three hours."

Chapter Five

THERE WAS HARDLY any time at all to prepare, but Cameron set his plans in motion. He sent word to one of his close friends to find out what could be done for Lady Rothburn. Then he sent a maid to buy a new wardrobe for Ashleigh, not sparing any expense. Though she'd requested a trunk of her own clothing, he suspected it would be too difficult to retrieve it without drawing notice. He would see if it could be brought with the marchioness. Last, he ordered Mrs. Cobb to prepare all manner of food and comforts for their journey.

He had nearly finished the preparations when his footman alerted him that the marquess's men had located his residence. Already Cameron could hear his butler arguing that they had the wrong address. Quietly, he gathered up his correspondence. He lifted a painting up from the wall and placed the letters in the hidden alcove. His servants would see to it that the messages were sent. Then he walked to the opposite wall, pulled back the brass sconce to open the hidden door, and walked up the narrow stairs.

Within minutes, he was outside Ashleigh's door. He knocked quietly, and when she opened it, he raised a finger to his lips. Without asking permission, he entered her room and closed the door behind him. Thankfully, she didn't protest but simply met his gaze.

"Your father has sent men to find you. They are here now, so it's time for us to leave."

"But how? If they have your house surrounded, how can we possibly escape?" she whispered. Already he could see her fears rising. But then, she'd never been protected by him.

"My coach is waiting outside, not far from the house," he said calmly. "All our belongings are packed. Bring whatever you wish, and we'll leave now while they're talking to my butler."

"But won't the servants say anything?"

He shook his head. "They would never risk losing their post." With a glance at her room, he asked, "Are you ready?"

She reached for her cloak. "Sarah already brought my ballgown downstairs. She said she had some other things I could take with me on our journey."

"Indeed," he answered. "And Mrs. Cobb has packed food and also more medicines to tend your face."

Ashleigh paled and reached up to touch it. "I suppose I look awful."

He didn't offer false compliments or tease her—instead, he offered his arm and said, "You're leaving all that behind. And in return, you'll be free of him."

She gave a nod and took his arm in hers. "What about my mother?"

"I've sent word to a friend of mine." He couldn't say more than that, for he didn't know what the outcome would be. But as Ashleigh walked with him into the hallway, he couldn't help but believe this was the right thing to do.

He revealed the hidden stairway, and her face brightened with interest. "How clever," she whispered. But instead of taking her to his study, he opened a different door inside the stairway and led her down a narrow corridor that opened outside where the coach was waiting. He paused at the entrance, looking for any sign of danger.

"Put on your hood," he advised, "and follow me."

Swiftly, he helped her into the coach, and within moments, his coachman drove them into the streets. Cameron glanced behind and saw the men still talking to the butler outside. Then, his servant allowed the men to enter the house at last where, of course, they would find nothing at all. He made a mental reminder to pay his butler a bonus.

Ashleigh appeared fearful as they began the journey. Which was to be expected. She had barely slept, she'd suffered at her father's hands, and now she was running off to marry a man she didn't know.

Later, she would have to become a mother to his three-year-old son. But he wasn't about to say a word about Logan. She'd endured too much and would undoubtedly refuse to marry him if he mentioned the boy.

Idly, he thought of Mrs. Harding's advice—that he should hire a housekeeper or a nursemaid to take the place of a mother. But Cameron knew full well what it was like to be unwanted. He'd never known a mother of his own. Or a father, for that matter. He intended to give his son the family he'd never had.

Ashleigh was a woman of good breeding, and when Cameron had witnessed the marquess's rage, he'd remembered his own childhood. He'd been beaten regularly in the orphanage until he'd learned to quietly disappear. It was a skill he'd carefully honed, being aware of his surroundings. He knew the face of every person, and his instincts for survival had served him well. The years he'd spent at war had made him valuable to the Crown as a spy.

And because of that, he had more money than most of the *ton*.

He smiled slightly, wondering what Ashleigh would think of all this. Part of him was eager for her to see his home in Scotland.

"I sent someone to fetch the trunk you wanted," he began, "but it may take another day or two to retrieve it."

"That's all right," she said. "I'm grateful to have this dress of your mother's to wear."

"It belonged to my wife," he corrected. Though at first, it had bothered him to see her wearing Rebecca's gown, he knew it was more practical for Ashleigh to wear something besides a ballgown for traveling.

Her expression shifted, and she studied him more closely. "I'm sorry. I didn't realize you were a widower."

"Rebecca died three years ago." He glanced outside the window, the familiar emptiness threatening to darken the mood. "I'm glad there were a few of her gowns left. But I'll see to it that you have new ones." With any luck, his staff had already purchased clothing for Ashleigh.

"If my clothes arrive, there will be no need," Ashleigh said. "I don't need that much, really. It wasn't my intention to cause you more expenses."

"It's nothing." He dismissed her concerns and changed the subject. "Are you hungry? We didn't have time for luncheon, and you ate very little at breakfast."

She leaned back on the opposite side of the coach. "I suppose I am hungry. It seems strange that we escaped without being caught. I don't think I imagined we would get away."

"I will always guard those under my protection," he said. Ashleigh had no idea how many close brushes with danger he'd had over the years. It was the reason why every house he owned had multiple ways to escape and many hidden passageways.

She drew her hands into her lap and eyed him. "There are so many things I don't understand. Why would you agree to marry *me*? We know nothing about each other."

"Then we'll learn," he said, avoiding the question as he opened the basket of food. "We have a week, after all." He saw the damp poultice Mrs. Cobb had made for Ashleigh, and he passed it to her. "You can put this on your bruises for now while I see what the cook packed for us."

She accepted the poultice and pressed it to her face. The bruises were darkening, and the sight of them angered him. In the basket he found fresh scones and a pot of jam, as well as strawberries, roast chicken, and other covered dishes. "What would you like to know about me?" he asked, passing her a scone.

She took it from him and asked, "Will you answer my questions honestly?"

"If I can," he hedged. It was better to keep some matters private, and some secrets were not his to share.

"Why do you wear your beard like that?"

He smiled. "Because people look at me with disgust and turn away. It's easy to disappear in a crowd when no one wants to look at you."

Her expression turned interested, and she lifted her head slightly, as if trying to imagine his face without the beard. "Why do you want to disappear among others?"

"Because one can learn a great deal on the edge of a crowd. People talk without noticing me. And I hear a lot." It was another reason why he'd acquired more wealth beyond what the Crown had paid him—he'd learned of investment opportunities others had ignored.

Ashleigh opened the jar of jam and spooned some onto her plate before handing it over to him. He took his own scone and added extra jam while Ashleigh ate daintily, barely dropping a single crumb.

"Tell me something about yourself," he prompted. "What is one of your happiest memories?"

Her face softened with a smile before it faded. "It's both happy and sad to me. It's a memory of my brother."

"I didn't realize you had a brother."

"He died when I was young," she said. Her expression grew shadowed, and then there came a wistful smile. "I remember one day when we ran away from our nursemaid and went to play in the fountain in our mother's garden. I couldn't have been more than five years old, and he was three. We splashed each other in the fountain until we were both soaked. I can't remember laughing so hard." Then her face turned wistful. "I miss him. Even though John died a few years later, I think of him all the time."

Her words stirred up memories he didn't want to face. He'd done everything he could to make Rebecca happy, but the only spark of joy he'd ever seen on her face was when they'd conceived Logan. It was his fault that she hadn't survived childbirth. She'd been far too frail to endure the agony. He never should have touched her.

"What about you?" she asked. "What is your happiest memory?"

It was the day he'd held his son for the first time. But he still wasn't ready to tell her about Logan. Instead, he shrugged and revealed a different memory. "I suppose the first time I had a full meal with enough to eat."

Her face paled, and she stared at him aghast. "You starved as a child?"

He took a bite of his scone. "I was an orphan. Starving happened to all of us." He'd grown accustomed to it.

"But someone adopted you? Is that when you had a full meal?"

He laughed and admitted, "No. It was on the day I learned to steal. I found a baker's shop where the back door was left unlocked. The baker had set aside old bread and cakes that he couldn't sell. He was going to throw them to the dogs. But I sat in the corner of the shop and ate nearly an entire loaf of bread. There was also a cake covered in syrupy honey with almonds. It was the most magnificent cake I'd ever tasted." He did smile, remembering the moment.

"And no one caught you?"

He laughed. "I was only seven at the time, and I fell asleep near the back door. The baker took me back to the orphanage. But sometimes when I escaped, he would send me on errands and pay me with food. He knew which cakes were my favorite and always saved extras for me."

She finished her scone and brushed away the crumbs. "Do you know, it almost seems as if you've lived an entire life that no one knows about. I don't even know how you earn your money."

"I was a soldier for a time," he admitted. "And I inherited a small house from my cousin. I rented it to a farmer while I traveled." But of course, that was only the start. He'd lived on the edge of ruin during the first few years, taking reckless risks that had thankfully paid off.

"How do you have enough wealth for another house here in London?"

He didn't want her to know of the true source of his wealth, so he evaded an answer. "My wife had her own dowry and funds that her father left her. It became mine after she died."

Understanding dawned in her eyes, and she nodded. "And without an heir, I suppose it would fall to you if she had no brothers."

He didn't answer but allowed her to draw her own conclusions.

"I understand why you came to London to find another wife," Ashleigh continued. "What I don't understand is why you want a celibate marriage. You need someone who can inherit your property."

Cameron didn't want to continue discussing the issue but instead decided to try a different tack. "I don't need a child in order to have an heir." He passed her some of the chicken to distract her from the subject. "Your turn to answer a question. If you do decide to wed me, what is most important to your happiness?"

"I want to be allowed to make my own decisions," she answered without hesitation.

It was a simple thing to offer, and he agreed, "You will be in charge of our household if you marry me. You may make as many decisions as you like."

"Tell me about your house," she said. "Is it similar to your townhouse in London?"

"Somewhat," he said, refusing to answer more than that. "You'll see it in time." He didn't want to ruin the surprise, but truthfully, he was looking forward to her shock at seeing Castle Kilmartin. "Would you like more to eat?"

She shook her head. "I'll be fine."

Cameron glanced outside the window and noticed that they were slowing down. There shouldn't be this many coaches on the road at this time of day, and they had only just reached the outskirts of London. His instincts tightened, and he wondered why so many vehicles were stopped. He stared outside the window and saw several men walking amid the coaches. Some were forcing the passengers to disembark while they searched.

Lord Rothburn had enough money to hire men or pay constables to search most of the coaches. When their vehicle came to a full stop, he moved to sit beside Ashleigh and lifted a hidden compartment below his seat.

"They're searching the coaches," he told her. "Get in and hide. It shouldn't be too long until we get past them." She looked as if she wanted to argue, but then his coachman rapped upon the window. "There's no time. Go now."

She climbed inside the compartment, and he gently closed it, replacing the seat. Then he sat upon it and said quietly, "Don't make a sound. I see them coming close now."

Within moments, a man jerked open the door to the coach.

ASHLEIGH KEPT HER knees tucked up while she remained inside the compartment. She could see through a tiny opening, and when the door opened, she heard Mr. Neill say, "What is the meaning of this?"

The man turned and called out, "We've found him!"

Ashleigh tensed, fully expecting the men to haul him away. Instead, Cameron never moved, behaving as if nothing were wrong. A few minutes later, she saw her father's face. She covered her mouth with her hand to avoid making a single sound.

"Where is my daughter?" Cecil demanded.

"Obviously not here," Mr. Neill replied. "Now if you'll be so kind as to remove your men, I'll—"

"You struck me," her father accused. "I ought to have you arrested for assaulting a peer."

"You were causing a scene in public, and you hurt your daughter," he answered. His voice held no fear at all, and he continued, "I merely freed her from you."

"Damn you, I will have you brought on charges of kidnapping."

"As you can see, she is not here. I don't know where she is. Now, you need to go."

"I won't—" her father started to argue, but then his words broke off. Ashleigh couldn't tell if Cameron had shoved him or what had happened, but a moment later, the door closed, and the coach began moving at a swifter pace. Cameron waited a little longer and said softly, "Once we're away from his men, I'll let you out."

"What did you do?" she asked. "How did you get him to leave?"

"With physical force," he answered. "He had no right to intrude on our space."

The coach continued along the road, rattling as it went, and she held on to the wooden seat to keep herself from hitting her head. At last, Cameron moved away and opened the compartment, helping her out. "Are you all right?"

She nodded and adjusted her skirts as she took her seat across from him. "What if he follows us?"

A gleam appeared in his eyes. "He can try. But I'm quite skilled at evading the enemy."

For a moment, he reminded her of a pirate, someone reckless and bold. She'd never met anyone with so many hidden doorways or compartments. Although she ought to be afraid of him, instead Cameron only intrigued her more.

"You're not who I thought you were," she admitted at last.

"Better or worse?"

"I'm not certain." But she continued staring at him, wondering how he was so skilled at evasion. Perhaps he really *was* an outlaw of sorts.

Before she could contemplate it further, he offered her a blanket and a pillow before taking one out for himself. "We'll be out of London soon, and I'm going to rest. You should try to do the same before we reach the countryside. The roads will be rougher. It's hard to sleep then."

"What about tonight?" she wondered aloud.

"We will stay at a local inn. You'll have your own room," he promised.

She believed him. Strangely enough, the more time she spent in Cameron's presence, the more she relaxed. He *had* protected her from being taken by her father again. And somehow, if anyone could rescue her mother, she believed he could do it.

He lay back on his own pillow, arranging himself so he was facing the door. He closed his eyes, giving her the opportunity to study him more closely. He still wore the long blond beard, and his hair rested against the edge of his collar. But his body filled out every inch of his jacket. It was not of fine quality, and it stretched tight upon him. She was starting to realize that he had a muscular form, like a man who had fought in many wars instead of just one. Everything about him reminded her of a fighter. The way he studied his surroundings, fading into the background. The way he could stop her father from beating her in one swift motion, so fast she still could hardly remember how she'd gotten into the hansom cab.

Cameron Neill was far more than she'd anticipated, but as he slept, she looked closer and saw scars on the backs of his hands. They were crisscrossed, almost like deliberate cuts. He'd mentioned being starved as an orphan. Was this a punishment as well? Had someone done this to him?

For a moment, she tried again to imagine him without his beard. He had a strong jawline and those piercing blue eyes didn't miss anything. He wasn't much older than herself, but it seemed as if he'd lived a very different lifestyle, one that made him wary of his surroundings.

He'd guarded her closely, and even when her father had been there, he'd defended her.

She closed her eyes and caught the scent of his skin. Almost a blend of pine, clean soap, and warm, male skin. A sudden flutter slid within her, and she had the sense that if he dropped the disguise, Cameron Neill would be quite handsome indeed.

What if they became more than friends within an arranged marriage? What would that be like?

The journey continued, but Ashleigh couldn't bring herself to fall asleep. Not yet. Instead, she let herself daydream, trying to decide what she thought of Cameron Neill. He seemed to drift into a deep sleep, but there was no peace upon his face—instead, he tensed. His fists clenched, and his breathing grew uneven, as if he were fighting within his dream.

Sweat bloomed upon his forehead, and she realized he was having a nightmare. Never before had he seemed afraid of anything—but in this dream, he appeared to be struggling.

"Mr. Neill, are you well?" she asked quietly, almost fearful of waking him. He didn't answer, but his knuckles whitened as he clenched his hands.

Something made her go to his seat—she couldn't say what it was. But she knelt beside him on the floor of the carriage and took his hand. In sleep, he grasped it like a lifeline. There was a sudden vulnerability about him, as if his past haunted his dreams.

When his breathing grew uneven and shaky, Ashleigh lifted his shoulders to remove the pillow and let his head rest in her lap instead while he held her hand. It was something she'd never done before in her life—getting this close to a man. But he seemed to grow calmer with her presence. She stroked his hair back, and his breathing became steady.

It should have been uncomfortable, or even awkward. Instead, it felt right to offer him comfort after he'd protected her.

For a time, she let him sleep, and his fingers laced with hers. The intimate moment was so unexpected. And yet, she could not deny that it felt good to be close to him. A prickle of apprehension flooded through her, and she studied every part of his features.

Up close, she could tell that he *was* handsome, though he tried to hide it with that terrible beard. She almost imagined what it would be like if she leaned down to kiss him. If he shaved, would his mouth be warm and firm beneath hers? Would he reach up and tangle his hands in her hair, pulling her body against his?

No. She shut the thought away, for he'd said many times that he did not want a true marriage. He wanted them to live apart with separate rooms. Perhaps he still loved his first wife and wanted nothing to interfere with that memory.

The question was, did she want to be wedded to a man who wanted nothing to do with her? At first, she hadn't hesitated—escaping was her only goal. But now, she was uncertain. Perhaps it was best to become better acquainted with Cameron and make the decision later.

But as she tried to close her eyes to sleep, she was afraid of letting herself imagine something more.

THE LIGHT SCENT of hyacinths awoke him from sleep. For a moment, Cameron questioned where he was. Beneath his cheek, he felt silk, and he was holding someone's hand.

He jerked upright before he realized he'd been sleeping in Ashleigh's lap. "Forgive me," he said. "What happened?"

"You were having a nightmare," she said. "You went back to sleep when I held your hand."

Ashleigh moved back to her own seat, her face crimson with embarrassment. For a moment, he was at a loss for words. Clearly, she'd recognized his discomfort and had come to soothe him.

Cameron didn't remember the specifics of the dream, but he was fully aware of his body's response to her nearness. He covered his lap with the blanket to hide the arousal. There was no denying Ashleigh's desirability. Her hair was mussed from the journey, but it only attracted him to her more. No longer was she the perfect debutante with the flawless manners and nobility bred into every line of her body. Instead, she seemed more approachable, almost human. She had reached out to him when the nightmare had disturbed him. He'd never imagined he would sleep in her lap. He had no idea how long he'd been asleep, but her gesture of kindness was like nothing he'd ever expected.

But then, he couldn't allow himself to entertain ideas of a real marriage between them. She didn't want a man like him. She was only using him to escape.

He raised up the invisible iron walls around his emotions. If she agreed to it, he would marry Ashleigh to provide a mother for his son. That was all. He didn't want a true wife or anything else from her. He'd experienced a failed marriage once before. This time, he intended to keep his distance and maintain only friendship between them.

He acted as if nothing had happened and inquired, "Are you hungry at all?"

"A little," she admitted.

"We'll reach the inn soon. In the meantime, there may be some biscuits in one of the tins. Mrs. Cobb packed a great deal of food." He distracted himself by searching for them, but he couldn't deny the reaction to her nearness. He could still smell the floral scent of her skin. When he passed her the tin, his hand brushed against hers. A flash of heat seemed to kindle between them, and he pulled back.

"Would you like one?" she offered.

He took the biscuit, not because he was hungry, but because it prevented him from having to talk. He couldn't remember the last time he'd been this distracted by anyone.

Time passed in companionable silence, and a few hours later, they arrived at the inn. The coachman opened the door, and Cameron stepped outside first to stretch his legs. Then he assisted Ashleigh from the vehicle. She was unsteady on her feet as well but braved a smile. "It's good to walk after so many hours of traveling."

"I'll arrange for a hot meal and rooms for both of us," he offered. "But stay with me until I know it's safe." He wouldn't put it past the marquess to send men to the inns along the main roads. Although Cameron had separated his staff and some would arrive later, his coach would still draw attention.

He led her inside the inn, and several people stared at them. Cameron spoke with the innkeeper and his wife, paying in advance for the two rooms. He lowered his voice and told the matron to bring up hot water so Lady Ashleigh could bathe. Although it was spring, the night air had grown cool, and he thought she might enjoy the luxury of a bath.

"Will you be wanting a meal here, sir, or will you and your wife want the food in your rooms?"

"We will dine together in my room," he said. "If you'll send someone up with it, we'll eat alone."

The innkeeper's wife inclined her head and gave him a candle. He carried it in one hand while Ashleigh took his arm as she accompanied him up the stairs. "One would think you're a nobleman with the way you carry yourself, Mr. Neill. You do know how to give orders."

"I've given my share of them as an officer," he admitted. "Are you comfortable joining me in my room for dinner?"

She nodded. "I'm grateful not to be dining downstairs. I'd rather be away from everyone else."

He understood that feeling well enough. "Your room is next to mine. If you need anything at all, you've only to knock on my door." He unlocked his room and led her inside. There was a small table by the window, and he lit the candle there before lighting the others.

A few minutes later, the innkeeper's wife knocked on the door and called out that she had food for them. Cameron opened it, and she brought them bowls of hot mutton stew with fresh bread and butter, along with two tankards of ale. The innkeeper bent down to light a fire at the hearth. He promised to do the same in Ashleigh's room to make the space warm.

Ashleigh stood by the fire once it was lit, holding out her hands to warm them. Cameron took a seat at the table and asked, "Will you join me?"

She did, and they ate for a time without conversation. She looked as if she wanted to ask questions but was holding back.

"Go on, then," he said. "Ask."

"What was your nightmare?" There was sympathy in her voice, and he tore off a piece of bread, wondering how to answer that. He'd witnessed torture, men dying, and bloodshed. Worst of all were the moments when he'd been unable to save someone. These were the moments that came most often to him in his dreams.

But that was nothing he wanted to share. At last, he decided that a simple answer was best. "War."

She gave a nod and tasted her stew. "How long were you there?"

"Months that felt like years," he admitted. "I'd rather not speak of that time, if you don't mind."

She seemed to understand and didn't press for more. Better to lock those memories away behind invisible bars. Instead, he preferred to ask her lighter questions. "What is your favorite food?"

Her smile turned guilty. "Any kind of sweets. Cake, puddings, biscuits. I love them all. What about you?"

"Warm bread, hot from the oven." The memory of the baker returned, and he thought again of the man's kindness. It had sustained him through years of misery at the orphanage.

"And your least favorite food?" Ashleigh asked.

"I don't care for fish." He'd been sick on it many times as a lad, when he'd eaten fish that had gone bad. But then, he hadn't had a choice in food at the orphanage. They'd been lucky to have much at all. "And you?"

"Porridge. I can't abide the scent or the taste of it."

"My Scottish ancestors might send you back to England if ye do say such a thing. 'Tis naught but a sacrilege," Cameron teased. He deliberately revealed his own accent, and her expression shifted.

"Mr. Neill, are you . . . a Scot?" Her question held surprise, but she didn't seem upset by it.

"I am." He dropped his English accent and admitted, "My true surname is MacNeill. I suppose my servants probably gave that away. I learned quickly that the *ton* despises any Scot who doesn't have a title. I disguised my speech, for they couldnae abide it."

"I thought you were English."

"When I was hardly more than a wee bairn, they sent me to a cousin who brought me to the orphanage in northern England. He didna wish to have the care of me."

"He abandoned you?"

"Aye, that he did." He shifted his speech pattern and continued, "So, I learned to speak like the English. But when I was thirteen, I made my way back to Scotland."

"Alone?" she asked. "How did you survive?"

"I paid a visit to the cousin who abandoned me," he said. "I had planned to work as a hired lad and reveal myself later. But Fate had a way of giving my cousin what he deserved. He died of a wasting disease, penniless." He drank his ale and then added, "I inherited his house, took what was left of it, and made it my own." And then, after he'd gone off to war, he'd rented it out. He'd used the profits, along with his meager salary, to buy another. And on again, over and over. Until at last, the Queen had rewarded him for his years of service by granting him the castle he'd truly wanted.

In fairness, Her Majesty hadn't really known much about

Kilmartin. It was in the Highlands, and the previous residents could no longer afford to take care of it after their chief had died. Cameron had asked for permission to buy it, and it had been granted. The people had appointed him Chief of Kilmartin after he'd offered to rebuild the castle and lands, and they'd pretended that he had a true claim because of his Scottish heritage. In all honesty, he suspected it was because of his money and the Queen's favor. His wealth had transformed their hardships, and the people had been grateful that he'd had enough to buy food and livestock. He understood what it was to starve, and no one had ever gone hungry under his leadership.

To be truthful, he didn't know what laws they'd twisted or what imaginary titles the Queen had bestowed to make it happen, but Kilmartin had been his home for the past seven years. He'd spent a fortune restoring it, and he'd earned the respect of his clan. When he died, he hoped the people would appoint Logan as the new chief.

Ashleigh took a sip of her own ale and winced at the taste. Then she passed it to him. "Take my ale, if you want it."

"Aye, lass."

She steepled her hands and studied him. "You've kept a lot of secrets. Your Scottish heritage, your life in an orphanage—it makes me wonder what sort of man you are."

He set aside his cup and leaned closer. "One who's had to fight to get what he wants." Nothing had ever been handed to him. He'd clawed his way out of poverty, using his wits and his instincts. He'd even fought for his education, learning to read and write at the age of thirteen.

Her blue eyes stared back at his before she blushed and looked away. "Have you done things that were against the law?"

"Many times." He spread jam over his toast, not apologizing for it. "I did what I had to do to survive. And then I did what I was commanded to do, as a soldier, and as a loyal subject of the Crown." She seemed unsettled by this, but he preferred honesty.

"If I agree to marry you, how do I know you're not a criminal?" Ashleigh asked.

"I would hardly be invited to gatherings among the *ton*, were I a criminal. I've connections and friends who trust me." When he had gained the Queen's favor, she had made introductions among the nobility. Else, he would never have gained invitations to balls or soirees.

It seemed to put Ashleigh's mind at ease, knowing that he did have friends. "You're right," she admitted. "I'm sorry for the accusation."

"If you'd rather not marry me, you can go back to your father and wed the viscount," he suggested, even knowing she wouldn't. "Or you can take your chances with me."

"You know I can't go back," she said. "That's impossible. But . . . I wouldn't mind staying with you for a little while, getting to know you better."

Though he understood her reasoning, there was more at stake than just this marriage. He didn't want Logan to care for Ashleigh, only for her to change her mind and leave. It wasn't fair to his son. But Cameron didn't know how he would talk her into marrying him immediately. In his mind, this was an arrangement. He would provide her with a home, whatever she needed, and in return, she would look after Logan.

He realized Ashleigh was still waiting for an answer, so he said, "I can grant you a little time." Then he stood from the table and added, "The innkeeper and his wife promised to bring you a hot bath. It may be ready for you now. I'll check."

The look of joy on her face illuminated her beauty. "I would dearly love a bath."

He escorted her to her room, and just as he'd hoped, a steaming tub of water was waiting. There was a towel nearby, and he noticed that one of the servants had already brought up the trunk of clothing he'd purchased for her. "There should be a nightgown and a clean gown in the trunk for you. Will you need a maid? I can ask the innkeeper's wife to help you."

She paused a moment and said, "If you would . . . just loosen my laces, I can do the rest. There's no need to hire a maid."

It was still about money, he realized. She was trying to be frugal. And though he could easily have paid someone, he was caught in a trap of his own making. She believed he had nothing at all because he lacked a title.

Ashleigh turned around, and a memory descended upon him. He remembered unbuttoning Rebecca's gown while she'd silently wept. It had made him feel like a monster, and he never wanted to feel that way again. "Are you certain?" he asked.

"It's all right. You've already said that I have nothing to fear from you."

"Not at all." He started unbuttoning her gown and saw the rise of goosebumps on her skin. The high-waisted gown had only a few buttons, and she wore short stays. The sight of Ashleigh's bare shoulders ignited a forbidden desire. He wanted to press his lips to her skin, to slowly pull out each of the laces until her clothing fell away. But he gritted his teeth and pushed back the longing, trying not to imagine her naked in the tub of water.

He untied her stays and loosened the laces. Once again, his body reminded him how long it had been since he'd been with a woman. After he'd finished, he turned away and strode toward the door. "Lock this behind me. And I'd advise you not to let anyone in unless it's me. We don't know if any of your father's men were among the guests."

She held her dress to her as she turned back. "Thank you, Mr. MacNeill."

"Cameron," he corrected. And when he heard the click of the lock after he closed the door, he could still smell the hyacinth scent of her skin.

Chapter Six

A SHLEIGH LEANED BACK in the bathtub, enjoying the heat of the water. She hadn't realized how cold she was until she immersed herself in the small tub. It was utter bliss. For a while, she washed away the travel grime, but her thoughts drifted back to Cameron.

More and more, she was making questionable decisions. She'd asked him to undress her when she barely knew him. And when his hands had been upon her skin, she couldn't deny the flare of interest. She'd liked it when he'd slid the laces free, loosening the stays. His hands had been warm, almost inviting.

There was no denying his thoughtfulness. Between the food, having her own room, and the hot bath—he'd given her everything she might need.

Still, at every turn, she discovered more secrets. He was a Scot who'd disguised his accent. He'd been an orphan abandoned by his own cousin, and he'd broken the law to survive. He'd openly admitted that he wore the long beard to eavesdrop and remain unnoticed by the *ton*, and there seemed to be endless hidden passageways in his home. What else was Cameron hiding?

The water was cooling down, so Ashleigh reached for a towel to dry off. There was a small trunk in the room, and she opened it, expecting to find other secondhand clothes. Instead, she found a nightgown, and it appeared to be new. The fabric was soft, the stitching perfectly lovely. There were other undergarments as well, along with a new day dress.

They probably weren't new, she told herself. Perhaps they'd simply never been worn by his wife. But when she pulled the nightgown on, she sensed that Cameron had ordered them for her to make her more comfortable.

Her room was warm from the coal brazier, but when she lay down upon the narrow bed, sleep would not come. Instead, she kept thinking about whether or not she would marry him. He'd already proven that he was different from the viscount. His actions were not those of a man who only wanted a dowry or her father's influence. No, this was something else.

Why had he changed his mind about wanting to marry her? At Gunter's, they'd both agreed that they weren't suited. But suddenly, he'd become her rescuer, and she didn't truly understand why. Was it pity? Or had something shifted between them? Ever since the night of the masquerade, he'd done everything to make her comfortable, spending far too much money on her. And what had she ever done for him, aside from letting him sleep on her lap? It made her feel guilty knowing how little she'd given in return. At the very least, she should try to see to his own comforts.

He'd done his best to appear ugly and unkempt to the world, a poor bedraggled gentleman with a terrible beard. And yet he'd protected her at every opportunity.

Once again, she thought of his broad shoulders straining against the cheap material of his jacket. When she'd held his head in her lap, she'd been fully aware of his strength. Behind the mask of his beard was a handsome face, if only he would reveal it.

He held so many secrets . . .

Ashleigh curled up on the bed, wondering why he was so careful to insist on a loveless marriage with no children. Was it because he didn't want to touch her? Or did he have other reasons? Then, too, she wasn't certain about her own feelings.

She couldn't deny the change in her perception of this man. Now, whenever they were close, she felt drawn to him. She didn't understand the unexpected attraction—but she yearned to know more.

She'd asked Cameron to give her time before she made her decision. But now, she was starting to reconsider. He'd taken care of her, anticipating her needs. Never had he pressed her for more—if anything, he'd been careful not to frighten her. She instinctively knew that she would never find another suitor like him. What was she waiting for?

She ought to marry Cameron MacNeill. It didn't matter that he was poor without a title. He'd given her freedom and had respected her wishes. Wasn't that enough?

The urge came over her to tell him, to let him know her thoughts about the matter. It was late, and he might have already gone to sleep. But she wanted to let him know.

Quietly, she went to her door and unlocked it. With a peek into the hallway, she saw that no one was there. She tiptoed barefoot to his room and gave a knock. For a little while, she waited, but there was nothing. Gently, she tried to open the door but found that it was locked.

Oh. He must have gone to sleep. She started to walk back to her room when his door suddenly opened. He wore no shirt, and she was stunned at the sight of his heavily muscled chest and abdomen. This man was no gentleman. He was a lean fighter, and his arms had the same tight strength. She stared at him a moment, disbelieving what she saw. A scar crossed his abdomen, and she itched to touch it, to run her hands over his skin.

Now where had that come from? He said nothing but opened his door wider. Ashleigh stepped inside, suddenly feeling vulnerable. What if he misunderstood her reasons for coming to his room? All of a sudden, she grew more nervous. He was half naked, and she wore only her nightgown and a dressing robe.

"Are you all right?" he asked. "Do you need anything?"

Her skin prickled with awareness, and she went to stand by

his fire. "I'm fine. I—I didn't mean to disturb your sleep."

"You didn't." He walked over, keeping a slight distance between them. "What's troubling you? Would you rather stay here, and I'll sleep on the floor?"

His words conjured up the image of sleeping beside him instead. She'd never done such a thing, but suddenly, the image of lying beside this man, of touching those rigid muscles, sent a rush of heat through her.

"I just . . . came to tell you that I changed my mind. I don't need to wait—I've made my decision. I will marry you once we reach Scotland."

There was a sudden gleam in his eyes before he masked his emotions. He didn't ask why she'd changed her mind, either. "Good. I'll send someone ahead to make the arrangements. It will be legal, I assure you."

Her throat had gone dry, and she returned to the table where they'd eaten supper earlier. She reached for the pitcher and poured ale, even though she didn't like it. The first sip wasn't any better, but she forced herself to drink.

"Ashleigh," he said quietly. It was the first time he'd ever used her first name, and it deepened her feeling of intimacy between them. "There's no reason to be afraid of me. I won't harm you."

"I know." But her voice held nerves she hadn't expected. Not because she was afraid of him forcing his way into her bed, but because she was afraid of her own feelings. A marriage to Cameron would indeed be safe and comforting. But with every moment she spent with him, she was starting to want more. She wanted to love someone and be loved in return. And hope was a dangerous emotion.

"I just—thought I should tell you."

He took her hand and held it a moment. "I'm glad you did." In the firelight, his blue eyes were almost violet, and she couldn't deny that she wanted him to kiss her. In spite of everything, she wanted to know if this unexpected spark was something he felt as well. She squeezed his hand, and he smiled before letting go of her hand. "I will see you in the morning."

It was the right answer, but she felt a pang of disappointment. He walked her to the door and asked, "Do you have everything you need?"

Not at all. She needed to be held right now, to be in his embrace. She wanted his hands in her hair, and she wanted to press her cheek against his heart.

But instead, she nodded. "Good night."

He waited until she had opened her own door and closed it behind her. After she locked the door, she wanted to curse herself. She didn't know what she'd expected, but it wasn't being sent to her room.

Ashleigh sat on the bed with her knees drawn up for a while. Then she lay back in bed, but her attention was distracted. In the darkness, she got beneath the covers, letting her imagination drift. She thought again of Cameron's hands upon her skin and the warmth of his touch. If he ever decided to consummate the marriage, she had no doubt he would never hurt her.

Instead, she suspected he would only tempt her. She thought of him again, and this time when she closed her eyes, she moved her hand to her own breast. Instantly, the nipple puckered, causing a sweet ache within her. She imagined Cameron touching her there, and the ache deepened between her legs. The sensations were tantalizing, and though she knew she ought to stop, she let her hand drift lower.

What was happening to her? Why was she dreaming of the man in the room beside hers, wanting his touch? She imagined his mouth upon her breast, and when she touched her nipple, she let out a soft gasp. The restless sensations only rose hotter, and when she pressed her hand between her legs, she was wet there. Her breathing grew unsteady, and when she touched herself, a storm of desire seemed to awaken.

Abruptly, she jerked her hand away, afraid of what she felt. She gripped the coverlet, squeezing her eyes shut tighter as she pushed away the sensation of impatient need. Though it took hours, finally she started to fall asleep. Even so, she could not deny her regret that she was alone in this bed.

Scotland

IT WAS LATE morning, and they had finally crossed into Scotland after many more days of traveling. Cameron had sent a few servants on horseback to ride ahead and make the necessary wedding preparations. Though he'd had time to make his plans and write out the instructions for his staff, he still felt a sense of wariness. In his first marriage, he'd been an eager young man, enchanted by Rebecca's beauty and her gentle ways. At the time, he'd believed he was in love with her.

This marriage was entirely different. He and Ashleigh were practically strangers and would remain so. Although she might be startled by the news of his son, he hoped she would come to love Logan as her own. In turn, he would grant her every wish. He'd spent a good deal of money to begin showing Ashleigh the sort of life he would give to her.

She would have a large estate, fine gowns to wear, and everything she could possibly want. Except a husband in truth.

After that first night, he'd sensed the danger of getting too close to her. The only way to curb his rising desires was to stay away from Ashleigh. He'd been careful to maintain the space between them on the remainder of their journey.

The coach came to a stop in front of the inn, and her expression turned confused. "We're not at your home yet?"

"No. But we've arrived at the place where we will be married. We're now in Scotland," he informed her.

"Oh." Her cheeks grew pink, and she looked downward. "I didn't realize we were—that is, I thought there was more time before we would wed."

"Have you changed your mind?" he asked.

"No." But it was as if she had to force herself to look at him. Cameron reminded himself that she didn't want to be married to him any more than Rebecca had. But he would do whatever he could to make the wedding better than a hasty elopement over a blacksmith's anvil. Many couples at Gretna Green had fled together and had been married by a blacksmith. Legend had it that if the bride and groom touched the anvil, it brought fortune and happiness.

He didn't know if Ashleigh held any faith in such beliefs. But when the footman opened the coach door, he helped her out.

"I've made all the arrangements you requested, sir," his footman said. "Lady Ashleigh's room is prepared, and we've done as you asked."

"Good."

"What sort of preparations?" she asked.

"I sent two of the men to ride on horseback ahead of us, to arrange our wedding. I thought you might wish to change your gown and refresh yourself before the ceremony."

A look of bewilderment crossed her face. "That's very kind of you. But I can wear the gown I have on."

"I bought a wedding gown for you in London," he admitted. "It was meant as a gift."

"Then you believed I would agree to marry you." In her voice, he heard a twinge of wariness.

"I hoped you would," he corrected. A sudden rise of nerves caught him unexpectedly, and he didn't know why. Perhaps it was because he wanted to believe that this marriage would be better. "But if you do not like the gown, you need not wear it."

He offered his arm, and Ashleigh took it. With each step, she seemed to grow more flustered.

"Our wedding is to take place in a few hours," he told her. "You've time to rest, or if you wish to have a bath, they can bring one to you. You've only to ask."

"Thank you," she murmured.

He led her inside, and the innkeeper brought them to their

rooms. "I hope all is to your liking, Chief MacNeill. Tell me if ye need anything at all."

"Chief?" she queried.

"Pay it no heed," he said. He hoped she would disregard the title. When he led her to her room and opened it, there were flowers everywhere. Bluebells, heather, and gorse. There was even a posy of roses, though he didn't know where they'd found them. Her wedding gown rested upon a chair, a deep blue that would contrast against her red hair and pale skin.

"Oh, Cameron," she breathed. "Where did all the flowers come from? They're so beautiful."

Her reaction pleased him greatly, but he suddenly felt ill at ease, as if she'd misinterpreted his gesture. "It's nothing. I only wanted you to have flowers for your wedding. I'll leave you now to your preparations."

He turned to go, but he heard her call out, "Wait. A moment please."

When he turned back, she embraced him. "Thank you for your thoughtfulness." The hug startled him, and he knew he'd stiffened up when her arms went around his neck. He couldn't remember the last time a woman had voluntarily embraced him, and he caught the hyacinth scent of her skin once again.

"You're welcome," he managed before he extricated himself and left her room. He opened the door to his own room and stared at the wedding suit that lay upon the bed. He'd worn the same blackcloth jacket and breeches to his first wedding, along with the red waistcoat.

What in hell was he doing? Already he was regretting the flowers and the gown. He had done it to make a good impression on her, to lift her spirits before he dropped the truth upon her. Instead, she might mistakenly believe that he wanted her to love him.

He sat down, resting his forehead in his hands. Memories of the emotions he'd felt on his last wedding day crashed into him. He'd held such hopes for a life with Rebecca. On the day they'd spoken their vows, she'd worn a pale yellow gown with a crown of white roses and her veil. She'd wept what he'd believed were tears of happiness. Now, he knew that she'd never wanted to be married to him.

Ashleigh doesn't want you either, the voice inside reminded him. He was providing an escape, and in return, she wanted her mother's safety. Thus far, he'd heard nothing about his efforts to help Lady Rothburn. He could only hope that the matron had decided to seize the opportunity he'd offered.

With a sigh, he reached for his clothing, hoping he wasn't about to make another mistake. Though he wanted to believe that this time was different, he didn't know. A feeling of uncertainty flooded through him, weighing him down with doubts.

He paused and caught a glimpse of his reflection in the looking glass. For a moment, he wondered if he ought to shave. He ran his hands over his beard, questioning the decision. Ashleigh had asked him to shave it, and he knew it made him look terrible. It added years to his age, but more than that, it provided another barrier between them. So long as he looked this way, she would never want more from him. She would be grateful not to have his touch. And at least, with this marriage, he would not disappoint his wife in the bedchamber.

For they would not be together at all.

LATER THAT MORNING, Ashleigh heard the knock on her door, and she rose from her chair. She wore the new gown Cameron had left for her, and she carried a posy of pink roses, heather, and bluebells. She'd decided not to wear her jewels from the ball on the night she'd run away. Somehow it felt like an insult to the efforts Cameron had put forth.

And he *had* done a great deal for her. The gown, the flowers—the way he'd been careful not to ask anything of her. She'd never imagined a man could be so thoughtful. But when she'd hugged him in gratitude, he'd seemed taken aback by the affection.

The more she thought of it, the more she believed he was unaccustomed to it. He'd been so careful to keep his distance, not to make her feel cornered or threatened in any way. Somehow, that courtesy had only drawn her closer to this man. She had a gut-deep instinct that Cameron would never harm her, would never do anything to make her feel uncomfortable.

She wanted to do something for him in return. But what? He lived such an ordinary life, revealing almost nothing about himself. All she could think of was offering a delicious wedding feast. And so, she'd spent a few of her own coins, asking the innkeeper's wife to prepare a special meal.

A knock sounded on the door, and she rose from her chair. Her nerves roiled in her stomach, and she wished her mother could be with her now. Georgina would have loved the ceremony, and Ashleigh had no idea whether the marchioness had managed to leave her husband. She suspected not.

But perhaps they could find a way. After she married Cameron, her father could no longer control her life. It wouldn't stop him from trying to annul the marriage, however. She could only hope that they would travel far into the Highlands where Cecil could not find them.

He can't annul the marriage if there is a child, her brain suggested. Before she could think on it further, she heard Cameron asking from outside, "Are you ready?"

She pushed away all thoughts and answered, "Come in."

He opened the door and stared at her as if transfixed. Ashleigh felt the color rush to her cheeks, but she walked to his side and tucked her gloved hand in the crook of his arm. "You look lovely." Then he switched into his Scottish dialect and added, "Verra bonny indeed."

His words had the intended effect, and she smiled. "You look fine as well, Cameron."

He rubbed the beard, and she caught a mischievous glint in

his eyes. It was almost a subtle challenge. One day he would shave off his beard, Ashleigh decided. She longed to see his true face. But his blackcloth coat and crimson waistcoat were eye-catching.

"Shall we go and be married?" Cameron asked.

"Yes." She took a deep breath and walked alongside him.

He led her outside and paused a moment. "You'll find that . . . my kinsmen have many superstitions. When we walk forward, you mustn't turn back. Keep your gaze ahead of us, and don't be turning your head."

Ashleigh hid her amusement. "So, it's bad luck, is it?"

"Disaster of the worst sort." Though his expression remained solemn, she detected a glint of humor in his eyes. She was surprised to see a large gathering of local villagers and some of their servants. There was a clergyman and . . . a blacksmith's anvil? She had no idea why that was there, but she supposed it was some sort of Scottish tradition.

"There are so many people here," she murmured.

"We Scots enjoy a celebration," he answered. "And I invited them to share in our food." He led her toward the waiting clergyman, and the people moved in closer to watch. She saw Mrs. Cobb, the housekeeper, and wondered how the woman had managed to meet up with them so swiftly. The servants must have traveled from London on the same day they'd left, in order to join them.

As the wedding began, strangely Ashleigh's nerves dissipated. She couldn't say why, but somehow this marriage felt right, as if she were marrying a friend. Cameron took her hands in his as he spoke his vows, and in his blue eyes, she saw the sincerity there. He would never forsake or harm her in the way her father had. He was a good man—she could feel it in her bones. And though she didn't know how they would save her mother or what sort of life she would have in Scotland, she made a vow of her own—to somehow find happiness in this marriage and to make Cameron happy as well.

Her smile was genuine as she spoke her wedding vows. He surprised her with a large sapphire ring and a gold band for her third finger. Before she could realize she didn't have a ring for him, he gave her a gold band to slide on his own finger. And when he leaned in to kiss her cheek, she felt a twinge of regret that it hadn't been a real kiss.

She didn't understand the turmoil of emotions, the sudden sense of longing. Where had that come from? He kept her hand in his, and a warmth spread over her.

Then she saw one of the servants pick up a large hammer, and he struck the anvil so hard that Ashleigh flinched as it rang out. The villagers cheered, and Cameron leaned in close to her ear. "The sound of the anvil seals our marriage and will bring us good fortune."

She laughed, and then bagpipes began to play a lively tune. Several men and women joined hands and started to dance. Ashleigh felt the joy rise up within her, followed by guilt that her mother was not here. It seemed almost wrong to be happy when Georgina was still trapped. Cameron took her by the waist and spun her around.

Ashleigh knew none of the steps, but it didn't matter. She stumbled, and several of the guests joined hands with her. It was unlike anything she'd ever experienced.

"My wedding ring is beautiful," she said.

"It belonged to my grandmother. No one has worn it since she died." He raised her hand up, and she admired it. Part of her was secretly glad to know that it hadn't been his first wife's.

"I feel terrible that I forgot to buy a ring for you," she apologized. "You shouldn't have had to provide your own wedding band. It's my fault, but everything was so sudden."

"It doesn't matter. I had my grandfather's ring that fits me well enough."

She took his hand and studied it. "So you didn't wear your former wedding ring."

He shook his head. "I would rather have a new beginning." In his eyes, she saw a flare of sudden emotion before he masked it. Almost as if he'd . . . wanted to marry her.

Her own feelings were skittish, and yet she was hopeful. There was a chance that they could make a good marriage together. And her own hopes rose higher at the thought of finding happiness with this man.

Before she knew what was happening, people were bringing out tables of food and drink. Even children were joining in with the dancing, and there were fiddlers who played with the piper.

She danced until she was out of breath, and Mrs. Cobb came forward, carrying drinks. "You'll both be thirsty, I'd wager."

"Thank you so much." Ashleigh took a drink, expecting ale, but instead tasted a sweet mead. It was better than she'd imagined.

"Married in blue, love ever true," Mrs. Cobb remarked with a smile and a wink. Then an older man whisked her away to dance, and she joined in the merriment.

Ashleigh felt a blush rise to her cheeks, but she said to Cameron, "The gown is quite beautiful. I hope it won't cause you any hardship with the expense."

"'Tis bad luck for a bride to wear a gown that isn't new," he said. "I wouldn't risk it."

She took his hand in hers. "I am grateful for all that you've done for me, I want you to know that. The rescue, the clothes, this wedding." All around her, she heard whistles and cheers. Ashleigh knew what it meant, so she stood on tiptoe and drew his face down to hers. She kissed his mouth for the first time, and the Scots applauded.

At first, she'd only meant it to be a quick kiss of thanks, but he caught her waist and held her for a moment. His beard and mustache were softer than she'd imagined, and he deepened the kiss. In that moment, everything seemed to fall away—all the deceptions, the secrets he held—and she was fully aware of the hard planes of his body. The kiss was pure heat, igniting her senses, and making her crave more.

He broke away from her and smiled, but it didn't meet his eyes. She felt as if she'd done something wrong, though she didn't know what it was. He leaned in and against her ear murmured, "Excuse me for a moment."

Then he released her hand and departed, leaving her to wonder what had just happened.

CAMERON RETURNED TO the inn, while several of the wedding guests clapped him on the shoulder in congratulations. Though he accepted their good wishes, inwardly, his mood had darkened. He kept up the façade of joviality until he reached the solitude of his room where he closed and locked the door.

He could hardly breathe. Memories assailed him, of his first wedding and all the hopes he'd been foolish enough to feel. He couldn't do that again. Ashleigh's unexpected kiss had awakened a storm of need he thought he'd buried years ago. When her lips had touched his, he'd been unable to stop himself from kissing her back. Even now, his body was alive with desire. He wanted to strip away the silk until he felt her skin beneath his.

It had been so very long since he'd lain with a woman. He'd buried himself in work, suppressing his urges, but one kiss had reminded him of what he'd been missing. And more than that, she had kissed *him* first. It was the kiss of an innocent woman who didn't know what she was starting.

But he couldn't allow it to go further. He didn't want to see her flinch with revulsion if he touched her—nor did he want her to turn away her face to hide the tears when he unintentionally hurt her. Rebecca had hated lovemaking, and he blamed himself for it.

He wished Ashleigh had never initiated the kiss, for it only opened up a Pandora's box of desires. He didn't need or want affection from his new wife. And the sooner she understood that, the better.

Cameron took several moments to calm himself, taking in deep breaths and pushing away the aching lust that had caught him. He would never indulge in it. Even tonight, he would demand that she remain in her own room, regardless of what the others might think.

A soft knock sounded on the door, and he heard her voice. "May I come in?"

He should have expected that she would follow him here. Though instinct urged him to tell her no, he supposed it was better to reestablish the boundaries between them. He went and unlocked the door, holding it open.

The look of concern on Ashleigh's face deepened his guilt, but she entered the room and closed the door behind her. Her beauty and the light in her eyes stole his breath. How on earth this rare creature had agreed to marry him was beyond all understanding. She deserved a far better life than the one he was about to give her. He could only hope that the wealth was a strong substitute for a husband.

"I'm sorry," she began. "I didn't mean to—that is, I shouldn't have kissed you. I let myself get carried away in the moment."

The urge to tell her that it was all right came to his lips, but he forced himself to say, "We need to keep to our agreement. Friends only, nothing more."

Her face fell, but she nodded. "Of course." He could see the disappointment on her face. He hadn't meant to ruin the mood, but he needed to put space between them. The last thing he wanted was to raise her expectations and make her believe that it could be a real marriage. Better to hurt her now than to break her heart later.

"I wanted to ask—is there any word about my mother?" she asked. "Did your men manage to help her?"

He shook his head. "I don't know yet. I may return to London soon to find out. Once you're settled in our home, that is."

"Thank you. I never meant to cause trouble for you in finding her," she said, "nor did I mean to cause hardship from the expense of our wedding. I have a bracelet I could sell, if that would help."

"No, it's not a hardship" he insisted. "I wanted to give you more than just a quick elopement." Especially as a way of atoning for what he was about to do, forcing her into motherhood.

"The wedding meant a great deal to me," she said, offering a smile. "You have given me so much, and I feel like I've given you nothing in return. I still wonder why you even agreed to marry me, after all the difficulties I've caused."

"As I said before, you needed my help. And I will need yours once we reach my home at Kilmartin. There is much to be done there."

"I will do whatever I can to help," she offered. She started to reach out her hand to his, but he didn't take it. Her expression faltered a moment, before she pulled her hand back. He regretted having to deny the affection, but there had been no other choice.

"Do you want to return to the feast?" he asked.

She hesitated and answered, "I suppose we should. Otherwise, the guests will wonder where we've gone."

Actually, the guests most likely knew where they were, though Cameron supposed they would endure teasing for returning. But he offered her his arm and led her down the stairs and outside. There were several knowing looks, but he answered their sly smiles with one of his own. Let them believe he'd carried his bride off for a taste of what was to come.

Someone handed them plates of food, and he brought Ashleigh over to a small table. She tore off a piece of bread, and he offered her cheese. While they ate, one of the Scots approached and asked him, "Should we pass the plate, my chief?"

"Nay," he answered. "Save your coins. I've already paid the piper and fiddlers. Tell everyone that when the feasting is done, all may take a share of the leftover food to their families." The man brightened and thanked him as he left.

"What did he mean by passing the plate?" Ashleigh asked.

"In some weddings, the folk pass the plate, and all will add a penny or two to pay for the musicians and food. All the rest goes to the bride and groom as a gift to begin their lives together." He met her gaze and said, "These people cannot afford any pennies to spare. I'd rather give them our celebration as a gift."

"I agree."

Cameron saw someone serving cups of mead and caught the man's attention. He passed the cup to Ashleigh and took another for himself.

"How far is it to your home?" she asked.

"I live in the Highlands, north of Fort William," he said. "We still have another two days to travel." He let his thoughts drift to his son, and he was eager to see Logan once again. More than that, he was curious as to what the boy would think of Ashleigh. Logan had only known nursemaids, never a mother.

"What should I expect?" she ventured. "Do you have a small staff there? Will I need to learn about farming or sheep or cattle?"

"We'll talk of it once we arrive," he told her. "There's no need to worry about it until then."

She sipped at the mead, but he could tell that her mood had gone pensive. Mrs. Cobb came over to offer them good wishes. In her hands she held a large shortbread cake. "May I, sir?"

Cameron nodded permission, and she spoke a Gaelic blessing before breaking the shortbread cake over Ashleigh's head. Then she gave each of them a small piece before bringing pieces to the other young women.

"Some will put a piece of the cake under their pillows in the hopes of dreaming of their future husbands," Cameron told her.

Ashleigh tried to brush the crumbs from her hair, and he helped her as best he could. But when his hand grazed her face, he grew aware of her skin, and the sudden shock in those blue eyes. His hand lingered on her cheek before he pulled it away.

Even so, he was captivated by Ashleigh's mouth. He wanted to steal another kiss, to taste those lips and lose himself in her.

But it wasn't a good idea. And as he forced himself to turn back to the other guests, he knew he'd have to leave soon.

Otherwise, he might not be able to keep his hands off his beautiful new wife.

ASHLEIGH HAD QUESTIONED whether she would share her husband's room after the wedding. But no, he'd kept his word, and after escorting her to her room, he'd gone back to his. She'd spent her wedding night alone, wondering if this was to be her new life.

He'd warned her that it was a condition of marriage. But part of her truly hadn't believed him. She'd never imagined that they would indeed live entirely separate lives within their marriage. It was almost . . . lonely.

For the next two days, they traveled north to the Highlands, and Ashleigh was beginning to feel as if they'd never reach Cameron's home. Though she'd adored the scenery, with mist-cloaked hills and groves of fir trees that lined the brooks, she was eager to see where they would live. He'd told her nothing at all about their home, thus far. She suspected it would be large enough to accommodate a small staff but smaller than her father's estate at Rothburn.

The coach appeared to be slowing down, and Ashleigh noticed that the road was growing narrower. She peered outside the window but could not see beyond the hedgerows.

"We're nearly there," Cameron admitted. Something about his demeanor seemed tense, almost as if he were looking for her reaction. Was it that terrible, then? Was he about to bring her to a broken-down cottage?

The folk had called him Chief MacNeill. Which meant he did hold a rank, though she wasn't certain whether it was the same as an English title. Did he own a larger manor house with tenants who farmed his lands? She let her imagination wander while the coach turned down another road heavily lined with trees. The shadows made it impossible to see anything, and when they made two more turns down other narrow roads, she was starting to wonder if they would live in the middle of the forest.

But no, they left the trees behind, and she saw a stone wall that lined the edge of land. A two-story cottage lay ahead, and she smiled at the sight of it. It was modest, yes, but large enough.

"Kilmartin is lovely," she said. "Is that ours?"

"Aye, but—"

"It will do quite nicely," she said brightly. And truthfully, it *would* be perfect. In many ways, she wanted to live a simple life. Here, she could be safe, away from the rest of the world. She imagined a small vegetable garden. Perhaps Mrs. Cobb would teach her to cook. It would be a good life, a peaceful one.

"That's not where we'll live," he interrupted.

"Oh." She didn't know what to think about that, but even if this wasn't their home, she would make the best of it. "Then where—"

Her words broke off when the coach continued around the bend. A large lake gleamed in the afternoon sunlight, a deep blue that faded into a rocky beach. In the distance, the water reflected a gray stone castle with six turrets.

Ashleigh's mouth dropped open, for she couldn't help it. "No," she breathed. "You're not serious."

When she looked over at Cameron, there was a mischievous gleam in his eyes. "Welcome to Castle Kilmartin," he said. His smile held triumph of one who was aware he was among the wealthiest men in London. And all the heiresses had snubbed him—Lady Persephone would have died had she known Cameron possessed such a fortune.

Perhaps it made her a terrible person, but Ashleigh felt positively smug. "Tell me you're not lying to me." Though she tried to keep her voice calm, inwardly, she was thrilled. As a girl, she'd dreamed of marrying a fairytale prince and going off to live in a castle.

And now, it seemed she'd done just that. Only Cameron had been a prince in disguise, wearing that terrible beard and ragged clothing. While she'd been worried about whether he was spending too much money on her wedding gown and the celebration, the expense must have been nothing at all to him.

"This is our home," he said as the coach pulled up inside the circle. "The other house is where some of my staff live. One day, perhaps your mother could—"

He never had the chance to finish his sentence when she threw her arms around him and hugged him tightly. "I cannot think of anything more wonderful, Cameron. Thank you so much!" Her exuberance overwhelmed her, and it was impossible to contain her joy.

Cameron had gone stiff beneath her embrace, but Ashleigh didn't even care. She simply couldn't suppress the need to show her happiness. "Forgive me." She released him and admitted, "I need to get all of my excitement out right now before I meet the other servants. I shall have to remain calm as Lady of Kilmartin Castle."

Before he could say another word, she gave a slight squeal of delight and seized his hands. "I don't know whether to be angry with you or overjoyed by the surprise. It's the most wonderful place I've ever seen. I cannot wait to explore every room. Will you show me everything?"

He only nodded, but she took comfort from the fact that he continued to hold her hands in his. "Now do you understand why I needed to wed a noblewoman?" he asked softly.

She grew serious at that. "Yes, I do. You must have a great deal of responsibility." And yet, she couldn't quite understand why he had hidden his wealth. "But you could have married anyone in London. Even Lady Persephone."

"I didn't want to wed a woman who only cares about wealth," he said. "And while I used to think you did, now I know that isn't true."

"No," she agreed. "The only reason I was trying to earn money was for my mother's sake. I would do anything to help her."

"Even wed a man like me?" he suggested. He started to release her hands, but she held them a moment.

"That isn't the reason I married you," she admitted. "You rescued me." She looked into his eyes and said, "Even if we had a house smaller than that cottage, it would be a better life than the one I left behind. I was prepared to live in poverty."

His blue eyes stared into hers, and he gave a somber nod. "I have obligations to the people here, Ashleigh. "And . . ." His voice trailed off as the coach drew to a stop. "Well, we'll get you settled in first before we speak of it."

One of the footmen opened the door, and Cameron exited first, holding out his hands to her. Ashleigh was glad she'd worn a soft plum-colored gown with long sleeves and a high waist. Though it was wrinkled from travel, she was presentable enough. She hadn't expected an estate of this size, but now, she was grateful to her mother for the years of training.

The moment Cameron helped her from the coach, she put on a quiet smile, taking in the sight of everything. She saw the familiar face of Mrs. Cobb, who had once again arrived first, and the older woman spoke to a matron whose gray hair was severely twisted into a tight knot. The matron wore a serviceable navy gown, but from the keys at her waist and the tilt of her chin, it was clear that she was the housekeeper at Kilmartin.

Ashleigh met the woman's gaze with a slight acknowledgment, but she showed no fear. Her mother had warned her that, when meeting staff members for the first time, it was important to be calm and assertive.

The butler offered a friendly smile and stepped forward with a bow. Cameron introduced her, saying, "Lady Ashleigh, may I present our butler, Hamish Kilmartin. Hamish, this is my wife and the new mistress of Kilmartin. See to it that she has everything she needs."

She gave a nod and greeted him, "I am pleased to meet you, Mr. Kilmartin."

"It's just Hamish, my lady," he answered. "All of us are of the Kilmartin Clan, so it makes it easier." He offered her a broad smile.

Next, Cameron introduced her to the housekeeper, Mrs. Carla Kilmartin. The older matron didn't smile, but she gave a quick curtsy, and they continued down the line of staff members. Ashleigh remembered her mother's guidance on how important it was to memorize names, and she did her best to at least learn the names of the older, more senior servants.

"You'll want to hire a ladies' maid," Cameron said quietly, "but Carla can be of help to you in choosing one."

When they reached the end of the servants, she asked him, "Will you take me on a tour of the castle?"

"Later perhaps," he said. "There's something I need to do first. Carla can show you to your room and you can rest before supper, if you like."

She hid her disappointment, wondering what it was that had stolen his attention away. But she tried to smile and act as if nothing were wrong. Cameron motioned to the housekeeper and said, "Please show Lady Ashleigh to her room." To Ashleigh, he said, "If there's anything you would like Cook to prepare for supper, tell Carla, and she will see to it."

Without another word, he hurried inside the house. Ashleigh couldn't understand what was so important that he would leave, but she kept her composure.

"I am glad to meet all of you," she said. "In the next few days, I hope we can become better acquainted." With a nod of dismissal, she returned to Carla. The older housekeeper appeared uncomfortable, but she managed to force her lips into the semblance of a smile.

"If ye'll just follow me, my lady."

Ashleigh did, but as she continued alongside the housekeeper, she turned back to glance at the staff members. They were nearly silent as they returned inside the house.

It seemed strange to realize that she had, quite literally, stepped into a fairytale. She was married to the prince in disguise, living in a castle . . . and somehow, she wanted more. No longer did she want a marriage in name only, with separate rooms and separate lives. She wanted a real marriage with a man she could learn to love.

It was worth fighting for.

Chapter Seven

C AMERON HAD GIVEN strict instructions to his staff not to speak of Logan. He wanted Ashleigh to get adjusted before telling her the true reason he'd married her. But right now, he was eager to see his son. While Ashleigh was off with Carla, he hurried up to the nursery. Logan's nursemaid Mary apologized, saying, "He's sleeping, sir. I would have brought him to meet you, but—"

"No, I'm glad you let him sleep," he murmured. With a nod, he dismissed Mary and slipped inside his son's room. Logan's blond hair was tousled, and he slept outside the covers, while clutching a stuffed bear. Cameron sat down on the bed, his heart aching at the familiar sight of his boy. He'd missed him more than he'd thought possible. Logan was innocence embodied, a child who deserved loving parents.

Not a father like him, who knew nothing about how to care for a young lad. Cameron had tried to give his son a good upbringing with all the comforts he'd never had. But his duties had kept him apart from Logan for many months—and sometimes, he thought that might be a good thing. He didn't want to make mistakes as a father, especially when he knew so little about what made a good parent. When he shifted his weight to get up from the bed, Logan's eyes opened.

Blue eyes stared at him in surprise, and a moment later, Logan crawled into Cameron's lap. He hugged his boy tightly, stroking the child's hair. "Hello, my lad. Did you have a good sleep?"

"Da," Logan said, gripping him in an answering hug. Cameron could see his son's confusion as he struggled to shake off the sleep.

"Do you want Mary to bring you some biscuits? Or milk?"

"I want milk," Logan answered with a yawn. "And biscuits."

"I'll send for some." Cameron started to stand from the bed, but his son refused to relinquish his grip.

"Stay, Da," Logan ordered. "Mary can bring my milk."

He extricated himself from his son's embrace and kissed his forehead. "I will see you later. You'll be wanting to go outside and play in the garden."

His son started to whine in protest, and Cameron walked to the door of the nursery. Mary was waiting outside, and he instructed her to bring milk to Logan, along with some biscuits. As he left, he heard his son starting to cry. He steeled himself against the sound, knowing he shouldn't have interrupted the boy's sleep. But he'd simply had to see his son.

Cameron crossed to the opposite side of the castle and returned to his chamber, needing time alone to figure out what to do next. To his surprise, he found Ashleigh waiting for him.

"I thought you were going to rest."

She gestured toward a teacart. "I asked Carla if she could order food for us. We have tea, sandwiches, and scones with clotted cream and jam. Shall I pour out?"

Cameron's mouth watered at the sight of it. He took a seat on a settee and answered, "I am hungry." But even as he eyed the food, he knew he couldn't avoid telling her about Logan for much longer.

Ashleigh brought him a cup of tea and asked what he wanted to eat. He accepted a scone with cream and jam, but even the delicious food tasted like dust in his mouth. She poured herself tea, and then asked, "I was wondering if we might talk about our marriage rules again. Your expectations and mine."

He sipped his tea and shrugged. "If you wish." Without even knowing it, she was laying the groundwork for him to tell her about his son.

"I know you have many responsibilities, and it will take me time to learn the castle and its needs. Am I correct in understanding that you want me to be Lady of Kilmartin and assume those duties?"

"Aye," he answered, setting the food aside. "And I will ensure that my staff obeys all your orders, whatever they may be."

She rose from her chair and moved to sit beside him on the settee. Her sudden nearness unnerved him, for he'd not expected her to come so close. Her leg was pressed against his, and she turned to him. "I wondered if we could . . . speak openly about other matters."

He didn't know what other matters she was talking about, but he was fully distracted by her touch. The scent of her skin made him yearn to unfasten that gown, to explore her bare body with his hands and mouth.

Damn it all, he needed to gather what was left of his wits and concentrate on their conversation. But then, Ashleigh reached for his hand and brought it to rest on her knee. "I know you said you wanted a marriage in name only. But . . . I wanted to ask why." Her cheeks flushed, and she continued, "Did something happen with your wife?"

The heat of her body was a distraction he hadn't expected. Although she probably meant nothing by it, she continued to rest her palm against his hand. His throat went dry with longing, and a rushing sound seemed to fill his ears. He could feel the round shape of her kneecap beneath her gown, and he imagined sliding his hands beneath the hem to explore her bare skin. Unholy desires and visions coursed through him, and he hardly knew how to answer.

"How did she die, Cameron? Did she grow ill?"

He shook his head. His thoughts had grown scattered, and he was fighting the desire to steal a kiss. Right now, he was holding on to his control by a thread, and she held the power to snap it.

"She . . ."

Ashleigh moved her hand to rest on his heart, and he covered her fingers with his. Then he faced her and admitted, "It's my fault Rebecca lost her life. She died in childbirth."

BENEATH HER HAND, his heart was pounding. She could feel his response and knew he was not immune to her touch. But the tragedy of his wife's death made so much more sense now. If he had lost her during childbirth—and blamed himself for it—of course he would not want to love a woman.

She moved her hand higher, to rest upon his shoulder. "I'm so sorry."

He held her hand for a moment before releasing it. "I don't want to get a woman pregnant again. Watching Rebecca die . . . and knowing she wouldn't have died if I'd never touched her . . ."

"You mustn't blame yourself," Ashleigh said. "What happened was a tragedy, but it wasn't your fault."

"It was," he argued. "Rebecca would have preferred the marriage you and I have—one in name only. Instead, I wanted more from her. I wanted her to share my bed, and I thought she would learn to love me. But she didn't and, in the end, it cost her everything."

Ashleigh was beginning to realize that this would be more difficult than she'd thought. His reasons for not wanting a true marriage were grounded in fear. And if he'd truly loved his first wife, she didn't know if he would ever feel anything for her.

"Believe me when I say it's better if we have a marriage only as friends," he said. "I would never want anyone to suffer what she suffered."

Ashleigh wanted to offer comfort, but she didn't. Instead, she tried to regroup her thoughts. "I understand that now. And your reasons do make sense." Even if they were extreme, she could sympathize with his tragedy of watching his wife and child die. "In some ways, I can see why you were reluctant to wed again."

She took a breath. "But what do you intend to do about Kilmartin? You will need an heir. And if I do not give you one, then how . . . ?"

His gaze turned sober, and he stood. "Come with me. I've something to show you."

She was curious but rose from the settee. "Another hidden passageway?" It was meant in teasing, but he didn't react. Which likely meant that there were indeed hidden rooms.

Instead, Cameron offered his arm and led her back into the hall. They walked to the other side of the castle, and he brought her to a winding set of stairs and then to one of the upper levels. Her heart began pounding, for she had the sense that he was leading her toward the nursery.

He opened the door and inside the room she saw a small boy sitting in his nursemaid's lap. The moment he saw Cameron, he bolted from the woman and ran, throwing his arms around Cameron's legs. "Da!" he called out.

In an instant, everything became clear. A sudden fear iced through her, along with the realization that she'd completely misunderstood Cameron's intentions. He had no need of an heir because he already had one. But why hadn't he told her? His secrecy felt like its own betrayal.

"Logan, I want you to meet someone," he told the boy, lifting him into his arms. "This is Lady Ashleigh. And she will be your new mother."

The frozen feeling spread all within her, numbing her emotions. The child never even looked at her, for he'd buried his face in his father's neck.

"This was why you married me," she whispered.

"Yes." His voice was clear and calm, making no effort to disguise his motivations. But Ashleigh had no one to blame but herself. She'd placed him in the role of a disguised prince, believing that she had wandered into her own fairytale. Yet he'd told her, from the very beginning, that he didn't want a real wife. Now it seemed he simply wanted a lady to be in charge of his castle while he was away and a mother for his son. But why would he withhold the truth about his own child from her? The shock permeated her, shattering her image of what their life would be.

"I will be leaving for London soon," he said. "I will find out what I can about your mother and whether my men managed to help her escape."

His words only confused her more. Though she was grateful that he had not abandoned her request to help Georgina, it felt as if he were abandoning her with his son. And she knew nothing about children or what to do.

"Thank you," she managed, though inwardly her emotions were tangled up. She wanted to be angry with him for this, but she was the one who had spun the tale wrong.

He tried to turn the boy to face her, but Logan kept his arms firmly attached to his father. In the end, Cameron gave up and said, "I'll leave you to become better acquainted with my son for now. I will see you at supper tonight."

He started to lower the boy, but Ashleigh said, "Wait." When he met her gaze, she asked, "Why didn't you tell me about your son before?"

"Because you never would have married me if you'd known my reasons," he answered honestly. "But it was a bargain you agreed to. You needed help, and I gave it. In return, you have everything you could ever want—a castle of your own, money, and servants. All I ask is that you be Logan's mother."

"We should talk of this more in private," she said. "Not in front of your son."

"Perhaps." With that, he held out the boy to her.

Ashleigh couldn't bring herself to take the child—for she sensed that he would not like being held by a stranger. And so

Cameron lowered the boy to sit upon a rocking horse. Then he left the room and closed the door behind him.

The boy began to cry, and Ashleigh fully understood that emotion. She wasn't ready to become a mother—not yet. And it did seem like Cameron was running away. Logan obviously wanted his father, and he ran to the door, pounding on it. Within a moment, his nursemaid returned. She was startled to see Ashleigh there, and she apologized, "Forgive me, my lady. I didn't know you were with him."

"It's all right," Ashleigh said.

"Would you like me to stay with the young master?" the nursemaid offered. Ashleigh considered it for a moment, for she had her own urge to go off and grieve the loss of the fantasy she'd imagined. But what good would that do? Crying would solve nothing at all.

She sympathized with the little boy who had been left behind, time and again. If someone had locked her in a room within a castle, she'd be howling, too.

So she refused. "No, I don't think so." Instead, she leaned down to the crying boy. Though she knew nothing at all about raising a child, perhaps taking him out of this room, providing a distraction, would stop his tears. "Should we go and find your father? Or perhaps you could show me the garden?"

Logan's tearstained face suddenly looked up at her. In those blue eyes, she saw the mirror of Cameron. His crying stopped, and he nodded, holding out his hand to hers. She took it, and it startled her to realize how small his hand was in hers.

"Wait a moment," she told him. To the nursemaid, she asked, "What is your name?"

"Mary, my lady."

"Does Master Logan have a handkerchief, Mary?"

The nursemaid went to a small chest of drawers and pulled one out. "Here we are." She leaned down and helped the boy dry his tears and blow his nose. "Shall I come with you on your walk, my lady?"

Though she suspected the nursemaid was trying to help—and really it was wise to bring her along—Ashleigh refused. "No, thank you." To Logan, she asked, "Can I rely on you to protect me? Do you have your sword if we need it?"

At that, he started laughing. "No! I'm too little."

Then he put his hand in hers and pulled her toward the door. "I want to go outside."

Me too, Ashleigh thought. But before they departed, Mary said, "Lady Kilmartin—it's very glad I am that you've come. Our chief and our young lad . . . the years have no' been easy."

Ashleigh gave a nod, and then opened the door, leading the boy outside his room. From his posture, she could tell that he was eager to run, and she asked him to lead her to the garden. He started to pull on her hand, but she slowed down. "I can't run as fast as you. Can you be a gentleman and walk with me?

He slowed his steps and walked alongside her. But as they made their way toward the garden, Ashleigh let her thoughts wander. Cameron had married her to be a mother to Logan. His travels took him away often, and the boy was desperate to be with his father. Something wasn't right. She couldn't quite tell what it was, but she could see Cameron loved his son. And yet, he seemed afraid to be fully a part of his son's life. Was it because Logan reminded him too much of his first wife? Or was it something else entirely? She didn't know.

But the more she thought of it, the more she was starting to believe that perhaps Cameron didn't understand what love was. After being abandoned as a child and widowed after his first marriage, he'd lost nearly everyone in his life. His insistence on a marriage in name only might be because he was afraid to love her—or anyone.

Her heart ached as she wondered whether there was any hope at all for their marriage to transform into a true one. She didn't know when or how her feelings had shifted, but she sensed that their life could be happy if Cameron would only consider it. He had done so much for her, giving her a life where she no longer had to worry about her father's rage. For the first time, she felt safe. And even though he had forced her into unexpected motherhood, it was a small price to pay for the sanctuary he'd given. It terrified her to reach out to him, for it was quite likely he would continue to spurn her.

But she simply had to try.

CAMERON STAYED WITHIN his study. He hadn't missed the look of betrayal in Ashleigh's eyes. But at least now she knew the truth. Although he had no wish to discuss it further, he supposed he couldn't avoid it indefinitely.

He studied his ledgers, noting that his estate manager had kept everything in order. All expenses were accounted for, all assets neatly tallied. Kilmartin was profitable, and his tenants had all that they needed.

Another letter lay waiting upon his desk. Although there was no name upon the letter, the burgundy seal told him what lay within. He broke the seal and found orders to return to London. The missive told him of several French officers captured at Waterloo last summer who had been brought to the Tower. He was needed to join them in prison and learn what he could about English prisoners of war or any further threats to the Crown.

So be it. He would leave within a few days. A grim sense of foreboding filled him, for he knew what lay ahead. Becoming a convincing spy meant that even the London guards would not know of his true loyalties.

He set the letter aside and stood from his desk. Though he didn't know how long he would be imprisoned, he intended to enjoy his last moments of freedom. He left his office and walked to the opposite end of the castle to the door that led to the terrace. The wide steps led down to the garden where a large fountain stood in the middle. His gardener was busy tending the beds, and several rose bushes were blooming. For a moment, he breathed deeply and drank in the sight of the peaceful flowers.

He walked down the steps toward the fountain, committing the scene to memory. Soon enough he would only smell the fetid odors of the Tower. He pushed back the dark thoughts and walked deeper into the garden. The sound of water splashing against the pool brought an air of calm. He continued past the hedgerows, until he reached a stone bench near one of the willow trees.

He'd done what he'd set out to do. He'd chosen a wife to govern Kilmartin in his absence. Ashleigh would become Logan's mother and give him the love and stability he needed. It was enough.

But the unrest crept beneath his skin at the thought of what lay ahead. They wouldn't know why he'd disappeared or why he wouldn't answer letters. He told himself that as long as he kept his distance from Ashleigh, she wouldn't miss him. He could be assured that she was safe and taken care of. And she would never know where he was.

The sound of a child's laughter broke through his dark mood. He remained behind the hedgerows but saw Ashleigh and Logan walking toward the fountain. She let him run around the garden, and the smile on her face warmed Cameron's spirits.

He'd made a good choice of a wife. Though she looked slightly uncertain, it was clear that Logan was enjoying himself. His son climbed up the fountain and began splashing the water. Ashleigh started to move toward him, and without warning, Logan splashed water over the front of her dress. For a moment, she looked horrified. Then his wife dipped her hand in the water and splashed him back. His son's face wrinkled up with surprise before he let out a belly laugh.

"I'm going to get you," Ashleigh warned. "You'd better run."

Logan laughed again and took off in the opposite direction. He rounded the corner and blinked in disbelief. "I found you, Da!" he crowed.

"Yes, you did," Cameron answered. "But I don't think you

can catch me." With that, he pretended to run away. Ashleigh caught up to them and watched with a smile as Logan continued trying to chase him. In the end, Cameron scooped him up and tossed him into the air before catching him again. "It seems I've caught you, instead." He ruffled his son's hair and met Ashleigh's gaze.

"I thought he would enjoy a walk," she said. "Do you want to join us?"

At first, he considered refusing. But then he reconsidered and decided there was no harm in spending the day with his family. God only knew when he would be permitted to return to Scotland. "All right," he said, setting Logan down. His son began to run ahead of them, laughing.

He walked alongside Ashleigh for a time before she said, "You should have told me."

"We both know you never would have agreed to the marriage." He saw no point in belaboring the issue.

"You don't know that," she said. "But you should have been honest with me. At least then, I would have known what to expect."

There was nothing he could say to change what he'd done, and truthfully, he held no regrets, deceptive as it was. Within only an hour, Ashleigh had proven that she could rise to the challenge of motherhood.

They continued walking along the gravel pathway while Logan ran and laughed. He stumbled and fell on his knees once, and before Cameron could reach him, Ashleigh lifted him up. For a moment, his son appeared confused on whether to cry, so Cameron reassured him, "You're fine, my lad. Go and play."

Ashleigh released him, and Logan continued on. Cameron moved to her side and said, "I'll be leaving for London within a few days."

"So soon?" Her voice held dismay. "Or is this about my mother?"

He didn't tell her the true reason why but let her draw her

own conclusions. "I'll find out whatever I can." It was true—both about her mother and about his work for the Crown.

"Do you think my father will find me here?"

He could hear the fear in her tone and answered, "I doubt it. Your father and most of London believe that I'm a merchant. There's little chance of him coming this far north."

"Will you ever tell me what it is you truly do?" she asked softly. "Or is that another secret you intend to keep from me?"

He didn't answer but kept his gaze fixed upon his son. She took his hand in hers, which startled him. "Cameron, I want to make this marriage a good one. Can you at least meet me halfway?"

"Some secrets are not mine to tell," he answered at last. He stopped walking and looked at her without saying a word.

Her eyes met his, and then she gave a single nod. "How long will you be gone?"

His only answer was to squeeze her hand for there was no way to know. Her expression held consternation, and as a distraction, he asked, "Do you find Kilmartin to your liking?"

"It's lovely," she answered. "But I would like to understand more about how to govern the estate in your absence. I need to know about the rents, the crops, anything you can tell me."

"We can go over it tonight," he offered. He was grateful for her willingness to take command. The more time he spent with Ashleigh, the more he realized how lucky he was that she had agreed to wed him. As the daughter of a marquess, she had been trained to manage an estate of this size, and her natural instincts for motherhood were outstanding.

It occurred to him that he should arrange a wedding gift of sorts. But as they continued to walk, he realized that the best gift he could give her was her mother's freedom. Somehow, he would find a way to make that happen.

They continued to walk along the garden path, and though he should have released her hand, he could feel her holding his. There was an undeniable connection. Had it not been for his previous marriage, he might have fallen into the trap of believing this marriage could be more than friendship.

But he would not take that risk again.

ASHLEIGH TOSSED AND turned in her bed, unable to sleep. She couldn't say what it was that had awakened her, but she suspected it was being here in this unfamiliar castle. She wanted to have a true conversation with Cameron about his son, but he'd rebuffed her earlier attempts. They also hadn't discussed estate management yet, though she had wanted to ask more questions.

Though it was entirely improper to seek him out at this hour, clad only in her nightgown, she decided to take the risk. Especially since he was leaving so soon. She took a candle and slipped outside her room. The halls were quiet, but she found her way to the opposite side of the castle. His door was locked, and she knocked softly.

No answer.

She faltered a moment, wondering if she should return to her room. But then she heard what sounded like a groan. It reminded her of the moment when he'd had a nightmare in their coach. She tried the door of the room beside his and found that it opened easily. From the soft rose colors and the furnishings, she suspected it had belonged to his first wife.

There was an adjoining door, and thankfully she found it unlocked. Quietly, she opened it and slipped inside his room. The fire had died down, and in the dim light, she saw that he was gripping his pillow.

"Cameron," she whispered. But he gave no answer.

She drew closer and saw that he was not wearing a nightshirt. Possibly he wasn't wearing anything at all. In the firelight, she saw his muscled torso, and it made her mouth go dry. She saw the scar across his stomach again, noting that every part of this man's body was lean and strong. She had the urge to run her fingers over his skin, to discover more. With each day she spent with him, she learned more of his secrets.

And now she was convinced he was a spy. It was the only explanation for his mysterious ways. He would tell her nothing about what he did—but how else could he have gained so much wealth? How else would he be a man of such strength?

His breathing was unsteady, and she decided it might be unwise to awaken him. Instead, she moved to the opposite side of the bed and sat beside him for a moment. He was sweating, his body tensed from the nightmare. Though he might be angry at her, Ashleigh couldn't simply stand aside and do nothing. Instead, she lay beside him and drew her arm around his waist with the offer of silent comfort.

Cameron gripped it like a lifeline, and she held him. He pressed her hand to his heart, and she could feel it racing. Whatever nightmare he was dreaming, it bothered him deeply.

"It's all right," she murmured. "I'm here."

Ashleigh couldn't tell whether he was awake or not, but he turned to face her, and pulled her to lie atop him. The shock of feeling the hard lines of his body against her softness made her tremble. The hem of her nightgown was hitched up to her thighs, and she was afraid of what she'd started. Was he going to claim her now as his wife? This wasn't at all what she'd expected. Her own heartbeat hammered in her chest, but she forced herself to remain where she was. She could feel the hot, hard length of his erection through her thin nightgown, resting against her belly. But he made no move to force her. Instead, his hands slid down her spine, and he wrapped his arms around her as if she were precious to him.

The gesture utterly undid her. She could feel his need, like a man who had been unwanted for most of his life. And though she was afraid, she touched his shoulders, feeling the raw strength of this man. He inhaled at her touch, and she felt his mouth move to her throat in a kiss.

The touch of his lips was silken, and her breasts tightened as shivers erupted all over her. His hands continued to caress her, and he reached down to cup her bottom. As he kneaded her there, she felt herself growing wet. A thousand sensations washed over her, as she hungered for more of his touch.

She rolled to her side, but kept her hands upon him, stroking his bare chest. She explored his hot skin, suddenly aware that she did want this man. She wanted to know him carnally, to understand the closeness between a man and a woman. And somehow, he needed her.

In the darkness, she felt his palms move to her breasts, and they budded beneath his fingertips. The aching pleasure as he stroked and tantalized her was overwhelming. She could feel something building within her, sensations and feelings that threatened to pull her under.

She was reaching for something, and as his hands moved over her, she craved more. She moved her hands lower, and her hands passed over his hard hips. Though she wanted to know more of him, she didn't know if he was truly awake. Was he aware of what was happening or was she taking advantage of him? She didn't know what she was doing, or even if he wanted this. And the fear made her pause.

But his hands continued to caress her breasts through the nightgown, kindling her desire hotter. Ashleigh loosened her nightdress, wanting his hands upon her bare skin. And when she guided his palm to her nipples, she couldn't stop her moan of need. She was aching for him, wanting him to touch her. Never in her life had she felt such yearning, and she pulled his mouth to hers, kissing him deeply.

For a moment, he kissed her back, and she felt the intimate slide of his tongue against hers. It was a prelude to what she desired, and she met his kiss with her own tongue. She tasted him, learning his mouth. His hands gripped her hair, and then abruptly, he broke away.

"Ashleigh." His breathing was harsh, and he moved away from her. "What are you doing?"

She suddenly felt uneasy, as if she'd come here to seduce him. It wasn't that at all, but her face reddened with embarrassment. "I . . . you . . . were having another nightmare."

"You need to leave," he said. The iron in his voice was unmistakable, and she scrambled from his bed.

"I'm sorry. I never meant—I only thought to comfort you." The humiliation washed over her, and she felt she could have died from it. She'd fallen beneath his spell, wanting so badly to feel his touch. And now, he'd made it clear that he didn't want her at all.

"Go." The words were unyielding, and she hurried to the connecting door, closing it behind her. Hot tears sprung to her eyes, and she let them fall as she hurried down the long hallway back to her room.

She couldn't believe she'd made such a mistake, believing she could push past his walls. He didn't want her. He'd been clear about that from the first, and he'd admitted his reasons why he didn't want to consummate their marriage. It was her own fault for daring to ask for more.

As she crumpled into her own bed to have a good cry, she couldn't stop the feelings of inadequacy. She'd reached out to Cameron, hoping to offer him comfort. But it hadn't mattered. He'd made it clear that he didn't want her at all. And now he never would.

Chapter Eight

"CAMERON, I NEED your help."

He glanced up from his list and saw Ashleigh in the doorway. Before he could ask her why, she continued and said, "You promised to talk with me about how I should govern Kilmartin in your absence. I need to see your ledgers, I need to meet with your estate manager, and you cannot leave for London before then."

Although he heard her words, he was far more distracted by his wife's presence. She had come over to his desk, and the hyacinth scent of her skin made him want to draw her into his lap. He wanted to taste that silken skin again, and the memory of her was driving him wild. She pulled a chair up beside him, and they were so close, her thigh pressed against his. "Teach me what I need to know."

But what he wanted to teach her was something far more physical. He gritted his teeth to push back the unholy desire she'd conjured. He could feel the heat of her skin against his, but he forced himself to open the ledger.

"These are the rents," he said, showing her the first column. "They've all been paid." He started to go over the figures, and she studied them, asking a few questions about whether any money was owed or what bills were forthcoming.

"Joseph Kilmartin is my estate manager," he said. "I'll introduce you to him before I go."

"I wish you didn't have to leave. We've only just arrived." When she met his gaze, an instinctive urge came over him to kiss her. He hadn't stopped thinking about last night when she'd come to his room. The memory of her hands upon his skin, her mouth meeting his—it was irresistible. He didn't know how any of it had happened. Most likely he'd been out of his head during the nightmare and had grabbed her without knowing what he was doing. But he hadn't been dreaming when she had touched him or kissed him back. And now, he wanted her desperately.

"I don't know how many weeks or months I'll be gone," he said, rising from his chair.

"Months?" she questioned. She appeared aghast at his words. "Then you're not just going on my mother's behalf."

"No. I'm not."

She expelled a long breath of air, though she didn't say anything. He could read her apprehension, despite the fact that he'd told her from the very beginning to expect this. "And you can't tell me anything about what you're doing, can you?"

Cameron shook his head. "Nor can you tell anyone else. As far as the rest of them are concerned, I've gone to see about your mother."

He repressed the thoughts of what was to come. The thought of returning to the Tower—even to be imprisoned among the French officers to gather information—was horrifying.

"Where can I write to you?" Ashleigh asked.

"Send any letters to my townhouse in London. My staff will see to it that I receive them after I return. Eventually." He closed the ledger and said, "You should have everything you need now."

She stood, and once again, he was drawn in by her presence. Her blue eyes stared at him, and she murmured, "Not everything." She remained in front of him and reached for his hands.

He froze at her touch. "Don't, Ashleigh. We made rules for this marriage and agreed to abide by them."

"Rules you've already broken." She looked into his eyes. "You never said a word about your son. Don't you think I deserved to know about him?"

He caught her hands and held them. "I don't regret the choice I made. You'll make a good mother to Logan."

But her eyes held a flash of anger. "You lied to me. Being a wife is one thing. Being a mother is another thing entirely."

"You'll adjust." He kept his voice cool and released her hands. But when he started to walk away, she stepped in his path.

"Kindness," she said. "That was one of your rules, wasn't it? And respect? How is any of this kind or respectful?"

Her face was flushed, and his attention fixated upon her mouth. His attraction to Ashleigh only heightened with every moment he spent at her side. "What is it you want from me, Ashleigh? I've given you everything you could possibly want."

"Everything except you," she said softly.

He couldn't think of anything to say to that. Then she stood on tiptoe and kissed him. God above, no one had ever reached out to him like this. Ashleigh snapped his threads of control, and for a moment, Cameron pressed her back against the bookcase, devouring her mouth. Her hands were in his hair, pulling him close as she kissed him back. Their tongues mingled, and he wanted so badly to give in to his needs and make love to his wife.

But if she became pregnant, he'd face the risk of losing her. He didn't want to be the cause of her death—not when he had the power to hold back. He broke the kiss, his breathing unsteady.

"Please, Cameron," she begged. "The way you make me feel—I need you."

His heart was pounding, for he'd never expected that their marriage would shift so quickly. It wasn't right to go back on the rules when he didn't know whether he could please her. Rebecca had never wanted him, no matter how hard he'd tried. Cameron was torn between his own desires and the fear that Ashleigh wouldn't like his touch. He didn't know why she desired him, but if he was about to spend weeks enduring imprisonment in the Tower of London, part of him wanted to take a memory with him.

"I'm leaving soon, Ashleigh. It's not fair or right." He tried to keep his voice rational, although he wanted her beyond all else. "We should wait."

She stared back at him, and he sensed her frustration. Slowly, she turned away from him and walked to the door. He let out the breath he was holding.

But instead, she reached for the key and turned it in the lock. Every muscle in his body went rigid. He swallowed hard as she faced him and walked back. Whatever rational thoughts had been in his mind earlier had transformed into fog. He had no idea what was happening, but his carefully laid rules were falling apart.

When she reached him, she brought her hands to his shirt. "Maybe I don't want to wait." She raised up on tiptoe and kissed him again. Against his lips, she whispered, "Maybe I want to break the rules."

He captured her mouth, surrendering to the dark desire she offered. He lost himself in her, barely aware that she'd removed his jacket and was helping him remove his shirt.

He brought her to a chaise longue and pulled her onto his lap. Hair pins scattered, and he dragged his hands into that silken red curtain. Her breathing was coming in soft gasps, and she pressed back against his erection, making him forget why he'd ever denied himself the pleasure of having a wife.

"Help me with my stays," she pleaded. "I can't breathe."

He began unbuttoning her gown, ripping the laces free, and she took a deep breath when he'd loosened the corset.

His brain warned him that a woman like Ashleigh didn't deserve to be treated like a lightskirt. This wasn't at all what a wedding night should be—not for a virgin.

But then, inspiration struck. He could keep his vow of celibacy and still give her what she desired while withholding himself.

Her breathing was still labored, but he could tell that she'd gone shy. She wrapped her arms around him, pulling him closer for another kiss. This time, it was softer. He took his time, learning the shape of her mouth, teasing her tongue with his own. Then he brought his hands to her chemise, cupping her breasts through the soft linen.

She flinched, and he pulled back his hands at once. Ashleigh broke the kiss and met his gaze. "You don't have to stop. It simply startled me." She took his palms and brought them back to her breasts, closing her eyes when he cupped them. "It's all right, Cameron."

It was the first time she'd used his name. Yet another barrier seemed to fall between them, and when he reached to touch her bare skin, she pressed back against his arousal. He began caressing her nipples, trying to learn what pleased her.

Her face flushed, and then she rested her hands upon his thighs. She squeezed him, arching her back while he touched her.

"You're beautiful, Ashleigh," he murmured against her nape. Then he bent to kiss her bare shoulders, savoring her silken skin. For a moment, he paused and then said softly, "If you want me to stop, I will."

"No," she whispered. "Don't stop." She turned to face him, straddling his lap with her knees. Her gown was falling down, and the swell of her breasts drew his attention.

For a moment, he tried to think of what he could do to bring her pleasure. He wanted nothing more than to fulfill her desires.

But you don't know what a woman wants, his mind warned. And that was true. So many times, he'd tried to touch Rebecca, but nothing he'd ever done had made her happy. Doubts plagued him, and he wondered whether he could find a way to please her. What if she looked upon him with fear the way his previous wife had?

Yet Ashleigh seemed entirely different. Even now, her breathing was uneven, and she reached out to touch his shoulders.

"May I touch you?" she asked.

Never had Rebecca ever wanted to touch him, and he hungered for Ashleigh's hands upon him. When she pressed him to lie back on the chaise longue, she shifted her position so her gown rode up higher. She sat upon him again, and a bolt of desire lashed through him as she pressed against his erection. He gripped her bottom, groaning slightly.

"I'm sorry," she said, sitting back. "I didn't mean to hurt you."

But her touch hadn't caused him pain—it had only intensified his need. He wanted her naked beneath him. And he wanted hours to explore her body with his hands and mouth.

"You didn't," he said. But it was probably better for her not to be so close. Right now, he wanted nothing more than to lift her skirts and sink deep inside her.

Her hands moved to his chest, tracing his skin. Then she followed his scar with her fingertip before replacing the touch with a kiss. "How did you get this? In battle?"

He nodded, capturing her hand.

"Ashleigh," he whispered.

She was breathing unsteadily, but she leaned in to kiss him again. The invitation encouraged him to explore her body. He wanted to caress her breasts, to learn every inch of her. He drew his hands over her chemise, cupping her warm curves. She gave a shuddering sigh, and he paused, wondering if he'd frightened her. He started to take his hand away, but she put it back. "No, it's all right. Touch me however you want to." Her gaze met his, and she added, "If you'll allow me to do the same."

Her words tantalized him, and he unbuttoned his trousers, allowing her to do as she wished. This time, he was gentle, but he reached up to the fabric of her chemise, touching her breast. Ashleigh bit her lip, shifting against him. "That feels good, Cameron." Her words encouraged him, and he stroked her warm skin, finding the swell of her nipple. With his thumb, he gently rubbed it, and she gave a soft moan.

Her encouragement gave him the courage to do what he truly wanted, and he sat up to take her nipple into his mouth. He swirled his tongue over her skin, and her nails dug into his back. "Oh my God."

In response, she slid her hands down his ribs, lower still, until they paused at his waistband. He guided her hand to his erect shaft, and she squeezed him gently, moving her hand in her own arousing exploration. She was pushing him to the brink, making him wild with need. He drew his hand beneath her skirts, caressing her thighs as he parted her legs. As he'd hoped, she was bare beneath her skirts. His fingers brushed against her intimately, and he felt the warmth of her wetness.

"Cameron." She spoke his name in a plea, but he was afraid she would push him away. Instead, she held his erection gently, as if not knowing what to do. "It's all right. You can touch me."

But he couldn't accept her invitation. They could tempt each other, but he would not cross that boundary of lovemaking. Instead, he continued to kiss her breast, giving the other one the same attention. She was moving her hand against him, and he showed her what he liked. Then he moved his fingers against her wetness, and she gave an almost violent start.

"Wait."

"I'm sorry." He took his hand away immediately and fastened his trousers. "I didn't mean to hurt you."

"You didn't."

But he sensed she wasn't telling the truth. Her sudden response had bordered on fear, and he would never press her toward anything that made her uncomfortable. He didn't know what would please her, so it wasn't surprising that he'd made mistakes.

"Cameron, I—"

"No," he insisted. "We'll stop." It was better if he didn't continue. Already he had crossed the boundary past friendship. He'd let himself get carried away, and it was better to go no further.

"There's no need to stop. I'm fine, really." She tried to take his hand, but he didn't allow it. Instead, he stood from the chaise longue and donned his shirt. Though his body was aching for release, he'd promised himself he wouldn't go this far. He'd broken his own rules, so he deserved whatever discomfort his body felt.

She sat up and lowered her head. "I've ruined it, haven't I? You're angry with me."

"Not at all. I shouldn't have started this when I have to leave." He helped her fasten her corset and then rebuttoned her dress. He knew his efforts were too hasty, and the staff would likely guess what they'd been doing, but it didn't matter. Her maid would help her fix her appearance.

"You don't have to go right now," Ashleigh insisted. "Take some time. Logan will want to see you."

"It's better if he doesn't. He'll only be upset again."

She looked as if she wanted to argue again, but instead, she grew quiet. "When will you be back?"

"A month or two," he predicted. "Possibly a little longer."

Ashleigh went to stand before him. She reached up to his face and traced the beard. "When you return from London, I want this gone. This is a disguise to push people away. You don't need it with me."

He especially needed it with her. Anything to distance himself. Her touch burned into him, and he savored the warmth of her hand. But it was best to keep the space between them, even if the memory of this moment with her would have to last him for weeks.

DURING THE NEXT fortnight, Ashleigh felt as if her life had become blurred. She spent time each day with Logan, but he often had nightmares and wouldn't fall back asleep unless she held his hand. The boy had utterly captured her heart, and she spent many hours with him, walking to explore the castle and enjoying the garden while he brought her pretty blossoms.

But as time dragged onward and there was no letter from

Cameron, she started to question whether he was all right. She spoke to the butler Hamish, asking how long he thought Cameron would be gone.

"He'll be fine, Lady Ashleigh. Nae need to worry. He's often gone for months at a time."

"I wish to speak with the estate manager Joseph," she told Hamish. "I want to see where things stand with Kilmartin right now."

"He's verra busy right now," the butler said. "But if there's something you're wanting, it might be that I could help you—"

Ashleigh gave him a smile that veiled her annoyance. "I can see that you have taken good care of the castle, Hamish. But it's the rest of the estate I need to understand. Please send word to Joseph that I wish to meet with him in the study." The butler appeared startled that she had pushed back, but she was not about to be dissuaded. If she was going to be mistress here in Cameron's absence, she needed to meet with the estate manager regularly.

"I will see if he can be found, Lady Ashleigh."

"Thank you." Then she added, "I will expect to see him at eleven o'clock." She left Hamish and returned inside the castle. Thus far, she'd found Kilmartin in good shape, and for the most part, the servants did an excellent job with the upkeep.

But the worry about Cameron knotted within her stomach. She returned to his bedchamber and closed the door. When she lay upon his bed, she could barely sense the scent of him. The tangled emotions sent a pang through her at the memory of the way he'd touched her. Would he ever cross the boundary and consummate the marriage?

The door swung open, and she saw the scullery maid, Blair. "Oh, I'm so sorry to disturb ye, Lady Kilmartin. I didna ken you were here." The maid began to leave, but Ashleigh stopped her.

"No, it's all right. You can go about your tasks." The young woman was one of the friendlier servants, and Ashleigh had enjoyed talking to her during the past two weeks. With a sigh, she admitted, "I was simply missing my husband, that's all."

At that, the maid's smile warmed. "He is a good master, is Chief MacNeill. We'd hoped he would remarry."

Ashleigh thought about asking questions about his former wife but stopped herself. Instead, she ventured, "Are you married, Blair?"

"Aye miss. Nigh on ten years now." The scullery maid was busy cleaning the hearth, but her tone was cheerful at the mention of her husband.

Ashleigh paused, wondering how to broach her own troubles without gossiping about their marriage. "Are you happy in your marriage, Blair?"

The woman turned from the hearth and smiled. "Aye, indeed. Stuart's a good man. He tends our land with me boys."

"Could I ask you a question?" Ashleigh ventured, feeling her cheeks burn hot with embarrassment. Though it probably wasn't wise to confide in a servant, she blurted out, "Have you any advice about pleasing your husband?"

At that, Blair laughed. "That's easy enough, my lady. Just give them a kiss and a good romp, and they'll be happy enough."

"I don't . . . really know how," Ashleigh confessed.

"Affection," the maid said. "Little touches, all the time. Show them you care. Kisses and a good bit o' temptation never hurts." She sent Ashleigh a wicked smile. "When he comes home, the chief might be wanting a hot bath. And if you're there to tend him, well . . ." She winked at Ashleigh. "I suspect we'll have a wee bairn within the year if ye tend him often."

Though she knew the prospect of another child terrified Cameron, Ashleigh wasn't opposed to the idea. Her greatest fear was that he would push her away. But the idea of affection wasn't a bad one. He *had* been eager to touch her. It had only been her nerves that had gotten in the way.

"I hope he returns soon," Ashleigh said. She did miss him in ways she'd never imagined. Even though she'd tried to fill the void with Logan, she caught herself staring at Cameron's empty chair in his office, wondering when he would be back. She sat at his desk, and sometimes if she concentrated, she could almost feel the touch of his hands upon her again.

"I supposed I'd better go and meet with Joseph about the estate." Ashleigh rose from Cameron's bed and thanked the maid before she left.

On the way downstairs, she heard the excited buzz of servants talking. Ashleigh hurried downstairs and heard them talking about the arrival of a coach. Had Cameron returned so soon? She went to the front door and opened it. A footman was there, escorting a woman from the coach.

It was her mother.

Tears of joy rose in her eyes as Ashleigh hurried to embrace Georgina. *He kept his promise,* she thought. Somehow, Cameron had found a way to bring her mother to safety. But the moment she reached her mother's side, there was only emptiness in her expression. She had the look of a woman who had given up on life.

"Mother, I'm so glad you're here." Ashleigh hugged her gently, but Georgina's frailty was shocking. "Come, and we'll get you settled."

She'd expected her mother to return the embrace or at the very least say something. But Georgina's silence frightened her most of all. No longer was she a frightened marchioness who did her husband's bidding without hesitation. Now, she was a woman who had been broken. There was no doubt that she'd suffered the wrath of her husband. And Ashleigh blamed herself for it.

Georgina walked slowly, and Ashleigh put her arm around her waist. She struggled with the stairs, but eventually Ashleigh was able to bring her into one of the bedchambers. She left the door open and asked Blair to come and build a fire in the hearth.

"Mother, come and sit down." She led Georgina to a chair near the hearth and remained beside her while the scullery maid lit the coals. Although her mother sat down, she didn't seem to truly hear or even see her daughter.

"Would you like tea or food?" Ashleigh offered. Still there was no answer. After Blair had finished lighting the fire, she murmured for the young woman to bring refreshments. For a moment, Blair caught her eye and offered her own silent sympathy.

Then she reached out and took Georgina's hands. "You're going to be all right now. I'm here, and we're both safe." Her heart warmed with infinite gratitude toward Cameron. She would ever be thankful to him.

If only he would come home.

Her mother's gaze was empty, but Ashleigh held fast to the hope that Georgina would recover once she felt safe again. She saw lines of weariness on her mother's face, but so much worse was the absolute silence.

"Do you need anything?" she asked her mother. "Just say the word, and I will bring it to you."

But once more, Georgina gave no answer.

Ashleigh didn't bother asking what had happened to her. She was unlikely to respond, and Ashleigh already knew the answer anyway. A hollow feeling welled up inside her, making her wonder if it might be too late to save her mother. Georgina appeared to be hardly more than a shell, as if there were nothing left to save.

She could tend her mother and offer her food and comforts. But there were other wounds that simply went too deep. There was a chance they might not heal.

And that terrified her most of all.

Chapter Nine

R ACHEL WAS SEATED at her desk when a gentleman knocked on the door to her study. He cleared his throat, and she glanced up. He looked to be in his thirties, rather good-looking, she had to admit. But who was he, and why was he here? Had Cedric arranged a meeting on behalf of one of their pupils?

"I'm sorry, are you looking for Mr. Gregor?" She set her letter aside, and he remained at the doorway.

"Forgive me, but no. Mr. Gregor told me I should come and introduce myself. He arranged an appointment and told me to come to the study." With an embarrassed smile, he added, "Or if I made a mistake, I could leave."

"No, it's all right." She hadn't been expecting a guest. Was he here to seek a wife? Or had he come for another reason? Rachel offered him a seat, noticing that he did have kind, green eyes.

"What can I do for you?" she inquired, taking out a sheet of parchment and a quill. "I presume you have spoken with Cedric about seeking a wife?" He was slightly older than she was expecting, but not so old that he couldn't be a possibility for either Miss Edwards or Lady Ashleigh. That is, if their current prospects did not end up as she'd hoped.

"Ah, yes," he admitted, a slight flush coming over his cheeks. "Although I know this is not the usual way of doing things. Mr.

Gregor did say he thought you might be able to help."

Rachel relaxed and began taking notes. "Let us begin by your telling me your name?"

He broke out with a startled laugh. "Forgive me. I should have begun with that. I am Sir Brian Lucas."

"A knight, then?"

"A baronet," he corrected.

She wrote down his name, and said, "Tell me, what are you looking for in a wife, Sir Brian?"

He cleared his throat and admitted, "I'm not actually certain. I know that I'm not the most exciting of gentlemen. I like to read, ride horses, and I am not especially fond of ballrooms. Though, if my wife wanted to go, I would certainly attend."

She wrote down that he would want someone quiet. "What do you hope we can do for you?" she asked. "Are you trying to improve yourself, or are you content and simply want our help with matchmaking?"

He paused a moment and seemed to think it over. "If I were only interested in a young debutante, it would be simple enough to attend a few balls. I am seven-and-thirty, and I do not think an eighteen-year-old miss would suit me at all. I am looking for a woman who is more mature."

A sudden rush of fear washed over her with uncertain nerves. Cedric wouldn't do this to her, would he? She had fully embraced the prospect of being a spinster for the rest of her life. She didn't want to open the Pandora's box of forgotten hopes.

Rachel dipped her pen in the ink and wrote the word *Mature* on the parchment. "All right." She was careful to keep her voice steady. It was entirely possible that she was mistaken about this gentleman. "Does she need to be an heiress?"

"No, not at all. I have enough to provide her with a comfortable living."

"And what about children?" she asked.

"I would welcome them," he answered. For a moment, he studied her as if he saw something interesting. Rachel had to fight back the sudden instinct to guard herself. She would never allow another man to court her again—not after the horrific marriage she'd endured.

"Have you been married before?" she asked quietly.

At that, an unknown emotion crossed his face. Then just as quickly, he shielded it. "No."

She was surprised to hear it, for he was an attractive man and seemed kind. Though she wanted to ask him more about why he hadn't married, something held her back. She had her own reasons why she'd avoided marriage, and perhaps he was the same.

"What do you hope to find in a lady?" she asked. "You mentioned someone older. What else?" She was torn between trying to remain neutral and being afraid that Cedric had set all of this up.

"Someone who knows her own mind," he admitted. She continued writing, and when he said nothing else, she glanced up to look at him. For a moment, she was startled by the look in his gray eyes. There was yearning there, and at the sight of his expression, her heart began to quicken. "You don't remember me at all, do you, Rachel?"

The pen fell from her fingers, and she sat back in her chair. "Sir, you've mistaken me for someone else. I am not who you think I am." Why had he called her by her first name? It was entirely too forward.

He stared a little longer before a chastened smile emerged. "So, you did forget. I don't know whether to be consoled by it or disappointed. No matter." His expression remained neutral, and it was then that they both overheard a commotion.

Sir Brian's expression turned uncertain and then suddenly, the door to the study flew open. Rachel barely had time to react before the Marquess of Rothburn strode into the room. His cravat was rumpled, and his eyes were bloodshot. Fury blazed in his expression as he moved toward her desk.

"What have you done with them?" he demanded. "First my

daughter, and now my wife."

He started to move toward her, but Sir Brian stepped in. "Sir, step away from Mrs. Harding."

"She's the reason they're gone!" he shouted. "And I intend to get them back, damn you."

Rachel flinched, cringing at his enraged tone. He lunged toward her, but to his credit, Sir Brian caught the man and held him back. There was no question the marquess was thoroughly foxed.

"I know Ashleigh was here, weeks ago. My driver told me everything. And now they're both gone. *You* are responsible for it," he accused Rachel. "I want to know where they are."

"I have done nothing with your wife or daughter," Rachel insisted. "You're mistaken." Though she tried to remain calm, her voice held a tremor she couldn't suppress. The marquess's fury reminded her only too well of the past she'd buried. She found herself falling back into the old habits of averting her eyes and softening her voice.

Don't argue, don't ask questions. Remain silent and maybe he won't hurt you.

She swallowed hard, forcing back the memories.

"Ashleigh ran off with that Mr. Neill, didn't she?" Rothburn insisted. "Where is he? I'll see him in irons for this."

"I don't know." Her emotions tightened, and she was entirely grateful that Sir Brian continued to keep the man away from her.

"It's time for you to leave, my lord," Sir Brian said. Within moments, Mr. Gregor joined him with another servant, and the three of them dragged Rothburn out of the study.

Shaken, Rachel covered her face with her hands while the marquess shouted and cursed at the men. She struggled to catch her breath, and it took everything in her not to cry.

A few minutes later, she heard a knock on the doorway. "Are you all right?"

Sir Brian's kind voice was her undoing. The tears escaped, in spite of her attempts to hold them back. "I'm fine." She kept her eyes closed and her face covered. "Thank you for your help, Sir Brian. I just—need to be alone right now."

She couldn't bear to see his sympathy, and she didn't look at him. He seemed to wait a few moments before at last he said, "Until next time, Mrs. Harding."

She waited until his footsteps had retreated before she lifted her head. When Cedric entered her study, she let the tears fall openly. "The marquess is not welcome here again."

"He won't return," Cedric said quietly. "I'll see to it."

She wiped her eyes and asked, "Why would you bring Sir Brian here, Cedric? You know I don't intend to marry again." She wiped her eyes with a handkerchief. The last thing she wanted was any man believing there could be a match between them. Those hopes had died a long time ago.

He leaned against the doorway. "I'm glad he was here to protect you, Rachel."

So was she, though she wouldn't admit it.

Then Cedric continued, "But I don't regret my own clumsy attempts at matchmaking. How can you help other young ladies fall in love when you've never been in love yourself?"

"I've been in love before," she argued, "but that love was a mistake. And I paid the price for my folly."

"Not all love is a mistake. And I think you should consider it. It took some digging through your past to find Sir Brian."

"Sir Brian wasn't part of my past," she protested. "This is ridiculous, and I won't be at home if he tries to pay another call."

Cedric took a step closer. "Stop hiding away from life, Rachel. The right man is worth waiting for."

But she wasn't willing to sacrifice her freedom for anyone. Not ever again.

THE STENCH OF suffering permeated the Tower. Cameron huddled among the other French officers, wearing rags. These men had been captured at Waterloo last summer but had only been brought here more recently. It seemed that there were a number of high-ranking British officers who had also been taken as prisoners of war during the battle and were still unaccounted for. Cameron had been instructed to learn whatever he could about the missing officers and about anything else he might pick up, anything that might constitute a threat to the Crown. The Tower guards treated him the same as the other prisoners, for only one man knew he wasn't an enemy.

Ever since Cameron had been placed with the officers, he'd not spoken a word of English. He'd mostly kept to himself, pretending to be a low-ranking French soldier. After he'd suffered a beating from the guards merely for asking for water, the men had accepted him as one of them.

But not before they'd questioned him.

"Who was your commanding officer?" one of the officers had demanded.

"Le Rougeaud," Cameron had answered in French, saluting the officer. At the orphanage, one of the nuns had spoken only French to him from the time he was a young boy. He'd grown up speaking the language with her, and thankfully, his accent was strong enough to deceive the officers. His language skills had value in espionage, and he'd grown accustomed to blending in.

"Where were you captured?"

"Quatre Bras, sir."

"And none of your fellow soldiers were brought in as well?"

Tread carefully, Cameron thought. *"Oui.* They were put in another cell, sir."

"Why would they put you with us?" he demanded. "You are not an officer."

Cameron lowered his head, avoiding an answer. The three officers began speaking with one another, and he overheard them speaking about Waterloo and other men who'd been taken captive.

The first officer turned back to him and continued the interrogation. Cameron gave him names, locations—everything they asked for. He knew the details because he had been to Quatre Bras before. His contact had given him a believable story to tell the officers, one no one would suspect. And thankfully, it seemed to satisfy them. At last, they concluded that it was likely a mistake that he'd been put with them.

Cameron remained as far away from them as he could, behaving as if he were unworthy to sit near them. During the next month, he listened every day, memorizing details. They gave him the scraps of their food, but it wasn't nearly enough to assuage the raging hunger. The officers continued talking in hushed voices about what would happen next, what they expected. Cameron kept gathering information.

He'd kept his head down, his face buried in his hands, as if he didn't care what they were discussing. As the weeks passed, they had grown accustomed to simply ignoring him.

But even as Cameron continued to learn everything he could from the officers, at night he thought of Ashleigh and Logan. He brought the image of her fiery hair and blue eyes into a vision that became real to him. He still couldn't believe she'd married him. There was no denying that she was the best impulsive decision he'd ever made. Logan had connected with her almost immediately, and it had filled him with such relief to see her caring for his son.

He'd never expected his own defenses to come crashing down. When she'd touched him, responding to him, it had awakened a hunger that could not be sated. No one had ever desired him, much less offered affection. He couldn't remember a time when anyone had willingly embraced him. And it humbled him to admit that he wanted her hands on him.

That day in his study, he'd lost all control, frightening her. In a way, he deserved this imprisonment. The weeks of separation were what he needed to regain his control. When he returned to Kilmartin, he and Ashleigh would be just as they were before— strangers. And with the information he provided to the Crown, he would earn more in a month than most men earned in a year. All he had to do was suffer among them.

His body ached with bruises, and dried blood marred his lip. The freezing cold and the rotten food were what he'd expected. He'd been careful to eat as much as possible before he'd met with his contact.

But that was many weeks ago now, and the scraps the officers had given him today left him feeling hollow. When at last they grew quiet and went to sleep, Cameron thought again of Ashleigh's smile. He remembered her touch on his face and the softness of her skin. God help him, he didn't know how he would keep his vow of celibacy. He yearned to touch her, to discover what gave her pleasure, and watch her come apart with ecstasy.

Just a little longer, he told himself. *Endure.*

In the middle of the night, two guards came for him. The taller guard was bald with a black beard and a scar across his forehead. "We're taking you for questioning." His smile widened. "My brother was killed by the French. I'm going to have some fun with you, French bastard."

Cameron didn't flinch when they pulled him out of the cell. It wasn't at all the right time for questioning, which made him believe this was the extrication that would happen. But when the guard struck him hard across the face and drew blood, he started to have doubts. Then the men locked him in a separate cell alone with the bald guard, and he realized that this attack wasn't planned. This guard knew nothing about his loyalty to England or why he was here. Instead, the man intended to torture him for his own entertainment.

Even if he revealed himself, the guard wouldn't believe him. The only reason why his espionage worked so well was because only a few knew who he truly was.

A cold fear iced through him as he took in every detail of his new cell, of his captor, and the key at the man's waist. His brain discarded escape plans as quickly as he conjured them.

His hands were bound in chains behind his back, and he suspected the guard believed himself completely safe. Not so. But for now, Cameron would bide his time and let his instincts lead him.

"Why?" he demanded of the guard, keeping his voice heavily accented.

"As I said before. My brother was killed by men like you." The guard's smile widened. "We put you in that cell to show the officers what we do to traitors. You'll be an example for them. After they see what we've done to you, they'll tell us whatever we want to know."

His skin prickled with the realization that this man intended to torture him. Possibly kill him. Cameron adjusted his grip on the chains, knowing he had only seconds to act. He would have to move so swiftly that the guard would never suspect.

But the weeks of eating hardly any food or drinking water had taken their toll. His strength was lacking, but he had to gather everything he had if he intended to make it out alive.

Without warning, the guard kicked him in his stomach, and Cameron stumbled to the ground, the air knocked from his lungs. He gasped to breathe, and the man withdrew his knife. Cameron tried to roll out of the way, but the guard's boot pressed against his throat, cutting off his air. The more he fought, the harder the guard leaned upon him.

So he stopped fighting, letting his body go limp until the boot lifted. It took every ounce of concentration not to gasp for air and reveal that he was still conscious. Cameron lay motionless, keeping his eyes closed. He relied on his other senses—sound and smell—to determine where the guard was.

Only the element of surprise could help him now. He waited for the guard to make his move. Every muscle tensed in anticipation.

"I think I'll take your sight first," the guard said. "Then you'll never know where I'll hurt you next."

His stomach churned as the blade descended.

Chapter Ten

LOGAN HURRIED DOWN the path ahead of her to the small cottage while Ashleigh followed. He struggled with the door handle, but Ashleigh showed him how to open it. When they entered, he called out, "Granny!"

Georgina didn't answer, so Ashleigh led the boy inside the cottage and saw that the back door was cracked open.

"I think she's in the garden," she told Logan. "Why don't you go and see?"

He raced to the back door and pushed it open. Georgina was sitting on a bench, repotting what looked like an iris. Logan raced over to her and said, "What are you doing?"

She smiled and rubbed her hands together to shake off the soil. "Hello, Logan. Would you like to help?" Then she murmured a good morning to Ashleigh.

It warmed her heart to see her mother slowly returning to normal. Though Georgina had barely spoken at all during the first week, she was now having tea in the castle every afternoon. She seemed to prefer the smaller cottage, and Ashleigh had made arrangements for her mother to take rooms there with a housekeeper and maid while she'd brought the other servants who had been living there to the main castle.

"He wanted to spend time with you," Ashleigh said. She took

a seat on the other side of the bench. During the past month, Logan had blossomed. He adored the attention he received from both of them, and aside from a few tantrums, the boy had eased his way into their hearts.

Nearly two months had passed, and there was still no sign of Cameron. Ashleigh had continued to send letters, but there had been no reply. She didn't know how long it would be until she saw him again, and her worry increased with every day apart from him. She had even begun sleeping in his bed at night in order to feel closer to him. She didn't truly understand why or how her feelings had softened toward Cameron, but she missed her husband dreadfully.

Ashleigh spent most of the morning with her mother and Logan, but around midday, the boy was starting to grow hungry and tired. He made no protest when Ashleigh suggested getting food. Although she invited her mother to join them for luncheon, Georgina preferred to stay at the cottage.

Ashleigh walked with Logan back to the castle, and although the boy held her hand, his mood darkened with every step. When they reached Kilmartin, he let go of her hand and raced up the stairs to the front door.

Hamish met her just inside the castle and brought out a silver tray. "There's a letter for you, Lady Kilmartin."

Ashleigh reached for it, tearing it open even though she didn't recognize the penmanship. To her disappointment, it was from Mrs. Harding.

Her spirits sank, and she noticed that Logan's expression had turned even more irritable. "I'm hungry," he whined. "I want to eat *now*."

There was no doubt her in mind that her stepson was about to start wailing. And she really did want to read the letter in peace, even if it wasn't from Cameron.

"Sweeting, I think you should go with Mary. I'll make sure you have your favorite sandwiches and scones with strawberries." To the footman, she said, "Please take him upstairs to the nursery. Send Mary along with the food."

"But I want to eat luncheon with *you*," Logan whined. "I don't want to eat in the nursery."

"I will join you for supper later," she said, giving him a swift embrace.

"No!" he shouted. To her surprise, he shoved her. "Now."

It wasn't the first time he'd thrown a tantrum, but between her worry for Cameron and the unexpected letter from Mrs. Harding, she stopped short. She was two-and-twenty, allowing a boy of three to scream at her. A sudden anger caught her unexpectedly.

But she was not her father. She would not yell back or strike him. And still, she could not let him speak to her this way.

Instead, she dropped the letter and picked him up. He began kicking, but she held him fast.

"My lady, are ye needing help?" Mary asked.

"No, I'm strong enough to carry him."

Logan continued fighting against her, but she gripped him with all her strength. She was out of breath by the time she reached the third floor, but she told Mary to open the door. "Wait here, please," she told the nursemaid.

"Don't leave me," Logan sobbed. His arms gripped her around the neck, and she suddenly felt his fears magnified within her. He'd been left behind most of his life, abandoned by the father who loved him—and now, they both were alone.

Tears caught in her eyes, and Ashleigh felt the same sense of isolation. She sat down on the boy's bed, holding him in her lap while he wept. Her own tears rolled silently down her cheeks. She'd never imagined she would feel this way about Cameron, but the months without him had taken their toll.

Was this to be her life now? Raising his son alone, never knowing how long he would stay before he left again? When she'd married him, she hadn't really understood what it would be like. But now, she was starting to realize just how lonely her life had become. Once, she'd believed if she and her mother were safe, it would be enough. But now, she wanted so much more.

Logan had begun to relax in her arms, and she realized he'd fallen asleep. She tucked a blanket over him, and after she opened the nursery door, Mary came inside. She promised to give him luncheon as soon as he awakened.

Ashleigh wiped her own tears away and went downstairs. Although it was time for her own food, she noticed that the servants were strangely missing. The footmen were absent, and there was nothing on the dining table.

She paid it no heed but sat down at the dining room table and tore open Mrs. Harding's letter. The matron had written to alert her that the marquess had hired Bow Street Runners. But it was her last sentence that held a clear warning: *He knows you are in Scotland.*

In a way, Ashleigh hardly cared any more. Her father would likely find her at some point, but he could hardly complain about the husband she'd chosen or the life she now led. As for her mother, she would never let him take Georgina. It would be better if he never discovered the marchioness was here as well.

If she did see her father again, it would be different. Here at Kilmartin, *she* was their lady, and she would never allow the marquess to bully her. Not anymore.

She folded up the letter and set it aside. The housekeeper cleared her throat. "Lady Kilmartin?"

Ashleigh turned, expecting her to announce that luncheon was ready. Carla's face was pale and fearful instead.

"Is something the matter?" she asked the housekeeper.

Carla seemed not to know how to answer the question. But she blurted out, "Lady Kilmartin, the chief has returned."

With those words, Ashleigh's heart pounded. She rose from her chair but realized Carla did not seem overjoyed—instead, something was very wrong. "Where is he?"

"The men are helping him from the coach," Carla answered. "He's hurt, milady. Very badly."

And then her own fear took hold. She started to run toward

the door, gripping her hands together to keep them from trembling. "Send for the doctor."

"We have, milady. He's on the way."

Ashleigh hurried outside, terrified of what had happened. The coach was just pulling away, but she couldn't see where Cameron was or what condition he was in.

She was out of breath and overheated from running, but she hurried up the stairs toward his chamber. The moment she reached his doorway, Hamish the butler blocked her path. "My lady, the chief is not able to receive any guests just now."

"I am his *wife*," she insisted, "not a guest."

"I ken ye are upset," the butler said, "but ye must allow the doctor to—"

"Get out of my way," she insisted. She couldn't believe he was barring her path. But when she tried to push her way past him, Hamish gently closed the door in her face and locked it.

Rage permeated her, and Ashleigh tried to enter the adjoining bedchamber, only to find it locked as well.

Words could not describe her fury. But since she couldn't break the door down, she forced herself to consider alternatives. She walked toward the stairs and saw multiple servants bringing up hot water, bandages, and all manner of things for healing. Mrs. Cobb hurried past her, and Hamish let her inside without question.

It occurred to her then that Cameron might have refused to see her. What if he had ordered them to keep her out? The thought bruised her heart, for of course the servants would not dare disobey him.

Woodenly, Ashleigh walked slowly along the hallway, wondering what to do now. Why wouldn't anyone tell her what had happened? He could be near death, for all she knew, and no one would let her see him.

Why had she ever believed this marriage could remain a friendship? Right now, she was near tears, imagining all the awful ways Cameron had been hurt. The sobs caught in her throat, and she gripped her fists as if she could hold her emotions together in the same way.

Mrs. Cobb hurried past her, and Ashleigh caught up. "How is he?"

The matron only shook her head and went down the stairs. What did that even mean? She was starting to understand that their loyalty to Cameron was indisputable. And while she could make demands of them, she understood that they were trying to help him, which was more important than all else.

She went down to his study, pacing as she studied the walls. Though she had explored the rooms during the past few weeks, wondering if there were any hidden passageways, the wooden panels made it impossible to tell. However, given what she knew about him, there had to be other ways around the castle—and other ways of breaking into Cameron's room. And if she had to tear the house apart, panel by panel, she would find them.

She hated being shut out like this, not knowing if he was all right or not. From the serious mood surrounding the servants' behavior, Cameron's life was in danger. She needed to be at his side. Her frustration mounted higher until finally, she released her tears.

She decided to change her strategy. As Lady of Kilmartin, she had the right to know what had happened to her husband—even if he had no wish to see her. Quietly, she dried her tears and steeled her resolve.

Deliberately, she walked back up the stairs. She found a chair in one of the bedrooms and carried it out into the hallway near Cameron's locked door. Then she sat down and leaned back against the wall, waiting. She listened but could hear nothing at all.

Hamish saw her on his way past and stopped a moment. "Lady Ashleigh, you cannot be here."

"Oh, but I can. And I will," she said, raising her chin. "All of you are treating me like a caller instead of a wife. I have a right to know what's happened to my husband, so I will simply wait until someone deigns to tell me the details."

"You cannot stay," he argued.

"To the contrary, I can. I live here, remember? And my belongings are in the chamber beside the chief's. Since you've locked my room, how do you propose that I sleep?"

The butler appeared confounded. "My lady, there are other rooms."

"No, I intend to sleep where I've slept for the past month." She crossed her arms and regarded him. "And there's naught you can do about it."

He tried a different tack. "And what about supper? You'll be wanting food."

She studied him carefully. "Do you really believe I'd be able to eat a meal without knowing how he is?" Hamish appeared unsettled by her declaration, so she continued, "No, I'm going to sit here until one of you lets me inside."

"Then I fear ye'll be waiting a long time. The chief has asked not to be disturbed."

She veiled her reaction, though it hurt to have her fears confirmed that Cameron didn't want her there. But Ashleigh could be patient if need be. And one way or the other, she was going to find out what had happened to her husband.

CAMERON LOST ALL track of time. He couldn't tell if he'd been in bed for days or over a week. He vaguely remembered Mrs. Cobb tending him, feeding him soup and giving him water. Though he was dimly aware that his body was healing from his wounds and the fever had gone, the torment of nightmares haunted him still. He awoke, shaking with fear, only to realize he was at home.

A faint scent of hyacinths invaded his dream, and he started to reach for Ashleigh, only to realize she wasn't there. Of course, she wasn't. He'd ordered them to keep her away since he didn't want her to see him like this.

Cameron clenched the pillow, and then he heard the unmistakable click of one of his hidden doors opening. Instantly, he tensed, waiting for the intruder to approach. He was about to attack when her scent struck him down. He heard her pull back the coverlet and slide into bed with him.

God above, he could feel the warmth of her skin. Why had she climbed into bed with him? And why had she used the hidden door? He wanted to say something, to voice the thousand questions that rippled inside. But every word simply disappeared when she reached for his waist and wrapped her arm around him. She nestled her face into his shoulder and sighed as if she were drifting off to sleep.

How long had she been sharing his bed? And why?

His body ached with so many injuries—the bruises from the beating, the numerous cuts where his torturer had sliced his skin. But all of it seemed to fade away at her touch. He didn't move, not wanting her to move her hands.

Her presence brought him comfort, pushing back the memories of torture. Even in the face of it, he'd never revealed his identity, letting the guard believe he was a French soldier. But it was through the grace of God that he'd kept his eyes.

An involuntary shudder broke through him, and Ashleigh's arm tightened around his waist. "I'm here," she whispered.

So she was still awake. He longed to say something, to turn over and pull her into his arms. But every muscle ached, and his flesh was sore from all the healing cuts. Mrs. Cobb had bandaged most of them so he felt rather like a corpse wrapped for burial.

His breathing grew unsteady as the unwanted memories intruded again.

I think I'll take your sight first.

The words made him shudder. But the guard sliced his cheek instead, a shallow cut that barely penetrated his skin. It was meant to terrify him, and Cameron flinched. It took all his discipline not to move—to wait for the right moment. Sweat bloomed on his skin, and still he waited.

When the guard moved the blade toward his eyes, Cameron flexed his shoulders, moving his chained hands from behind his back, over his head to the front. The guard jerked with surprise, and Cameron used his chains to choke the man.

He didn't kill him but waited until the guard lost consciousness. Then he summoned the last of his strength to escape the Tower—a challenge for him, even if he did know every cell and every corner. It was a matter of finding the right guard who knew him, the guard who had initially placed him in the cell.

He allowed that guard to "recapture" him before taking him to a private chamber where he met his contact and gave all the details he'd learned, especially about two other English officers who were being held in France.

Cameron had earned a small fortune for the information, along with compensation for his wounds and starvation. He'd been offered a carriage back to his townhouse and a chance to heal and recover in peace.

But he sensed that if he stayed in London, they might want him to go back to the Tower. He'd fulfilled his task, but he wasn't willing to sacrifice more time after spending nearly two months away from home. They had other men who could go. He simply couldn't bring himself to do it.

Instead, he'd allowed a healer to bandage him up, and he'd accepted a swift coach and driver to bring him home to Kilmartin. But on the way, some of the wounds had become swollen. He'd developed a fever, and he couldn't remember much about the journey, except that it had taken almost a week to reach the Highlands.

But now, his wife was willingly sharing his bed. A wife whom he'd promised never to touch. A harsh lump caught in his throat as he wondered what Ashleigh wanted from him.

She wouldn't understand the horrifying moments he'd suffered. Though his wounds were painful, they would heal. But the Tower had conjured the ghosts of his past—memories he could never share.

Her body was pressed against his, and he was grimly aware of the soft curves of her breasts, the touch of her knees against his legs.

He wanted her so badly, he could hardly bear it. Then he heard the sound of her weeping softly.

And God help him, he turned to her.

ASHLEIGH DIDN'T KNOW what had been done to Cameron, but he'd gone willingly. It nearly broke her heart to feel all the bandages. She was torn between wanting to offer him comfort yet being afraid of hurting him. No one had told her how badly he was wounded, so she'd simply guessed that it was awful.

Then he'd turned to face her.

"You're awake," she murmured. God above, could she have said anything more stupid? Why hadn't she said *I'm glad to see you* or even *Thank goodness you're home?* No, she'd spoken the obvious.

Cameron said nothing in return, and she wondered whether she'd been mistaken about him being aware of her presence. Her face flushed with embarrassment as she wondered whether she should dare to reach out to him. Her heart hammered, but in the darkness, she touched his shoulder.

For a moment, he seemed to stiffen beneath her fingertips. Then he caught her hand and drew it away. "Why are you here, Ashleigh?"

His voice was rough, as if he'd endured horrors she could only imagine. And now, she'd interfered with his sleep and healing.

Stubborn tears rose up in her eyes. She'd taken a risk, in the hopes that she'd been mistaken when Hamish had kept her out. Now, it seemed as if Cameron hadn't wanted her at all.

"I'm sorry. I've just been worried about you," she said. "You've been gone for so long." But her words couldn't capture the emotions in her heart. Each day, she had hoped he would return. And she'd feared that he might never come back. "Do you want me to leave?" she asked.

"You'd probably be more comfortable in another room," he said quietly. But it wasn't quite an answer to her question, which gave her a glimmer of hope.

"Is that what you want?" She kept her voice gentle, trying not to push past the invisible boundaries he'd raised.

Cameron hesitated. But then, he continued, "It's what we agreed on when you married me."

Once again, it wasn't a true answer. She took a risk and said, "That isn't what I asked you." Her heart was beating rapidly, but she needed to know the truth. "If you want me to leave you, I'll go. But if you want me to stay . . ." She let her words drift off, letting him make of them what he would.

When he didn't answer, her hopes fell. And so, she pushed the coverlet aside and swung her legs to the edge.

Only to have him catch her wrist. He held it loosely, but answered, "I've barely slept at all during the past months, Ashleigh. And when I do . . . there are nightmares. I don't want to disturb your sleep."

Ashleigh didn't ask what the nightmares were, but she admitted, "I haven't slept well, either. I've missed you." She lifted the coverlet and slid her feet back beneath the blanket. "Hamish barred me from entering. He said you didn't want me here."

"It's been difficult . . . while I was gone. I thought it would be easier on you if you didn't see my injuries."

She held his hand in hers. "It's been far worse staying away. I kept imagining what happened to you. No one would tell me."

"They had their orders," he said. "And I thought it would be better this way."

"Not for me. It's been terrible not knowing." She added, "It took me a long time to find the passageway to this room." She'd searched for days before finally finding the correct panel to press. He fell silent for a time, and then she asked, "Do you want me close, or do you want me to stay on my side of the bed?"

He didn't answer, as if trying to decide. Then finally, he said, "Do as you will."

Ashleigh drew closer to his body heat and brought her arm around his waist again, pressing her face against his shoulder. "Am I hurting you at all?"

"No." His voice held weariness, and she could hear the pain within it.

"Where were you for so long? In London?" Though she wasn't certain whether he would answer, she wanted to know.

He expelled a sigh and leaned back against her body. "I was in hell, Ashleigh. And I pray to God, I never have to go back."

DAYLIGHT STREAMED INTO their bedroom, and Ashleigh leaned on her side to look at Cameron. A slash cut across his cheek, but she stared at his features, admiring him.

Sometime in the morning, Mrs. Cobb came to tend his wounds. She said nothing to Ashleigh but checked a few bandages before she gave him a strong sleeping draught.

"Let him rest, my lady. It's what's best for him now."

"I'll stay with him while he sleeps," she promised. "I'm not leaving."

"And what about Master Logan?" the older woman chided.

"He has Mary," Ashleigh answered. Raising her chin, she added, "I'll ring for you when he awakens later."

After Mrs. Cobb left, it didn't take long for Cameron to fall into a deep sleep. Ashleigh studied him, and then her gaze turned to a basin of warm water that the matron had brought. And near that, she saw a razor.

Perhaps the Devil had coaxed her into this, but she was thoroughly sick of his disguise. It was nearly impossible to tend the cuts on Cameron's face, and so she made the decision to shave off his beard while he slept.

It was far more difficult than she'd imagined and took nearly an hour. Even with soap and warm water, she'd found it challenging to shave him without awakening him. Thankfully, whatever potion Mrs. Cobb had given him to drink had made him oblivious to what was going on.

Now that the long beard was gone, she could see how incredibly handsome he was. Her husband had a strong jawline and a sensual mouth. His blond hair framed a face that reminded her of a pirate. Or maybe that was the shallow slash on his cheek. Although she should probably feel guilt or remorse over what she'd done, the truth was, she didn't.

Cameron MacNeill was a man so handsome, it nearly hurt to look at him. Without the beard, she wanted to run her fingers over his cheeks. He stirred in his sleep, and she indulged the urge, tracing the line of his jaw. And now, he was awake and staring at her.

She ventured a slight smile. "Good morning."

He appeared confused for a moment before he reached up to his face. After he felt only bare skin, his eyes hardened. "Why is my beard gone?"

"Your cheek had a cut that needed to be cleaned," she said calmly. "It was necessary."

It wasn't, but she held no regrets about the lie. Oddly enough, his mouth tightened into a line, and his blue eyes turned stormy. It was the first time she'd ever truly seen him angry. But why? It was only a beard.

"You didn't have to take it all off," he argued. "Was this your idea?"

She nodded. "It was. And you look far better because of it."

"You had no right to shave it off," he accused. "The beard was a necessity."

Part of his mysterious work again. And yet, she wasn't sorry. If removing the beard meant he had to wait for it to grow back, keeping him safe longer, so be it.

"After what you suffered, maybe you shouldn't go back," she

insisted. "They hurt you."

"I have responsibilities, Ashleigh—"

"Responsibilities be damned." She sat down on the bed beside him. "If shaving the beard off will grant you a few more months' respite, then it is worth it to me. And I like your face. You're handsome."

"You don't understand what you've done." His voice was tinged with ice. "This wasn't a decision based on what I look like. It's meant to keep people away."

"Including me?"

Cameron gave no answer. Instead, he sat up from the bed and jerked the sheets aside. He turned his back on her and gave her a magnificent view of his naked backside while he pulled on smallclothes and his trousers. The wounds on his back had healed into bruises, but once again, Ashleigh grew aware that this man was a fighter.

She slipped out of bed, wearing her nightgown, and went to stand by the fire. "You were badly hurt. And I hated it when the servants kept me away from you."

He turned to face her. "It's better if we remain apart."

"Is it?" Emotions gathered within her, forming a tight ball that caught in her throat. It didn't seem to matter what she said or did—he continued to keep himself separate.

Yet, at night, he clung to her.

She wanted to hold him, to sleep in his bed with his arms around her. In spite of everything, she was drawn to this man. Beneath his disguise, he was honorable and strong—everything she wasn't.

And God help her, she was falling in love with him.

Cameron put on a shirt and had just opened the door to leave when Logan came running down the hall. The young boy threw himself at his father in an embrace. "I missed you, Da!" Logan said, squeezing hard. Cameron flinched, as if the hug pained him, but he ruffled his son's hair. Then Logan's expression turned confused. "Your beard is gone."

Cameron ignored the comment. "I missed you, too, son."

Logan reached out to touch his cheek and smiled. "Mother and I went to visit Granny every day while you were gone."

Ashleigh paled at Logan's words, for it was the first time he'd called her mother. The ache in her heart caught her unawares, not because it bothered her, but because the young boy had captured her heart. His nursemaid Mary had cared for his needs, but Logan had craved love and affection.

"I played in the garden and picked her flowers," he told his father. "I could pick you some if you want."

"I would like that," Cameron said quietly, meeting her gaze. In his blue eyes, she saw a strong emotion, almost gratitude.

She couldn't stop the tear that escaped her, but she swiped it away. "Logan, go and see if Mary will take you to see Granny. Your father and I will join you there soon."

"I want Da to walk with us now."

She bent down and dropped a kiss on his forehead. "I have to finish getting dressed. I cannot see Granny in my nightgown."

Logan giggled at that, and she bade him, "Go on now, and perhaps Granny will have cakes waiting for you." He brightened and hurried off.

After he'd gone, Cameron stood. His gaze was inscrutable, making her nervous. Was he still angry about the beard? She couldn't read his expression, but she felt the need to say something. "He—he's never called me Mother before."

"He's not the same boy I left behind." Again, she couldn't read his emotions. His words were toneless, almost disbelieving.

"Well—I spent time with him. I read stories to him and took him out to the garden." Ashleigh studied him, uncertain what to think. When he didn't respond, she offered, "If you'd rather he calls me something else, I'm sure I—"

Before she could continue, Cameron caught her in his arms and kissed her. Her mouth drifted open in surprise, but she kissed him back. Heat flared between them, and she wrapped her arms around his neck.

This was what she'd wanted—to be held by her husband and to feel the sudden prickle of need. Her body ached as she yielded to his touch. She reached up to his shaved cheek, caressing his skin.

She couldn't help but remember how he'd touched her before, and she wondered what had prompted the kiss. He'd been so angry with her before—why the sudden change in emotion?

Her unspoken question was answered when Cameron said, "I haven't seen my son this happy in years. I'm grateful to you. You held up your end of our marriage bargain."

That was all it was? Gratitude for their bargain? Dismay filled her, but she hid her feelings. Instead, she managed, "So have you. Thanks to you, my mother is safe."

For a moment, their breaths mingled, making her long for so much more. She wanted him to kiss her again, but although she kept her mouth close to his, he didn't move.

She murmured against his mouth, "Are you still angry with me about the beard?"

He gave a single nod. "But it's too late to change it."

"I'm not sorry for what I did. As I said before, I find you very handsome." He appeared disconcerted by her words. And to prove her point, she stood on tiptoe and took the kiss she wanted.

The moment she did, something shifted within her husband. His tongue slid against hers, as if he couldn't get enough. Desire slammed into her, and she could hardly catch her breath. She wanted his hands on her skin, and she wanted to lose her innocence to him.

"Cameron," she whispered against his mouth. "I don't want to only be your friend anymore." Although she was afraid to expose her desires, she blurted out, "I want to be your wife in body, as well as in name."

She started to remove her nightgown, but just as she'd feared, his demeanor cooled. He gently took her hands, and his face grew serious. "Don't ask that of me."

Embarrassment flooded through her, for after that kiss, she

hadn't expected him to deny her. Her cheeks were crimson as she turned and found a dress and her stays. She removed the nightgown with her back to him and put on a clean chemise and petticoat. Then she reached for her stays. "I'll need you to send for Sarah. Or you can help me with my laces."

She fully expected him to ring for her maid. But after a brief hesitation, he drew closer. He stood behind her and helped tighten the stays. Her heartbeat quickened at his touch, and she wished more than anything that he would change his mind about consummating the marriage. She wanted his hands upon her bare skin.

But instead, he helped her button up the back of her day dress.

"Where is your mother now?" he asked. The conversation was a subtle distraction, and she supposed it was necessary.

"She's staying in the cottage. She felt more comfortable there."

"Then we'll go and see her. And Logan." He offered his arm, but even as Ashleigh took it, she felt the sting of rejection. It was her own fault. Cameron had only ever been honest with her about this, and she should have known better than to hope for more. Her husband didn't want her in the way she wanted him. Or perhaps he was still afraid of her conceiving a child and wasn't willing to take the risk.

They walked along the gravel pathway that led to the cottage where her mother now lived. Although the house was visible from the castle, it was still a long walk, and Ashleigh noticed her husband's occasional pauses, as if his wounds still hurt. She shouldn't have asked him to go such a distance; it had been thoughtless of her. Ashleigh trudged beside her husband, wishing she'd ordered a carriage.

Along the walk, he finally admitted, "I was imprisoned these past two months."

His words shocked her so badly, she stopped walking. "For what reason? Did they accuse you falsely of a crime?" Worse came the thought of her father. In a matter of months, he had lost both his daughter and his wife. The marquess would never give up so easily. Perhaps this had been his doing.

"No. I was ordered to share a cell with French prisoners of war. They wanted me to learn what I could from them."

She let out a shaky sigh, suddenly realizing how awful it must have been for him. "So you agreed to endure it. For months."

Another nod. She tried to read his expression but couldn't. "You don't speak French, do you?"

"*Oui,*" He answered. "One of the nuns at the orphanage was kind to me. She didn't speak English, but I learned how to speak French from her. I think I was the only person who ever talked to her."

"You must have spoken it for years," she said. Yet another piece of his life revealed.

"I did, yes," he said. "Very few people know of this."

And she understood then that he was trusting her with the knowledge. It made sense why Cameron would be so desirable to work for the Crown if he'd been a soldier and could speak the language well. She had learned a little French as part of her own education, but she could not dream of discussing topics such as war or battlefields.

He reached out and took her hand. His large palm covered hers, and it felt like a silent apology. She held it in return and tried to push away her longing for more.

"Did you see my father when you were in London?" she asked. "Before you were . . . taken?"

He shrugged. "I made inquiries. Lord Rothburn spends most of his days and nights drinking from what I've heard. He hired a Bow Street Runner to find you and your mother. But thus far, they have not found anything."

"That's not true. Mrs. Harding wrote a letter, warning me that Papa knows I'm in Scotland. He very well may find us." The thought made Ashleigh shiver as she spoke the prediction.

Cameron slowed his walk and turned to look at her. "By law,

he cannot touch you. You have nothing to fear, even if he does find you."

"And what about my mother? What if he finds her?"

"I will try to keep her hidden," he answered. "But both of you should be careful."

She tried not to think of what would happen if her father somehow found them. Scotland had become the sanctuary she'd never known. And she didn't want to lose this life of peace that she'd built.

They finally reached the cottage, and Ashleigh led him back to meet her mother. Georgina wore a gown the color of butter, and her hair was pulled up. Strands of gray tinted her red hair, and she smiled at the sight of Cameron. "So, you are the scoundrel who carried away my daughter." The words were spoken with amusement.

"And the one who brought you here," he finished. "Or at least, arranged it."

Georgina crossed the small parlor and reached out to take his hand. "For which I shall be forever grateful." Her smile softened. "And your son is a pure delight. I am proud to call him my grandson. Had I known what a treasure you were, Cameron MacNeill, I should have ordered my daughter to wed you sooner."

Was her mother flirting with Cameron? Ashleigh could hardly believe what she was hearing. In the nearly two months she'd been at Kilmartin, her mother had transformed from being a terrified, silent woman into one who had begun to live her life again.

They spent the remainder of the afternoon having tea in the garden, and soon enough, Mary brought Logan to join them. He devoured the sandwiches and cakes that Georgina gave him. Then he crawled into Ashleigh's lap, where he cuddled against her. Her heart gave another silent tug. It surprised her to realize she wanted to have many children. But despite the expression on Cameron's face, she knew he wouldn't agree.

How could she reconcile herself to years of marriage to a man who didn't want to touch her? On the surface, everything seemed fine enough. He'd given her a beautiful castle to live in, servants, safety, everything she could ever desire.

Everything except him.

"I KNOW WHERE they are."

Cecil glanced up from his glass of brandy and stared back at the Bow Street Runner. "Where?"

"In Scotland. Kilmartin Castle."

"Cameron Neill has them, doesn't he? That low-born bastard took my daughter and now my wife." The familiar rage curled up inside him, brewing a resentment that made him reach for his glass.

"That lowborn bastard is the Chief of Kilmartin," the Bow Street Runner corrected. "His name is Cameron *Mac*Neill, and he has far more wealth than any of us imagined."

Now this was unexpected. Cecil took a swallow of brandy, his mind turning over the information. "If he indeed has this— wealth, then he will have to compensate me for the loss of my daughter's virtue."

"He married her," the Runner said. "And shortly thereafter, Cameron MacNeill filed papers that would grant her a generous settlement and another house that would be hers, should anything befall him."

That can be arranged, Cecil thought to himself. Victor Colfax, the Viscount Falkland, might be convinced to help him. His mind turned over the details, and for the first time in months, his spirits lifted.

The marquess lifted his hand in dismissal. "My secretary will see to it that you're compensated for your information."

After the Runner departed, Cecil pulled out a quill pen and paper and began to make his plans. Georgina was his wife and property. Any man who dared to take her ought to face severe punishment. And if Ashleigh was the beneficiary upon the death of her husband, so much the better.

Satisfaction flooded through him. Soon enough, he would have both of them back.

WEEKS PASSED, AND Cameron's wounds were now fully healed. But the nightmares remained. He tried to maintain boundaries with Ashleigh, but every day became a torment. She had left him alone, which was what he'd wanted. A restlessness had settled within his bones—the knowledge that this marriage had become something more.

He was acutely conscious of his wife's presence at every moment. The way she touched his son's hair before she took Logan's hand in hers. The hyacinth scent of her skin as she walked past him. And the aching desire that only worsened with each moment. He'd made a personal vow not to touch her, to give her the celibate marriage of convenience he'd promised.

But at night when he awakened from a nightmare, he wanted her in his bed. He wanted to lose himself in her, to push away the horrors.

During the day, he simply existed, as if real life were a waking dream. At night, he thought of the Tower, of the rancid odor that had permeated the stones and the utter sense of hopelessness. He'd endured these conditions before, and the nightmares were familiar. Yet something was different this time. Perhaps it was because he now had a family to live for. He didn't want to go back to a life of momentary suffering for the sake of money. The more he thought of it, the more he understood that it was because of Ashleigh. She had filled the emptiness inside Logan, giving him a mother. And though Cameron had thought he could leave them both behind, satisfied that they were safe together, he was starting to realize that he didn't want to.

He wanted his wife's warm body pressed up against him in bed. He wanted to see his son's smile.

He didn't know if he could ever go back, but perhaps he wouldn't need to anymore. As far as the outside world knew, his role didn't exist—that person could simply disappear. And Cameron knew that if he hadn't managed his own escape from that Tower guard, he would have died that night.

His skin sometimes itched at the memory of the way the guard had carved his skin with his blade, as vengeance for something Cameron hadn't done. He tried to lock the memory away, to remind himself that he was free, but it didn't stop the visions from breaking through his slumber. It was easier not to sleep.

Last night, he'd remained in his bed, but he'd awakened nearly every hour as the clock chimed. Although he'd tried to pretend as if everything was all right, his mind and body still ached with exhaustion. And now it was early evening again, and he wanted nothing more than a dreamless sleep—but it wasn't possible.

In the next room, he heard his wife speaking to her maid Sarah. Only then did he realize that the adjoining door of Ashleigh's bedroom had been opened slightly. Then he heard the sound of water being poured into a tub. He remained seated in the chair, and then he heard the soft splash as his wife stepped into her bath.

"Do you need anything else, Lady Ashleigh?" Sarah asked.

"No, thank you. You can go now."

He ought to close the door. Surely, she didn't know it was open. But when he moved to a different chair, he had a clear view of her profile.

God help him. Only a voyeur would stare at a naked woman in her bath. Even if it was his own wife. He saw that her hair was caught up, but a few wet tendrils rested against her shoulder. She had a bar of soap between her hands and was lathering it.

Ashleigh leaned back against the tub and lifted one leg, soaping it from foot to calf. From his vantage point, he could see the curve of her breasts, and he hungered to touch her.

"Cameron, could you bring me that cloth?" she called out to him.

She knew he was there. Probably, she suspected he'd been watching her. But why would she want him to intrude on her bath? He didn't know what to think.

Yet, nothing would tear him away from this opportunity. He opened the door wider and stopped a moment. The words of apology caught in his mouth, but he didn't voice them. He wasn't sorry that his wife had invited him into her room. Nor was he sorry when he saw the water droplets skimming down her creamy skin.

He grew instantly rigid with arousal. He wanted to kiss her deeply, to trail his mouth down to her breast and pleasure her.

Instead, he went over to the chair where she'd left the towel.

"No, not that one," she said. "The one over here."

It was a cloth well within reach of her hand. She could easily have fetched it herself. But her blue eyes had gone dark, and she made no effort to hide herself from him. He openly gazed at her, admiring her beautiful breasts and the coral nipples that bobbed in the water.

"Will you wash my back?" she asked, holding out the soap. "There's a stool you could sit on."

He slid the stool over behind the tub and took the soap from her. Then he dipped the small linen cloth into the water.

All their marriage rules seemed to disappear. She'd invited him into her room and had asked him to touch her. Rebecca would never have done such a thing. She would have shrieked and demanded that he go. And he knew the moment he touched Ashleigh that he was lost.

Her skin was smooth like the surface of the water, silken from the soap. He took his time, washing her neck, then her shoulders. He stroked circles around her shoulder blades and followed it by wringing out the wet cloth to rinse the soap away.

"Do your wounds pain you anymore?" she asked. "How are

you feeling?"

Like he wanted to lift her from the tub and carry her off to bed, he thought darkly. If he wasn't going to sleep peacefully again, at least he could spend the hours with something far more interesting.

But instead, he answered, "My wounds have healed."

"I'm glad," she murmured.

"When did you move your belongings to this room?" he asked, soaping his hands before washing her waist.

"The day after you left for London," she answered. "I had been sleeping in your bed until—"

"Until I returned."

She nodded but didn't turn to look at him. When he washed her waist again, she caught his wrists in her hands. Slowly, she drew his soapy palms to her breasts.

He hid his sharp intake of breath. Her nipples had gone erect, and she moved his hands over her breasts. "I miss sleeping in your bed. It made me feel close to you."

"Ashleigh," he warned.

"This has gone on long enough," she said. "I have been patient, and I've done everything you asked. But there is more you can give me, even if we don't make love."

His hands stilled at that as her meaning became clear. And then she continued, "And there is more that I can give to you."

He couldn't bring himself to speak, especially when she stood from the water, naked before him.

"Hand me the towel, won't you?"

Cameron didn't know where she'd gathered such courage, but desire roared through him with the force of a storm. He brought her the linen towel, and as he wrapped it around her, he lifted her from the tub. He didn't ask for her consent but carried her back to his bed. Gently, he laid her down, and she held the towel around her.

"Will you build a fire in the hearth?" she asked quietly. "It's cold."

He obeyed, desperately needing the distraction while he tried to think of how he could keep his control. He feared that if he allowed her to touch him at all, he would lose command of himself like a green schoolboy.

Thankfully, the servants had already set up the fire, and he struck the tinderbox to light it. In time, the flames took hold, and he turned back to face her.

"Take off your clothes," she ordered. "I want to see you."

She kept the towel covering her own form, but he removed his shoes and stockings, then his jacket and waistcoat. He walked back to the bed, unfastening his cravat and finally removing his shirt. He kept his breeches on for now, but then she sat up and let the towel fall away.

Ashleigh's body stunned him with its beauty, and he wanted nothing more than to spend the rest of the night worshipping her. There could be no barriers between them—only skin to skin.

He unbuttoned his breeches and removed his smallclothes until he was naked before her. She flushed but never took her gaze from him.

This time, he had no intention of leaving.

Chapter Eleven

THOUGH SHE TRIED to behave with confidence, inwardly Ashleigh was trembling. She didn't know what she was doing or how anything would work. But the scullery maid Blair had given her good advice.

"If ye're wanting yer husband and he's being stubborn, ye've only to offer yourself. Let him see ye wearing naught but the clothes God gave ye, and he willnae be able to resist."

The maid had given her other instructions on how to drive Cameron wild, and Ashleigh had been both tempted and afraid. What if she didn't please him? What if he turned her away? But thus far, it had worked. And from the hunger in his eyes, she suspected he wanted her as badly as she wanted him.

His erection, in particular, fascinated her. She'd never seen him naked before, and she wanted badly to touch him. But she was afraid that if she did, it would send him away again.

"Ashleigh, I—"

"No." She cut him off, not wanting to hear excuses. "I'm not asking you to take my virginity. I'm only asking for us to . . . learn one another."

It made her feel foolish, but Blair had told her other ways of temptation. The maid had promised she would like it, though Ashleigh had no idea what to expect.

Cameron moved to sit upon the bed, and she sat beside him. Despite her earlier desires, now she felt awkward and uncertain of herself.

"If we do this, I need your honesty," he said.

She nodded, not really understanding what he meant by that. Then he admitted, "I . . . wasn't a very good husband to Rebecca. She never liked it when we . . . were intimate." His expression grew embarrassed, but he admitted, "I want to please you. But I need you to tell me what you want. Or if you don't like something."

She was starting to understand his uncertainties. It sounded as if his first wife hadn't wanted him in the same way. "Will you start by kissing me? And touching me?"

She turned to face him, still sitting beside him on the bed. He reached out to her face and slid his fingers down one cheek. Then he bent and claimed her mouth in a searing kiss. She kissed him back, welcoming his tongue inside her mouth. She cupped his cheek, delighted that he'd continued to shave. She loved looking at his handsome face, knowing that he was hers.

As he continued to kiss her, a restless ache rose between her legs. The sweet ache intensified, and she murmured against his mouth. "Please touch me, Cameron." She moved his hands to her breasts, leaving no doubt what she wanted.

He moved his fingers to caress her, still kissing her. She grew breathless, loving his hands upon her, and she explored his chest with her fingers.

"Are you all right?" he asked. "Can I do more?"

"Yes, please," she breathed. He kissed her throat, lowering his mouth. She sensed he was about to kiss her breasts, and she drew her own hands down to his stomach. She was timid, afraid to cross the boundary, even though his erection rested just below her fingertips.

"Is it all right if I touch you?" she asked. He guided her hands lower and took one nipple in his mouth. It was like touching a match to oil. Her body ignited, and she arched against him, digging her hands into his hips. She grew wet between her legs, remembering how it had felt when he'd tried to touch her the last time. Even though she was afraid of her own response, she guided his hand there.

His fingertip stroked her lightly, and a spiral of pleasure curled within her. She instinctively reached for his manhood, wanting him to feel the same. But he inhaled sharply, and she pulled back.

"It's all right," he said, guiding her hand to touch him. Slowly, she explored his hot, velvet skin. In turn, he moved his fingers against her wetness. Her body was instantly responsive, and she felt her breathing grow unsteady. It was both exhilarating and terrifying, not knowing what he wanted.

She took a moment to slide her hand over him intimately, to learn the swollen shape of his shaft. His expression was fierce, as if he could not bear her touch, and she shied away, pulling her hand back. "Am I hurting you?"

"No, don't stop."

She sensed that this was new to him. Perhaps Rebecca had never explored his body the way Ashleigh yearned to. "Tell me what you want," she urged.

"Kiss me," he said in the barest whisper. "Everywhere you want to."

She was afraid, but her instincts suggested that he was willing. And so she moved atop him, parting her legs and resting her knees on either side of his waist. Cameron pulled her close until she was seated against him, and the hard length of his shaft pressed against her wetness. She felt a quake of longing, but she started by kissing his mouth again.

Her husband took her lips hungrily in response. She felt him press against her, and the desire seemed to grow hotter between them. Though she was afraid of what was to come, she did want to feel him inside her.

A darkness bloomed within her, and she wondered if she could coax him to change his mind. He'd said that his first wife didn't like lovemaking. But every time Cameron touched her, she felt her body rising with need.

She lowered her mouth to his throat, kissing him there. He jolted at her touch and then reached between her legs to the wetness. "May I?" he murmured.

"Y-yes." She could hardly breathe as his clever fingers slid against her seam, finding a fold of flesh that made her cry out.

He stilled his hand instantly, but she didn't want him to stop. She guided his fingertips to the sensitive place, and whispered, "Gently."

He obeyed, and as he circled the fold, she felt a deep, powerful surge of desire. Her breathing shifted, and he found a rhythm that made her quake with need.

"Don't stop," she begged. "It feels good." She reached down to touch him in turn, and he showed her how to stroke him. Upon the head of his shaft, she felt a bead of moisture, and she rubbed him until he, too, shivered.

"Cameron," she whispered, as he found an ebb and flow that was driving her closer to the edge. She clenched him, wanting so badly to guide him inside. But he interrupted her thoughts when he slid two fingers inside her. She shuddered and began to move her hand up and down. He echoed her own gasp, and her breathing grew ragged.

No one had ever touched her like this, and she wanted more. Her body was seizing up, reaching for something she couldn't name.

And then, the rhythmic intrusion of his fingers pressed her to the edge. She felt herself coming apart, and she dragged his mouth to hers, sliding her tongue inside as he continued to invade and withdraw with his fingers. She arched against him while the shimmering pleasure broke over her in a wave. Her fingers dug into his backside as she tried to take him inside her, but he moved away.

For a moment, she felt spurned, wishing she could do something to bring the same pleasure to him. His erection strained against her, and without knowing what prompted her, she moved lower and took him into her mouth. The salty warmth of his shaft was unfamiliar, but she loved the power of bringing him pleasure. As she licked him, she grew aware of him changing their position.

This time, she, too, was exposed to him. As she suckled at him, she felt his warm tongue move to her folds, and she gripped the coverlet as he tormented her in the same way. With every stroke of her tongue, he echoed it against her own flesh. The shattering pleasure gripped her again, but she was determined that he would feel the same release. She took him into her mouth as if it were between her thighs, and as she did, she felt him tense. He reached to her breasts, stroking her nipples as he slid his tongue against her folds.

He was breaking her apart, the wave cresting again and again. She surrendered to the mind-searing release, and finally, she pushed him over the edge where he lost his own control.

Then he gathered her close where she heard his heart thundering against her ear. But he didn't speak a word.

CAMERON GREW RESTLESS in the night. Past and present blurred, and a film of sweat covered his body. Invisible hands held him down, and he struggled against the covers.

I'm going to take your eyes, the guard's voice taunted. Cameron could feel the kiss of the blade against his face, and he struggled to free himself. Cold sweat appeared upon his forehead, and his wrists burned from the chains.

The guard shoved him against the wall, and when Cameron kicked at him, the man held him against the stone *"My brother died because of men like you."*

I'm not French, he wanted to say but didn't. He'd made an oath of secrecy to the Crown, one he had to keep. His eyes were closed, but he was fully aware of the Tower odors of filth and suffering.

Then a new scent caught his attention. The hyacinth fragrance blended with the acrid prison smells. For a moment, he was confused.

It must have been a hallucination. He thought he heard someone trying to soothe him, saying, *"It's all right. I'm here."*

But the words weren't real. Only the hands on his shoulders were real, along with the threat of the blade. With all his strength, Cameron shoved the hands away, fighting against the visions. He couldn't allow himself to fall prey to false dreams.

He wanted peace. He wanted to be home. But this guard was trying to keep him from his wife and son. He had only seconds before the man would carve out his eyes.

When a hand touched his face, he lashed out at the guard, striking fast. His fist connected with flesh, and he heard a cry. He swung his fist again, but this time it connected with nothing. He didn't know how his chains had broken or how he'd managed to free himself, but he didn't waste time wondering.

Ice cold water struck him in the face, and he sputtered at the shock. A candle lit the darkness, and he saw his wife clutching her face. In one hand, she held an empty pitcher.

"Ashleigh—" he started to say, before he realized what had happened. His nightmare had made him believe that *she* was his captor. He'd struck her, not the prison guard.

God help him, the sight of her swollen cheek filled him with shame and self-loathing. But more than that, he saw fear in her blue eyes. And when they welled up with tears, he lowered his head with guilt.

His nightmares had caused him to lose control—something he'd never wanted to happen. And despite his efforts to guard her, Ashleigh wasn't safe around him. Not anymore.

"I'm so sorry," he said, flipping back the coverlet. "I never meant to—"

"I know," she answered. "It was an accident. You were dreaming." But still, she took a step away.

In her eyes, he could see the same terror that Rebecca had felt toward him. He was nothing but a monster, a man incapable of pushing back the darkness. And now he'd harmed the one woman who had tried to help him.

"Go back to your room," he ordered. "I'll ask Mrs. Cobb to bring a compress for your face."

She managed a nod, but her fear remained. He despised himself for losing control, even if it was a dream. Ashleigh had already endured her father's mistreatment—and now she likely believed her own husband was the same. It didn't matter that Cameron had been unaware of his surroundings; the result was the same. She'd been hurt by his own hands.

After she'd left the room, Cameron donned his clothing, hardly caring what he wore. He needed to put distance between them so she would feel safe again. It was barely past dawn, but he rang for a servant and gave orders for them to pack a few days' worth of clothing and prepare a horse. It might be best if he visited one of his smaller estates, giving his wife time and space.

He knew he was running away. But what other choice did he have? He couldn't endanger her—especially not now. It was his one hope of earning her forgiveness.

He sank down in a chair, remembering the forbidden night they'd shared. She had invited him to touch her, giving him a glimpse of the heaven in her arms. She'd wanted to consummate the marriage, and last night, he'd been stunned at the feelings she'd conjured. No one had ever touched him in that way, and it only deepened his hunger for Ashleigh. Even now, he wanted to pull her back into bed and explore every secret of her bare skin.

Which was yet another reason why he should leave. If he stayed, he would surrender to his own carnal needs. He didn't want any chance of Ashleigh conceiving a child—for he didn't want the risk of her dying. He'd already lost one wife, and he wasn't about to lose another.

A few days ought to be enough time for her to forgive him for the accident, he told himself. He didn't want to awaken Logan because he had no explanation to give.

Instead, within the hour, Cameron was on horseback, journeying south.

As he stared out at the gray landscape, it mirrored his own bleak frustration and guilt. Why had he ever believed he could make her happy? His first wife had never known marital happiness, and now he'd accidentally hurt Ashleigh.

He blamed himself for it. It didn't matter that he'd been haunted by the imprisonment—he should have known better than to share a bed with her. He wasn't safe. He only wished that he had done a better job of his apology, soothing her so she wouldn't see him as a beast.

He wanted her forgiveness. But God knew, he was unworthy of it.

ASHLEIGH FELT LIKE such a fool. Cameron had already left, giving her no time whatsoever to make sense of last night. Only hours ago, she'd fallen asleep in his arms after experiencing the greatest pleasure she'd ever imagined. He'd made her feel treasured, but then his nightmare had surprised her with its intensity.

From the moment he'd started thrashing, she should have moved away from him. He hadn't been aware of his surroundings, and the blow to her cheek had caught her by surprise. In that split second, she'd remembered her father, and she'd cowered in memory only to realize Cameron was still a prisoner of the dream.

The past still haunted him, and it would take time for him to rid himself of the memories. She had so many questions, and yet he could not give her the answers.

At breakfast, she dined with Logan, making excuses for Cameron's absence. Mrs. Cobb admitted that the chief had traveled on horseback along the southern road. "I'm certain he'll return in a few days, Lady Ashleigh. Naught to fret about." But the housekeeper's eyes held wariness.

Ashleigh's own restlessness was getting the better of her. She didn't want to spend the rest of the day worrying about her husband or when he would return. He'd left, believing he'd hurt her. And after the night they'd shared, she wanted him to know that she didn't blame him. It had been entirely an accident—she'd simply been in the wrong place at the wrong time.

A thought occurred to her. She didn't *have* to remain at Kilmartin. There was still time to catch up to him if she made haste.

She stood from her chair and Logan asked, "Where are you going, Mother?"

"I'm going to find your father and bring him home." As soon as she spoke the words, a sudden thrill rushed over her. Cameron might not like it, but it was the right thing to do. Whatever demons were bothering him, they would face them together.

"Can I come too?"

"No, sweeting, I need you to stay here and protect the castle." She touched his nose, and a laugh escaped him. "Can you do that?"

He bobbed his head up and down. "Yes, Mother."

"Good. I hope to be back later today."

She didn't bother packing anything, for she intended to simply bring him back. Instead, she gave orders for the groom and driver to prepare the fastest carriage or coach they had. Her patience wore thin while they readied the horses and vehicle. But her instructions to the driver were simple—*Find the chief.*

As they drove past Kilmartin Castle, she tried to think of what she could say to her husband. Would he agree to come back with her? Could she make him see the truth, that she understood it was an accident?

He'd endured so much, and the sacrifices he'd made had taken their toll. She hoped to convince him to return home, to let her build a life for them. And perhaps one day, he would set aside his vow and make love to her in truth. She wanted a child of her own, one with Cameron's eyes. Last night, they had come so close. He had so much to give, and she hoped she could find a way to make him see that.

They reached the main road, and the driver turned right to take them south. Ashleigh remembered Cameron saying something about another property southeast of Kilmartin Castle. Perhaps he'd gone there.

It had rained last night, and she saw tracks in the road from Cameron's horse. Surely, he couldn't be too far ahead of them. But the mud made it difficult to drive any faster. It seemed that the farther they drove, the worse the roads became. She should have taken a single horse, just as he had.

At last, the driver Malcolm was forced to stop. He got down to investigate the mud, and Ashleigh opened the door. "How bad is it?"

"Bad enough that I dinna think we can go any farther, Lady Ashleigh." He glanced up at the sky. "More rain is coming. We should go back."

"How far away are we from the house?"

Malcolm shook his head. "Nigh an hour. The chief took a horse, so he willnae have the same problems as us."

"I should have done the same." Ashleigh sighed. "And we can't unhitch the carriage, take the horses, and leave it?"

He shrugged. "We've no saddles."

She was beginning to realize that she should have accounted for the weather and the bad roads. "Do you know where the chief is?"

"Like as no', he's gone to the house at Lochmore," Malcolm said. With a sympathetic look, he offered, "I can bring you back to Kilmartin, and we can try again in the morning."

Ashleigh wanted to curse with frustration. "I suppose you're right." She closed the door, and he began turning the carriage back toward the castle. Though she knew it was their only choice, it bothered her that she could do nothing to continue her journey.

They had only traveled a few minutes when she heard the sound of approaching horses. Malcolm pulled their carriage to the side, to allow the vehicle to pass. But instead, the other coach stopped. She paid little heed to them, waiting for her driver to take her back.

But strangely, she heard the men talking. A moment later, someone opened the door to her carriage, and she inhaled with surprise.

"Lady Ashleigh?" a man asked.

"Yes?" She wasn't certain who had stopped them, but the man only smiled.

"Good. You've saved us a great deal of trouble." He called out orders, and a moment later, she heard a gunshot. Oh God, had Malcolm been shot?

Fear and shock flooded through her, but he blocked her from exiting the vehicle. Instead, he seized her arms and pulled her out. Ashleigh struggled, not knowing who these men were or what they wanted, but the sight of her driver bleeding on the ground filled her with terror. Was he dead?

"Who are you?" she demanded. "What is this?"

"Your father wants to see you," was his answer. It was the last thing she heard before the world went dark and she crumpled to the ground.

At first, Cameron wanted to ignore the pounding at the door. He'd come to Lochmore under the pretense of inspecting the house and lands, but truthfully, he wanted some time alone. Ashleigh wasn't safe around him, and he needed a chance to sleep alone and push back the vivid memories of her.

The pounding continued, and finally, he rose from his chair and went to answer the door. One of his drivers had fallen to his knees, and blood covered his shirt.

"Malcolm?" he asked. "What's happened?"

"They took her, sir. Lady Kilmartin."

Instantly, his mood hardened into fury. "Who took her?"

Ashleigh was under his protection, and any man who dared to harm her would not live to draw another breath.

"I heard one mention her father."

Cameron helped the driver up and put pressure on the man's wound as he brought him inside. "Where did they take her?"

Malcolm shook his head. "I dinna ken. But it seemed they were traveling north again."

Then he could track their coach and horses. He helped Malcolm sit down at the table and brought the man a length of clean linen for his wound. "How badly are you hurt?"

"I'll live," Malcolm managed. "The bullet passed through. Though it hurts like the Sassenach bastard tried to peel the skin from my bones."

"I'll ask some of the tenants to come tend you," Cameron promised. "But I have to find Ashleigh."

The driver nodded. "There were six men." He described them, and from what Cameron heard, it sounded as if the marquess had not been among the assailants.

He hurried to call some of the tenants to help the driver, but even as he arranged for a healer, his mind shifted into a military approach. He would need men of his own—maybe some of the tenants.

Horses, supplies, weapons—and time was of the essence. One way or another, he would get his wife back. And God help those who had dared to take her.

Chapter Twelve

ASHLEIGH AWAKENED TO a terrible headache. She didn't know quite where she was, but it resembled a byre. Her hands and feet were bound with rope, and there was no door. Outside, the rain pummeled the earth, making it difficult to see, but she guessed it was late afternoon or perhaps early evening. Two men guarded the entrance, and she shivered against the stone wall.

Inwardly, she was numb. Malcolm was likely dead because of her. She shouldn't have been so impulsive. Her heart ached with anguish, for she also didn't know what would happen to Cameron. Did he even know she'd been taken? And why?

"What is happening? Why did you take me prisoner?" she asked the taller man standing by the door.

"Your father paid us to bring you home," he answered.

Her heart sank, as she realized Mrs. Harding's warning had come true. "I am married to the Chief of Kilmartin," she said firmly. "I don't care what my father paid you. I am going nowhere."

The man smirked. "You'll go wherever we take you, miss."

"It's Lady Kilmartin," she said. "And if you dare try to take me anywhere, my husband will—"

"He doesn't know where you are," the man said. "At least, not until we send word to him. And once he comes to claim you, it'll be his last day alive." His smile turned chilling. "We were also paid to kill him. You'll be a widow soon enough."

Her skin turned to ice. Though she fully believed Cameron could rescue her, how could he manage against six men? It was too much for anyone. But she wouldn't let this brigand see that his words had frightened her.

"You're foolish if you believe you can kill my husband. He's the strongest man I know. And when he comes to find me, it will be *your* last day alive."

The man seemed to dismiss her warning. "We'll see then, won't we?" He turned to the other guard and said, "I'm going to take a piss. Make sure she doesn't move."

Ashleigh struggled to loosen her ropes, but they were wet, which made it even more difficult. Her gown was also sodden, which worsened the chill that permeated her skin.

Cameron had endured far more than this. She couldn't imagine how he had survived two months of such misery. He'd gone hungry, slept in the Tower, and he would carry the scars of those months for always. She closed her eyes, wondering if there was any means for her to save herself. The last thing she wanted was for him to attempt a rescue, only to die at the hands of these men. The thought terrified her.

Time dragged onward, and she realized the first guard had not returned. The second had noticed it, too, and was eyeing her with frustration. Finally, he called out to another guard. "Go and find Benjamin. He's been gone too long."

At that, Ashleigh straightened. Her heart began pounding, as she wondered whether Cameron had somehow found her. *Be careful,* she prayed silently.

She glanced around the byre, wondering if there was any place to leave, save the main doorway. But no, there was nothing except a small opening near the roof. She couldn't reach it if she tried.

Her remaining guard wasn't looking at her, so she managed to get to her knees. Using the stone wall for balance, she managed to push herself into a standing position. Slowly, she inched her way along the wall, shifting her bound feet as she tried to get closer to the doorway.

She heard the sound of men talking, and it seemed that another man had gone missing.

"It's like he was taken by a ghost," one voice said. "I don't like it. Both of 'em gone. No sound, no footprints."

"It's not a ghost," another said. "The pair of them might have gone off with the whisky."

"Go and find them," Ashleigh's guard ordered.

"Won't be me. I'm not going to be taken by a ghost. You go and find them."

Ashleigh's mood lifted, for it did sound as if Cameron was here. She tried to get closer but suddenly lost her balance and fell hard on her side.

"Where do you think you're going?" the guard demanded. He took several strides inside, and Ashleigh tried to move back. He hauled her back to her feet, using the ropes to drag her hands up.

A moment later, she heard the faint gasp of a man outside. That was only the sound before silence fell. Her guard stiffened and kept his hand on Ashleigh's ropes. He jerked hard, and she fell forward, unable to walk. He dragged her to the doorway where the rain was still pounding.

"Did you come for your wife?" the guard shouted. "She'll be dead before you can take another step forward. He pressed his blade to her throat, and Ashleigh went motionless.

"Sam!" a man's voice shouted. "Is that you?"

"Get in here and take the woman," Sam demanded. "We're losing men, one by one. He's coming for her, so we'll wait and take him here."

The other guard slipped inside, and Sam ordered. "Stay with your back to the wall. When he comes, you stab him."

"What about her? She'll warn him."

"You're right. We'll gag her."

Before they could move, Ashleigh spied movement in the

darkness. Though she wasn't certain it was her husband, she couldn't risk anyone seeing him. She turned her face so both men would have their backs to the intruder as they moved to gag her.

The first man dropped so suddenly, Ashleigh's stomach churned. She tried to throw herself to the ground, but her captor seized her and put her body in front of him as a shield. He started backing out the doorway. Rain poured over them, and Ashleigh felt the sharp blade at her throat once more.

And then she saw his face. Gratitude poured over her at the sight of Cameron, and she couldn't stop the tears. He was here. He'd come for her, and she trusted he would keep her safe.

"Let her go," he said to the guard.

"No. You're going to drop your weapons."

The blade pressed into her throat, and abruptly, she felt the weapon slide into her skin. She felt the guard falling backwards, taking her with him.

And the moment he fell, he was going to slit her throat.

CAMERON WATCHED IN shock as his wife started to fall backwards, the knife cutting into her skin. His butler Hamish had tried to help by stabbing the man from behind, but as the guard died, his body weight dragged her down.

Terror flooded through Cameron as he realized she could die within seconds, leaving him powerless to help her. "Catch him!"

But he already knew Hamish couldn't. Cameron threw himself forward, seizing the man's arm and ripping the blade away from her throat. But blood welled against her skin, and he had no idea how deep the knife had gone. He pulled her free of her attacker, but her face had gone pale with shock, and she fainted.

"Sir, is she—?" Hamish's words died off, and Cameron didn't answer. Swiftly, he untied his cravat and used it as a makeshift bandage. It didn't seem to be bleeding enough to soak through the linen, so he had hope that it wasn't too bad. He sliced through her ropes and lifted her into his arms.

Rain pounded both of them, and he ordered, "Bring the horse. Now!"

Hamish hurried off, and he cradled Ashleigh's limp form. *Please let her live,* he prayed. He didn't know if she'd collapsed from her wound or shock, but he needed to bring her to safety.

His butler brought over the horse, and Cameron lifted Ashleigh onto the saddle, swinging up behind her. "I'm bringing her to Lochmore. Ride hard and fetch a doctor!"

The butler ran and mounted his own horse. Cameron turned his gelding toward the smaller estate and quickened the pace, not knowing how bad Ashleigh's injuries were. Inwardly, he felt every emotion rise to the surface. All she'd ever wanted was to love him. And like a fool, he'd pushed her away, time and again. She'd offered herself to him, wanting a loving marriage, but he'd refused.

Somehow, he'd believed that by keeping to this celibate marriage, he was protecting her. Instead, he'd made her marriage into a misery. He'd let his nightmares get the best of him and had struck her in his sleep. And now, when she'd relied on him to rescue her, she'd nearly died at the hands of her assailant. Familiar guilt flooded him, and he held her close while he rode as fast as he dared.

He didn't want to imagine what would happen if she died. The very thought filled him with dread. Ashleigh had slipped into the cracks in his life, filling up the lonely, empty places he hadn't known were there. Though he'd tried to distance his heart, now he couldn't imagine a life without her.

He couldn't lose her now.

When he reached Lochmore, he threw the front door open and brought her inside to one of the bedrooms. Her gown was soaked from the rain, and he needed to get her warm.

Quickly, he undressed her, and she stirred as he pulled the wet clothes from her. "I'm so c-cold," she whispered. He wrapped her up in a warm blanket and laid her back on the mattress, retying the cravat to stanch the blood. Even so, seeing the crimson against the white made his guilt twist even deeper.

"Hamish went for the doctor."

"I'll be all right," she said. "I don't think it's deep."

"I blame myself. I should have disarmed him before he ever got close to you."

She was trembling hard and pleaded, "Cameron, will you hold me?"

"Let me put on dry clothes first so I don't make you cold again." Quickly, he changed his attire and then joined her on the bed.

He sat up against the headboard and pulled her into his arms, stroking her wet hair. "I'm going to fix this. The doctor will make you well again. We'll stay here as long as you need."

She managed a nod, but he didn't like the sickly pale color of her demeanor. She'd lost blood, and he was terrified of watching her die.

Eventually, the doctor arrived and examined her wound. He cleaned and bandaged it, reassuring them, "Lady Kilmartin will be well enough in a few days. If she develops a fever, call me again. Otherwise, she should make a full recovery."

"I want to go home," Ashleigh whispered. "Logan will be worried about us."

"Later," he said gently. "You need to rest."

But the real reason was that he wanted to keep her hidden. If the marquess had tracked her to Scotland, then his men had likely followed Ashleigh from Kilmartin Castle. If there were remaining assailants, they'd go back. It was safer for Logan if neither of them was there.

He spoke with Hamish and gave orders for Georgina and Logan to be heavily guarded. "I want more men here to keep Lochmore safe. Send Mrs. Cobb and a cook, and we'll remain here until Lady Kilmartin's wounds have healed."

"Yes, my chief." Hamish inclined his head and hurried away. After he'd gone, Cameron checked all the locks to ensure the house was secure. When he returned, he found Ashleigh shivering in the bed. He moved in beside her, offering his body heat. She sighed with contentment, and eventually her breathing grew even and deep.

Though he was glad that her wounds were not life-threatening, he was still shaken by what had happened. He should have protected her better. As he watched his wife sleeping, he realized what a fool he was for not accepting the gift she'd given him.

And when she had healed, he promised himself that everything would be different.

ASHLEIGH WASN'T ABOUT to leave Logan alone, and she insisted on returning to Kilmartin the next day. She felt far safer in the large castle, though Cameron insisted that she should remain in bed until she was stronger. Her throat was still sore, but the wound was beginning to heal. Mrs. Cobb had given her so many poultices and healing herbs, she rather felt like she'd been basted and seasoned. But in time, she began to feel better.

Logan came to visit her every day. One morning, he brought her a handful of weeds with a few colorful flowers mixed in. He cuddled on her lap but was careful to avoid her bandage.

Every night, Cameron slept with her. She was conscious of his body heat, and the strong, lean planes. She wanted more from him, but after he'd left her the last time, she didn't dare reach out to him.

Ashleigh began to sense that something had changed. He'd been attentive, looking after her needs. But there was a tension within him, almost like a dormant hunger. She didn't know if she was imagining it or not.

A few more days and she was finally able to remove her bandages. Although the red line remained, she hoped it would fade in time. Sarah had already helped her undress for the night, and she wore a thin linen nightgown. It was cold in her room, but she noticed that the adjoining door to Cameron's bedchamber was open. He was already kneeling beside the hearth, adding coal to the fire.

Slowly, she opened the door and saw him look back at her. "May I come and warm myself?"

He stood and nodded. His jaw seemed to tighten, and his gaze slid over her body as she came further into the room, as if he remembered everything he'd seen beneath the nightgown.

"How are you feeling?" he asked.

"Much better." But even though physically she was well, she hadn't forgotten what her father had done. This wasn't over yet. Anyone who would hire six men to kill her husband would not give up so easily.

It had been borne in on her again that life could change in a single moment. She wanted to make the most of the time they had together, but she was so afraid of hearing his reasons why they should not consummate the marriage.

Ashleigh took a step closer to him, and he reached out to touch her waist. His palm warmed her skin through the linen, and she closed her eyes, savoring his touch. Neither spoke, but she rested her hands upon his chest. He wore only a shirt and his trousers, and he'd shaved again. She reached up to touch his cheeks, and it was only natural to put her arms around him. His mouth descended to hers, and in his kiss, she tasted the echo of her own yearning. She'd fallen in love with Cameron MacNeill, and right now, she wanted nothing more than to be in his embrace.

"I was afraid I'd lost you," he said. "You can't know what that felt like." His voice was hollow, and in his eyes, she saw an unspoken pain.

"But you saved me." She rested her hand on his face. "And those men can't hurt us anymore."

Her heart was pounding as he covered her hand with his own. "I will never let anyone harm you."

She stood on tiptoe and kissed him. Though she wanted to tell him the words in her heart, she held them back, afraid that if she said the wrong thing, he might leave again.

His hand moved back to her nape, sinking into her hair. She had it in a single braid, and he untied the ribbon, loosening her hair until it spilled over her shoulders. "You're beautiful, Ashleigh."

Her cheeks flushed, and she ventured a smile. Slowly, his hands moved lower in a silent question. She turned her back to him and brought his hands to the buttons of her nightgown. One by one, he opened them until the gown slid from her body, leaving her naked in front of the fire. She felt vulnerable to his gaze, wondering what he was thinking. But then his hands moved to cup her breasts, and she felt the rise of desire as he caressed her nipples. He bent to kiss her shoulder, and then he turned her to face him. His eyes were heated with his own needs, and she moved her hands beneath his shirt to touch him. He helped her remove it, and in the firelight, she saw the shadow of his scars.

"I despise the men who hurt you," she murmured. "And I pray you never have to go back."

His gaze drifted to her throat. "I swear, I will kill any man who dares to lay a hand on you." In his voice, she heard the regret and guilt.

And so she asked, "What if I want *you* to lay your hands on me?"

In silent answer, his fingertips skimmed over her body. Past her ribs, lower still, until they slipped between her thighs. She was wet, aching for his touch, and she parted her legs.

"I am at your command." He touched her intimately, and she suppressed a gasp. "Look at me, Ashleigh."

She did, and his fingers continued to delve against her folds. He was slow, wickedly tempting her with his touch. There was an ebb and flow that made her knees weak. He bent to kiss her breast, and his tongue swirled over her nipple.

"I want you inside me," she whispered, pleading for him to

make love to her. Though she was nervous, she sensed that their marriage would never truly be real until they consummated it together.

He slid two fingers into her depths, and she let out a moan. In response, she unbuttoned his trousers and reached for what she wanted. When her hand closed over his hot length, he quickly removed the rest of his clothes. A moment later, he lifted her in his arms and carried her to the bed.

To her surprise, he lifted her to straddle him. It was strange being in such a position of power. But she understood why he'd done this. He wanted her to be empowered—not to take from her, but to give instead.

Ashleigh cupped his length, caressing him. He pulled her so close, his shaft nestled against her wetness. She was startled at how good it felt, and she rose up onto her knees. He guided himself to her entrance and remained there, letting her take the lead.

"I am yours, Ashleigh."

She could feel the thickness of him stretching her, but it felt good to take part of him inside. Nerves caught up inside her, and she hesitated, not knowing what to do. But when he sat up slightly and took her nipple in his mouth again, she felt the echoing pleasure deep in her core. Slowly, he moved against her, and she began to lift herself up and sink down again. She felt awkward at first, not really knowing the rhythm. But as he continued to suckle at her breast, her breathing grew uneven.

She found it easier to take more of him inside, and he penetrated the barrier of her innocence abruptly. She gasped when he was fully embedded inside her. For a moment, she was afraid to move, but he continued to touch her. His hands moved down her spine, then he cupped her bottom, squeezing it lightly. She felt a sudden throb within her legs, and she sensed that this was only the beginning.

"Cameron," she whispered. "Show me what to do."

In answer, he rolled her to her back, still inside her. He lifted one of her legs and began to slowly penetrate and withdraw. The motion teased her, and she clenched her inner muscles around him.

"Careful," he warned. "Or I won't be able to last."

He praised her, gliding his hands over her breasts, against the dip of her waist, and then he rested his hand on her hip.

But she wanted more from him. She remembered how good it had felt to have his thumb against her hooded flesh. She guided it there, showing him how she wanted to be touched.

"Like this?" he asked.

"Yes." She showed him how to press against her, and when he continued his thrusts, she felt her body rising to his call. She lifted her hips, meeting him as he entered and withdrew. "I never knew it would be so . . . arousing," she whispered. "I feel like I don't ever want you to stop."

He continued his strokes, penetrating her until she grew restless. She reached for his hips, wrapping her legs around his waist. Though he tried to be gentle, she couldn't stop herself from arching her back, quickening the pace.

Cameron kissed her deeply, and she slid her tongue into his mouth. He was so rigid within her, she could hardly bear it. Over and over, he drove her to the edge, making her crave the fulfillment she needed.

And though she'd never meant to speak, she couldn't help herself. Against his lips, she said, "I love you." The words had an immediate effect on him. He sheathed himself deep inside and used his fingers to torment her. She was rising to the edge, floating higher as he found the secret place that made her break apart. The pleasure shimmered through her, and she arched, feeling the rush of wetness against his body.

"Come with me," she pleaded, and he resumed his thrusts, his body meeting hers as she convulsed around him. It took only moments to see the tension rise in his face before he penetrated a few more times and flooded himself within her.

This was what she'd wanted. To join with this man in the

most intimate way, to feel their bodies intertwined. The physical release had been everything she'd ever imagined.

She only wished that he could have said the words of love in return.

Chapter Thirteen

CAMERON HAD NEVER imagined married life would be like this. He'd made love to Ashleigh all night long, learning what pleased his wife. She was particularly sensitive, and he'd never imagined she would be so responsive to his touch.

Even now, her legs were twined with his, and she traced one of the scars on his chest. "I want to stay here all day in this bed." Her smile turned wicked.

"Do you?" He rolled her beneath him, and she wrapped her arms around his waist. He was already hard again, and she reached down to touch him.

"The only problem is food. And Logan will want to know where we are."

"Thank God for doors that lock." He guided himself between her legs, and she took him inside her body. The sweet heaven of joining with her drowned out all logic. He knew there was still a risk of making her pregnant. And yet he also understood now her desire for a child of their own.

He could imagine a little girl with Ashleigh's smile. Or a little brother for Logan with her eyes. He'd never imagined having other children, but it humbled him to realize he wanted them with her.

He knew it was fear holding him back. Fear of losing her, fear of losing a child. But he'd come to realize that each day was a gift, and tomorrow was not promised. Even with all his rules and precautions, he'd still nearly lost her during the attack. If she'd died, he never would have shared these moments. And even though he was terrified of her dying in childbirth, neither did he want to live a life governed by fear.

She began to move beneath him, and he used his mouth and tongue against the sensitive part of her neck. Gooseflesh covered her skin, but she met his thrusts with her hips.

"Cameron," she murmured. "I don't want anyone to threaten this life we have together."

He knew she was speaking of her father, but he was entirely too distracted by his wife's sweetness. He balanced his weight on one arm, lifting her leg over his shoulder. The new position gave him deeper access, and within moments, she was gasping, digging her nails into his shoulders.

"No one will *ever* take you from me again," he swore, driving deep within her. "I promise you that, Ashleigh."

Tears came to her eyes, and he saw a tremulous smile before she came apart, her body squeezing him tightly while she erupted with her release.

He thrust a few more times, savoring the way her body felt beneath him, the way he was sheathed deep inside. Then his own release crashed through him, and he shuddered as she clung tightly, her legs wrapped around his waist.

"We should go to London," she suggested. "Together, so we can face him. My mother should stay here."

"Your father holds a great deal of power in London. And to the rest of the *ton*, I'm a man of little means."

Ashleigh laughed before she turned more serious. "And weren't they mistaken?" She leaned in and kissed him softly. Cameron responded to her, taking her lips slowly, as if he could savor the taste of her mouth.

"I don't want you to go back to . . . whatever you were doing before," she said quietly. "I don't want you to risk your life again."

He wanted to agree with her, but he couldn't. Not yet. He'd barely made it out alive the last time, but he was one of the few men who could infiltrate the French. It wasn't so easy to say no when it meant serving his country.

But he did agree with her that they needed to resolve the issue with her father. "We cannot simply face your father at your home. He will try to have me arrested and claim that I took your mother."

"She can't go back to him," Ashleigh insisted. "Even if he doesn't hurt her...he would shatter her spirit completely. She's happy for the first time in years, Cameron. I can't take that away from her."

"But he won't grant her a divorce," he pointed out. "A separation is the best she can hope for. And we'd have to convince him to let her go."

She sobered at that, and he rolled to his side, facing her. "I don't think he will ever agree to that." For a long moment, she thought. Then she said, "My father is a proud man. He would never want anyone to believe his wife would leave him."

Cameron considered her words. "Then we need to invent a story that she's ill and has gone to one of the lesser estates to live a quiet life. If it's for her health, no one would think anything of that."

"Except that, to him, she's a possession. He's furious that we both left, and he wants to punish us." She buried her face in his chest. "He already tried to kidnap me and kill you."

Cameron comforted her, holding her close. "But I'm alive. And we'll find a way to resolve this." A man like the marquess wouldn't give up easily—not when he had money and resources. But Cameron wasn't about to let Ashleigh be endangered again.

"I don't know what to do." Her voice was a whisper, revealing her fear.

He withdrew from her body, holding her close. "Do you trust me, Ashleigh?"

She nodded. "It's my father I don't trust. He has enough money to hire as many men as he wants. I don't want you to leave for London without me. I want to help you with this."

Though he understood her reasoning, he couldn't consider it. "He tried to hurt you, Ashleigh. I'm sorry, but I can't let you go with me to London. You're safer here."

She stiffened in his arms. "Six men kidnapped me only a few miles from here. I hardly think I'm safe."

He wanted to argue that if she hadn't left, it never would have happened. But she'd been pursuing him, so he held his tongue. Even so, her words were a sharp reminder of her injuries. Aye, he'd caught up to her and rescued her from the men—but she'd still been hurt.

His wife rose from the bed, giving him a breathtaking view of her naked body. He was disappointed when she pulled on her chemise and then set out her corset, petticoats, and a morning gown.

"No, I am going with you to London," she insisted. "This was an act of war, and I intend to answer it."

ASHLEIGH HAD NO intention of waiting around while her husband disappeared for another two months. This was a battle for her freedom, as well as her mother's. And going to war meant gathering allies.

"What do you plan to do?" His voice held wariness, as if he didn't trust her.

"We need allies if we're going to fight this war," she announced. Her father's greatest weakness was his pride, and it made sense to strike him where he was most vulnerable. "We should speak to the most powerful members of the *ton* and ask for their support of our marriage."

She saw the moment his demeanor shifted. "Ashleigh, no one can know who I am. It's too dangerous."

Although she understood that, she continued, "They don't need to know your secrets—only that we're married and are happy together."

She could see the doubts on his face. "Hear me out. My father values his friendships. Everything he does is to gain power and standing. If anyone learns what he's done to challenge our marriage, then it will force him into a difficult position. We might threaten how the *ton* sees him. And he would do anything to avoid losing face."

"But someone who is trapped will fight harder to escape," Cameron pointed out. "He becomes more dangerous."

Before she could argue further, he pushed back the covers and stood. Ashleigh felt her cheeks flush at the sight of him. Never in her wildest dreams had she imagined a man as handsome and strong as Cameron would belong to her. She gave him an appreciative glance while he reached for his own clothing.

"Keep looking at me like that, and we won't leave this room," he warned with a wicked tone.

Ashleigh turned her back and hid her smile. She still believed if they could gain the support of the most powerful peers in London, her father could do nothing to dissolve their marriage.

"I still think our best hope is to gain the favor of the most powerful families in London." Then, if her father threatened them, it made him look bad among his friends. "I could speak to Mrs. Harding," Ashleigh offered. "She might have even more connections."

"Not the kind we need."

"Do you think Violet Edwards and Lord Scarsdale could help us? Or even his father, the marquess?" That is, if Violet had forgiven her for what she'd done. It still bothered Ashleigh deeply that she'd behaved like such a terrible person during the dancing lesson that day.

"Scarsdale?" he mused. "Are he and Miss Edwards . . . ?"

"I think so," she answered. "They certainly couldn't keep their eyes off one another during the masquerade." She hesitated a moment and ventured, "Or if you aren't opposed to it, perhaps Persephone's father, the duke, might come to our aid."

"I don't trust them," he admitted. "I would rather avoid that alliance, if possible."

She understood his reasons, though she was willing to beg favors from the Devil if it meant protecting their marriage.

"I could try to gain an audience with the Prince Regent or the Queen," he said softly. "A royal intervention would be the strongest alliance." He paused and added, "I suspect the Earl of Dunmeath might also help us."

"I don't know the man," Ashleigh said.

"Cormac has a reckless side," he said. "I've met him on several occasions, and he enjoys being rebellious. With the right incentive, he may be helpful." He finished buttoning his trousers and stood before her. Ashleigh reached up to trace the firm muscles of his chest, and his arms slid around her waist. "I'll begin making arrangements to leave in the morning."

"For *us* to leave, you mean." She wasn't about to let him leave her behind again.

"I mean *I* will go. Ashleigh, I'm going to keep you safe. It's too dangerous in London."

The iron look in his eyes frustrated her, and she simply couldn't stand aside. She wanted to push back, to demand that he let her go. And yet, she suspected if she didn't yield, he would only tighten his resolve. She was struggling to find the words, to find her voice, but then he unraveled her anger when he leaned in to kiss her.

"I can't let you be hurt again," he said against her lips. She yielded to him, and he crushed her in his embrace. "It would break me if anything happened to you."

His words rushed through her with a different understanding. He wasn't taking her freedom out of a desire for power or control—this was fear. For a long moment she held him close, breathing in the scent of her husband. She was conscious of his breathing, the heat of his skin, and the way she needed this man.

Cameron took her mouth in a possessive kiss, and she answered it with her own. He belonged to her, just as she belonged to him.

"You're not alone," she said softly. "I don't want you to feel as if you have to fight my battles for me."

His eyes burned into hers. "I would fight every battle for you, Ashleigh."

And again, the ache in her heart spread throughout her body, wishing he would say the words of love she wanted to hear. But he didn't, and she hid her disappointment.

Instead, she changed her tactics. "Let me start by writing letters," she said. "We'll ask for help from all our friends. Then we'll set our strategy and plans. Together."

He pulled back and cupped her face between his hands. In his eyes, she saw the emotions, even though he couldn't speak the words. Somehow, she would have to find a way to work with him to solve their problems.

But she still had no intention of being left behind.

IT WAS RATHER like planning a military battle, Cameron decided. They knew their enemy, they understood what he wanted, and now it was a matter of facing the marquess. In the past week, Ashleigh had written nearly twenty letters to every friend she had, announcing her marriage and telling them she hoped to return to London soon to host a celebration.

"Lord Dunmeath will let us have the ball at his residence," Cameron said.

"How do you know? It's too soon to have a reply to our letters," Ashleigh said.

"Because he's been asking me to invest in his wool." Cameron sat back in his chair. "If he hosts the gathering, then he knows he'll get what he wants from me."

"You don't want to have it at your London house?"

He shook his head. The last thing he wanted was anyone

knowing where he lived. He'd managed to keep a quiet residence no one knew about, and he had no intention of bringing the *ton* into that life. "It's too small."

Ashleigh sealed the last letter and crossed the room to sit in his lap. The floral scent of her skin tempted him, and he leaned in to steal a kiss while she put her arms around his neck. "When do we leave for London?"

He hesitated a moment, wondering what to tell her. Those few seconds darkened the expression on her face. "I'm not staying behind, Cameron. If I do, we cannot win this battle. We must go together and face him."

"I want you to wait at least three days before you join me," he corrected. "Give me time to find out what your father has been doing."

At that, her anger seemed to ease. "Reconnaissance, then."

"Yes. And I'll need time to ensure your safety, make arrangements for the ball, order clothing for us, ensure that Prinny can come, and—"

"I can help you," she reminded him. "You don't have to shoulder all of it alone."

He gave a nod, but he wasn't concerned about the ball. His greatest worry was keeping her safe. Ashleigh was right that there had been six men who had tried to take her, not just the four he and his men had dealt with. Though it was possible that the other two had run away and abandoned their job, he couldn't deny the possibility that they were still a danger. During the past few days, the dogs had barked more often than usual. He was convinced that someone was watching the castle, waiting for an opportunity.

If he pretended that he and Ashleigh were journeying together, packing all manner of trunks and belongings, then perhaps he could lure the men to attack the coach. It was easier to defend himself than to worry about his wife. If Ashleigh followed a little later, she could travel with some of his stronger servants for protection.

"You're worrying again, aren't you?" She traced her hand against his beard stubble, and her touch warmed him. He craved her affection, and it reminded him again of the differences between her and Rebecca.

"I am concerned that your father will try to charge me with kidnapping," he admitted. "It wouldn't hold, but it could make our lives inconvenient. Too many questions."

"We're married," she argued. "I would tell the magistrate that we eloped. And as for my mother, we'll simply say that she came to visit me in Scotland."

Though she was only trying to justify what they'd done, he knew the truth. While he could shield Ashleigh from her father, the law was clear enough that the marquess had the right to demand that his wife return home. And unless Cameron could find a way to coerce the marquess into letting her go, Georgina's fate might be out of their hands.

"I'll do what I can," was all he could promise. "But it would be easier if your mother remains hidden."

A commotion in the hallway caught their attention, as if someone were running. Ashleigh stood up from Cameron's lap, and he pressed her behind him to protect her. Her trepidation heightened, but instinct kept her in place. Whatever was happening had not alarmed the servants.

A moment later, her mother burst into the room. Her eyes were wild, and her hair had fallen about her shoulders. But it was the tears running down her cheeks that made Ashleigh run to her mother's side.

"What's happened?"

"He's gone." Tears streamed down her face. "I went to wake him from his nap. At first, I thought he'd run away or that he was playing a game, hiding in the cottage. But those bastards took him." Georgina sobbed and held out a crumpled piece of paper. "Look."

Ashleigh's heart went cold, but she took the note and showed it to Cameron. In scrawled handwriting were the words:

Come to London if you want your son back. Bring your wife and her mother.

Her knees went weak, and when she turned to Cameron, she saw that his face had become something else. No longer was he the kind, loving husband. Instead, his face held cold rage. His blue eyes were ice, and his mouth had tightened into a grim line. In that moment, she wondered if he intended to kill her father for what he'd done.

"How long ago was this?" he demanded of Georgina.

"L-less than an hour," she said. "Logan ate luncheon with me, and he went for a lie down at half one."

"And you didn't notice that someone took him? You left him alone?"

Her mother blanched at his words. "I—I was only outside in the garden. Cook was in the house, along with one of the maids. I don't know how it happened. None of us saw or heard anything."

Ashleigh reached for her mother's hand. She didn't know what to say, but on her husband's face, she saw only fury. He jerked the bell pull so hard it nearly came off. A footman came running, and Cameron ordered, "Prepare my fastest horse, and ask for four volunteers from among our men. We're leaving now to find my son."

"I'll come with you," Ashleigh started to say, but he lifted a hand.

"You're going nowhere. You'll stay here with your mother while I bring Logan back." The razor edge to his voice took her aback. She'd never seen him like this before, commanding and fierce. She had the feeling that if he caught up to the men who took Logan, they would be dead within minutes. Her fears were confirmed when he unlocked a desk drawer and took out two pistols and ammunition.

"He's my son too, Cameron," she said softly. "What can I do to help?"

"You can stay behind and not be in my way," he answered.

"But whatever you do, don't try to interfere."

She had no opportunity to say anything else before he strode from the room. Her mother leaned against the wall, weeping softly. "This is my fault."

For a moment, Ashleigh felt dazed and uncertain. She hardly knew how to react or what to say. But she tore from the room, running to the entrance hall after her husband. "Cameron, wait."

He was already reaching for the doorknob, but she caught his arm. "What are you going to do?"

"He's my son, and I'm going to bring him back tonight."

He started to push past her, and she called out, "But what if you can't find him? What then?"

He stopped and looked her in the eyes. "I won't come back until I do find him, Ashleigh."

And with that, he opened the door and left.

"MY LORD, YOU have a caller." The footman paused and added, "One of your men has returned." The servant appeared uncomfortable, as if he didn't know quite what to say.

Cecil straightened in his chair and regarded his footman. "Did he succeed? Are my wife and daughter with him?"

The footman appeared uncomfortable. "Not exactly." He glanced into the corridor and signaled for the man to come forward.

Cecil wrinkled his nose when he saw the Scot he'd hired. The man smelled as if he hadn't bathed in weeks. His eyes were bloodshot, and he stumbled into the drawing room. "Well, where are they?" the marquess demanded. "And what happened to the rest of your men?"

"All but one are dead, my lord."

Though it wasn't unexpected, Cecil didn't like the turn in this conversation. It implied that they'd failed in their task.

"I took their boy instead. They'll come for him."

At that, some of Cecil's mood eased. It was a good plan to use the child as bait. "Bring him inside. I want to see him for myself."

The man returned to the corridor and a few moments later, he brought in a large wooden box. Cecil heard the sound of crying from within, and though he supposed he ought to feel guilty for the kidnapping, he didn't.

Cameron MacNeill deserved this. The Highland chief had stolen from Cecil, and it was only right that he should endure the same frustration and annoyance of losing his family.

The marquess lifted the box lid, and inside was a small boy, bound and gagged. Tears streaked the child's dirty face, and there was a strong scent, as if the boy had wet himself. For a moment, he studied the child.

"How do I know he belongs to MacNeill? You could have stolen another child and tried to pass him off as the chief's."

"It's his son," the Scot insisted. "And ye'll know it's his because MacNeill will be here within a day. He's been tracking us, and it's only by the grace of God that I'm alive."

Cecil reached down and untied the gag, pulling it out of the boy's mouth. The child started to scream, and he gripped the boy's hand.

"You do not talk unless I tell you to."

The boy flinched and lowered his head, whimpering.

"Good. Now what is your name?"

The boy didn't answer, but kept his head down, his shoulders trembling.

"Answer me!" The marquess had little patience for this. He seized the boy by the ear and jerked him up. "What is your name?"

"L-Logan."

"And who is your father?"

The boy started crying harder, and Cecil tightened his grip. He raised his other fist in a silent threat, and Logan pleaded, "Don't hurt me."

"His *name,*" Cecil demanded. "You'd better tell me what I

want to know or—"

"MacNeill," the boy sobbed.

The marquess tied the gag back in place and pushed the boy into the box. Then he reached for a handkerchief to wipe the boy's filth from his hands. He rang for a footman and ordered, "Have one of the maids take care of this boy. Bathe him and lock him in the nursery for now."

The servant appeared aghast, but he murmured, "Yes, my lord," and reached into the box to lift the boy up. The child struggled against him, trying to scream against his gag. It didn't matter. Once he was cleaned up and fed, the child would settle down. Or if not, laudanum would shut him up.

"What about my payment, my lord?" the Scot asked.

Cecil shrugged. "I'll see to it that my secretary pays you half the money. You'll have the rest when my wife and daughter arrive."

"I want all of it," the Scot argued. "I did as you commanded."

"No, you didn't." Cecil had no intention of letting this brigand make demands. "Until my wife and daughter are here, you'll wait. Return to me in one week, and if both are here, you will be well rewarded." The Scot's expression grew stony, but he was wise enough to hold his silence.

Cecil intended to keep the boy here until Ashleigh arrived with Georgina. After he dismissed the Scot, who went back into the hallway with his secretary, he leaned back in a chair, feeling satisfied.

Members of the *ton* had been gossiping about him for weeks behind closed doors. Not only because of Ashleigh's running away, but also because of Georgina's disappearance. It had taken the Bow Street Runners weeks to find them, and Cecil blamed MacNeill for all of it. The man had made him into a laughingstock. But no longer.

At last, he'd gained the upper hand against MacNeill. He was in control again, and he would gladly trade the boy for Ashleigh and Georgina. And the two of them would be sorry they'd ever left.

Chapter Fourteen

I T HAD BEEN a grueling week of travel, but Ashleigh and her mother finally reached the outskirts of London. They had waited days for Cameron's return, and when he hadn't come back, she and Georgina had decided to face the marquess at last.

Their determination didn't make the prospect any less frightening, but they had to force Cecil to stop. Her father had tried to kidnap her and kill Cameron—which had been horrifying enough. But he'd dared to harm her son—and she could never forgive him for that.

Emotions welled up within her, the fear and devastation pushing against the boundaries of her control. She couldn't cry—not yet. She had to remain strong for her mother and pretend that she had the strength to endure this. If she kept pretending long enough, maybe she would start to believe it.

But the very thought of those men taking Logan was enough to push her up to the edge. She had to stop thinking of it and concentrate on one hour at a time. It was the only way to keep from losing her mind.

Georgina sat across from her, and with every mile, her spirits dimmed. Her face was drawn, and during the journey Ashleigh had had to coax her to eat. The truth was, neither of them was looking forward to what lay ahead.

On impulse, she reached across the space of the coach and took her mother's hand, squeezing it. "It's going to be different this time."

"Will it?" Georgina didn't sound convinced. "He's going to force me to live with him again. And I don't know if I can endure it. Not this time." She gripped her hands together. "But he has Logan. And we have to get him back."

"We will," Ashleigh said. She wished her mother hadn't come on the journey, but Georgina had been adamant. She blamed herself that Logan had been taken, but Ashleigh didn't, not any more than she blamed the cook or the maid who had been in the cottage. It could just as easily have happened to anyone.

She believed her father would give Logan back. Not because he would feel any sort of remorse, but because he had no use for the boy. He was the bait, and although Ashleigh had taken the lure, she had no intention of being caught.

It was nightfall by the time they reached Mrs. Harding's house. It took only moments for the headmistress to usher both of them inside.

"Have you eaten?" Mrs. Harding asked. "I could have Cook warm up some soup or give you sandwiches."

"We ate on the journey," Ashleigh said. "If my mother could stay here for the night, I will gladly pay you." She planned to continue onward to Cameron's townhouse.

But it was Georgina who surprised her when she spoke. "I should like to stay a little longer than one night. And I also would be glad to pay you for your services. Only . . . I think *I* am in need of lessons."

"Lady Rothburn, my lessons are for young ladies seeking husbands," Mrs. Harding said gently.

"But you do teach them more than etiquette and social graces," Georgina continued. "I saw what you did for Violet Edwards. You transformed her from a quiet mouse into someone powerful."

"I transformed her into a countess." The headmistress smiled.

"She married Lord Scarsdale not long ago."

Ashleigh couldn't stop her smile. So she'd been right about Scarsdale. "I am happy for her," she admitted. And she was. "Mother, why do you want the lessons?"

Georgina continued clenching her gloved hands together. "I need to learn how to stand up to Cecil. He doesn't listen to anything I say. I have no voice in the marriage, and I cannot live with a man who never lets me speak my mind."

Mrs. Harding's expression turned gentle. "I can help you with that."

Ashleigh sobered, realizing what her mother meant. She'd made the same mistakes while growing up in her father's household. Every time she had tried to face his wrath, she'd failed. And now, with her own husband, she was beginning to follow the same pattern of remaining silent.

"Mother, I really should be going. I need to speak to Cameron and find out what he's learned about Logan." She embraced Georgina and gave Mrs. Harding a banknote for fifty pounds.

The matron thanked her quietly. "Are you certain you don't want to join your husband in the morning?"

Ashleigh shook her head. "It's best if I go now." If there was any chance Cameron had already managed to rescue his son, she wanted to be there. "Thank you for protecting my mother."

She said her farewells and then returned to the coach. Though she tried to pretend that everything was fine, inwardly she was afraid. Cameron had warned her not to interfere, and she didn't know if he would be angry with her. He might try to send her away.

Hot tears gathered in her eyes as she feared what lay ahead. Not just facing her husband, but—what if he hadn't rescued Logan? What if their boy was still in danger? Logan wasn't her son by birth, but she loved the child, nonetheless. She loved his impulsive hugs and kisses, the way he curled up on her lap, and how he'd stolen her heart.

They had to find him and bring him home. She couldn't bear

it if anything happened to their son. Without warning, her tears came, and she sobbed in the coach. She had held herself together for over a week, but now that she was alone, all the terror and guilt crashed through her.

But if anyone could find Logan, it was Cameron. She fully understood his fury and the way nothing else mattered except finding their son.

A sobering thought filled her at the thought of her father. Though she wanted to believe that Cecil hadn't harmed the boy, she couldn't be certain. And more than that, she couldn't blame Cameron if he wanted to murder the marquess for what he'd done.

The coach came to a stop at Cameron's townhouse, and she hastily dried her tears, trying to keep herself together. Nerves tightened in her stomach, but she gathered her courage. The driver helped her out of the coach and kept close as she walked to the front door and knocked. Ashleigh waited a moment, but no one answered. She knocked again. And still, no one came to the door.

"My lady, do you want to return to the Harding residence?" the driver asked.

"No, not yet." She stared up at the darkened windows. If her husband was here and did not want to be disturbed, of course he would not open the door, and he would command his staff not to answer. But perhaps she could go through the servants' entrance.

"Follow me," she commanded.

He obeyed, and she went to the entrance where they'd escaped the last time they'd been here. The door was nearly hidden, but she tried the knob. At first, it didn't budge, but when she shook the knob, the door suddenly swung open. At that, she smiled.

Ashleigh paid the driver and dismissed him to return to her mother, then she walked inside the townhouse. She bolted the door shut behind her and went up the narrow stairs. Though she wasn't certain what she would find, at least she was home.

Inside, the house was mostly dark, except for a faint light coming from a room at the end of the hallway.

Her husband was here, after all. Ashleigh guessed it was his study or the library perhaps. She continued quietly down the hallway, wondering what she would find.

She opened the door and said softly, "Cameron?"

But there was no one there—only a desk with papers all over it and a burning candle.

"What are you doing here?" came his voice from behind her.

She spun and saw him standing in the hallway. Of course, he'd heard her approaching. She wanted to embrace him, but the look in his eyes held a warning.

He wasn't at all happy to see her. His demeanor was cool, and she saw that his beard and mustache were starting to grow back. Likely he hadn't shaved since he'd left Scotland.

"Have you found Logan?" she asked quietly, even as she already knew the answer.

"Your father has him."

Which was just as she'd guessed. "Have you seen him? Is he all right?"

Up close, she could see that his eyes were bloodshot. It looked as if he hadn't slept since he'd left Scotland either. "No. I've been unable to see him yet."

She wanted to ask how he knew Logan was there, but from the fury on his face, she didn't risk voicing the question. Instead, she said, "Then I will go to my father's house in the morning. I'll bring him back myself. Then you can take him back home." She reached out to take his hand, but he pulled it back.

Startled, she raised her eyes to his and saw the coldness in them. "Choose a room, Ashleigh, and go to sleep. I have plans to make."

CAMERON COULD SEE the hurt in her expression, but he saw no

choice but to set down invisible boundaries. He'd asked Ashleigh not to leave Scotland, and she'd ignored him. She believed she could walk up to her father's door and rescue Logan—to easily accomplish what he'd been unable to do since he'd arrived.

There were constables guarding every entrance to the marquess's house. Cecil expected him to attempt a break-in. And Cameron knew, the moment he came close to the house, they would arrest him.

No, it wouldn't work. Instead, he'd been trying to use one of his servants to infiltrate the marquess's household. One of his maids had gotten close—and had confirmed Logan was there—but thus far, she'd been unable to flee with the boy.

The marquess could not continue this game for too much longer. Cameron had been watching the house every day, and he'd hired others to do the same. Soon enough, he would break through.

Ashleigh was a complication he didn't need right now. Even if he managed to get Logan out, he suspected the marquess would lock her away and punish her for eloping.

He started to walk away, but he heard her speak from behind him. "I've been bullied all my life, you know."

He paused, not turning around. But he did listen to her words.

"First and foremost, by my father. I was never allowed to have an opinion of my own. And if I dared to speak out against his orders, he punished my mother."

He heard her soft footsteps drawing nearer. "Hurting her was his way of hurting me. And I saw her slowly dying from that marriage. I didn't know if I could ever get her out.

"Then he arranged a marriage for me, with a man who wanted to do the same thing. But you stood up for me. You defended me against the men who wanted to hurt me." Her hand reached out to touch his shoulder. "You accused me of standing aside when Persephone bullied Violet. And you're right. I was a coward then." She turned him slowly to face her. "But I will be damned if

I stand aside after that monster took our son."

He saw the tears streaming down her cheeks, and the rage in her eyes. "I'm not a coward now, Cameron. I will fight to bring him back. And my mother is in London as well, to help ensure that my father doesn't make false accusations against any of us."

Her auburn hair was falling down from its arrangement, and her blue eyes were shadowed with grief that mirrored his own. Her beauty haunted him, for he sensed that their marriage hung in the balance, based on what he chose to do now.

"I am going to bring Logan home, and you are going to help me," she insisted. Her tears continued, and he wanted to brush them aside. God help him, he wanted to hold his wife. He wanted to lose himself in her body, to forget all his failings. But he didn't want to see the disappointment in her eyes, as he had with Rebecca. His first wife had been miserable, and he didn't want that to happen with Ashleigh.

He'd wanted to shield her from all this, for her to remain safely in Scotland while he figured it out. But instead, his actions had caused her to view him in the same controlling light as her father. The realization sobered him, for he'd never intended her to feel mistreated. He'd spoken harshly out of adamance at keeping her away and protected.

"I won't stand aside," she continued. "And I won't let you treat me like my father has done all these years. I am your wife, and I will not wait in the shadows for you to fight my battles for me. We fight together."

She locked her gaze with his, and her nearness aroused him to the point of physical pain. He yearned to take her to bed, to taste her skin and feel her softness all around him.

"Look at me, Cameron," she whispered. "Will you let me help you?"

He didn't know how to answer her, but when she reached up to touch his cheek, he could bear it no longer. He crushed her mouth with his, pressing her back against the wall. In the kiss, he unleashed his pain, needing her touch as a healing balm. She responded to him, wrapping her arms around his neck, threading her tongue with his.

"I blame myself," he admitted when they broke apart. "He was taken because I didn't guard him closely enough."

"Don't," she insisted, loosening his shirt from his trousers. "The past doesn't matter anymore. All we can do is bring him home."

His fingers unbuttoned her gown, and he lost all sense of patience. He tore at her stays, trying to free her breasts, but he struggled to loosen her bodice. Right now, needed to be inside his wife, and when she unfastened his trousers and reached for him, he let out a groan.

"Ashleigh, you're killing me." He started to take her toward the stairs, but she shocked him when she sat down on one of the treads. She pulled her bodice lower, lifting her breasts free of the chemise and lifted her skirts.

"I want you, Cameron," she said. "Please. I don't want to wait." She spread her legs apart, and he saw the slit of her drawers. He freed his erection, and she reached for him, guiding him inside.

He couldn't believe how wet she was, and when he filled her, she guided his thumb to stroke her intimately. She let out a gasp and showed him what she wanted.

He sweetened her pleasure, watching as she arched against him, her eyes falling closed. "Touch me."

He could feel her squeezing him within her depths, and he kept the pressure of his thumb against her while he moved inside her.

"Slowly," she urged. "And not too deep."

He found a rhythm of shallow penetrations, and she encouraged him, telling him how much she loved feeling him inside her. He covered her nipple with his mouth, and she let out a ragged cry of ecstasy. "I love it when you kiss my breasts. It feels so good."

The words washed over him, and she said, "Do you know

how much I missed you? How empty our bed was without you?"

He swallowed hard, trying to protect her as he thrust against her on the stairs. She wrapped her legs around him, and it didn't take long before her breathing came in short gasps, and she gripped his hair, crying out as her orgasm flooded through her. Her body spasmed around him, and he lifted her up from the stairs, bringing her to the wall. He supported her weight, still inside her while she quaked. God above, but he needed her.

Her eyes opened, and her lips were red. Her skirts were tangled above her waist, and then she whispered, "Your turn."

He didn't know if he could continue the shallow, slow thrusts, but she moved in counterpoint to him, sinking down as he drove against her.

"Cameron, don't hold back now," she insisted. "I want you to let go." She leaned in to kiss him. "Do whatever you want with me."

He penetrated her deeply, feeling her silky wetness surrounding him. And he found his own rhythm, increasing the speed of his thrusts while she ground against him. He could feel her rising again, her throaty cries as he quickened.

Then he surrendered to his darkest desires, taking her hard against the wall. He ignored everything except the savage instincts that demanded he claim her. Her breasts bounced, and she reached for one nipple, fingering herself as he pounded over and over.

The release ripped through him, and he held her against the wall as he emptied himself deep within. His body convulsed against hers, and his knees nearly sagged with the force of his pleasure.

Somehow, he managed to carry her up the rest of the stairs. When they reached his bedchamber, he withdrew from her body and lowered her to stand before him.

"Don't leave me behind again," she whispered, pulling him to kiss her. "You're not alone. You don't have to carry the burden by yourself."

Slowly he helped her undress, and they climbed into bed together. With her skin against his, he realized that the emptiness he'd embraced was out of habit. He'd relied on no one but himself all his life. And after Logan had been taken, he'd pushed everyone else away.

Ashleigh lifted her leg over his hip, gazing at him. His beautiful wife had surprised him in every way. He'd underestimated her. And as he thought of what she'd said, he realized that she was right. He needed her to get Logan out safely. She knew the house as well as she knew her father and could easily get inside.

All he had to do was help her escape. He stole a swift kiss and said, "You're right. I'm not used to having anyone to help me. I was wrong to leave you behind."

She stroked his cheek, and he covered her hand with his own. "I have an idea of how we can get him out. Will you tell me what you think of it?"

After he did, she stole a kiss of her own. "It's very clever Cameron. But what if we try this instead?"

And after he heard his wife's plan, he smiled. "I like it."

"ARE YOU READY?" Rachel Harding walked alongside her in the hallway.

Georgina nodded, but it was a lie. Her insides were twisted up in knots, and her skin had grown cold. "Yes, I suppose so."

"Good." Rachel guided her toward the drawing room and opened the door. In a low voice, she said, "Your first task in standing up for yourself is to face the barrister who is bringing charges of kidnapping against Cameron MacNeill. You, yourself, are being charged with desertion of the marriage."

Georgina had no time to respond before Mrs. Harding gave her a light push into the room. A gentleman was waiting for her, clad in blackcloth, and his expression turned grim the moment he saw her. Fear and anger warred within her at the realization that

Mrs. Harding had called the authorities. The act of betrayal infuriated her as much as it terrified her. She wasn't ready to face them now.

Before she could turn around, he spoke. "You are Georgina Pryor, Marchioness of Rothburn, I presume?"

"I am." Her voice came out with a quiver she couldn't hide. "And you are?"

"Robert Worley, barrister." The gentleman gestured for her to have a seat. "I have instructions to bring you back to your husband, the Marquess of Rothburn."

Georgina shook her head. "No, I cannot."

He laughed softly. "This isn't a situation in which you have a choice, Lady Rothburn. By law, you are his marital property. Unless you have proof of life-threatening injuries, I have my orders to take you back."

It occurred to her that if there were ever a way of forcing her to confront her worst fears, of standing up for herself, then this was it. The urge to cry came over her, but what good would tears do? It had done nothing in all the years she was married. If anything, Cecil had enjoyed seeing her weep. It had given him the power he craved.

She couldn't go back to the shadow of herself. Ever since she'd arrived in Scotland, she'd enjoyed being a grandmother, working in her garden, and finding peace.

She took a moment to calm herself. In her mind, she imagined what a powerful woman would say or do. Someone the opposite of herself. A duchess, perhaps. And so she straightened and regarded the barrister. "I hardly think that's necessary."

His expression darkened. "Madam, you have no right to abandon your marriage. By the law, you must return."

She was well aware of this. And yet, a duchess would not let a mere barrister tell her what to do. Though her stomach clenched with nerves, Georgina took a deep breath and said, "But the law does not say *when* I must return. I have been visiting with my daughter these past few months. One could not call that desertion."

"If you do not have your husband's permission, you cannot—"

"Do not be ridiculous," she cut him off. "I hardly think a court would convict me for visiting my daughter and grandson."

The thought of Logan bolstered her courage. She loved her little lad, and there was no doubt he was in Cecil's household right now. Her husband was likely holding him captive as a way of baiting Cameron.

She would not let Cecil hurt her grandson. It didn't matter what kind of controlling games her husband was playing—her grandson meant everything to her.

"Go on your way," she told the barrister. "I will be returning home tomorrow to pay a call on my husband. And we will discuss his so-called accusations."

"But Madam—"

"Good-bye," she said, walking to the door. "A footman will show you out."

"I have the authority to bring you to the marquess right now," he insisted.

Georgina hid her fears and pushed them beneath the surface. Instead, she put on her haughtiest expression and said, "If you do, I will see to it that your reputation in London is utterly ruined. No one will hire you again. I have a great deal of money at my disposal, and I won't hesitate to use it against you."

From the hallway, she heard the sound of applause. Mrs. Harding was smiling, and strangely enough, so was the barrister.

"Lady Rothburn, you have no need of lessons," Mrs. Harding said.

Georgina stared at them both in confusion. The matron continued, saying, "Allow me to introduce you to my partner, Cedric Gregor. Forgive our deception, but we wanted to see if you were ready."

"Then you're . . . not a barrister?"

"I am not," Mr. Gregor said. "But you did very well indeed. I think you are ready to face your husband."

Georgina could scarcely believe what had happened, but she felt a slight swell of pride within her. Whether or not it would work with Cecil, she didn't know. But at least she had taken the first steps toward reclaiming her own life.

Chapter Fifteen

ASHLEIGH STOOD UPON her father's doorstep, escorted by her footman, who kept a safe distance behind her with his head lowered. The door swung open, and one of the servants stared back at her in surprise. Without waiting for an invitation, Ashleigh stepped past him and said, "I am here to pay a call upon my father. I presume he is here?"

The servant inclined his head. "Yes, Lady Ashleigh."

"I am Lady Kilmartin now," Ashleigh corrected. "I would like tea and refreshments in the drawing room." She needed to establish authority immediately to set the right tone. "Tell my father I am here." She gave her footman her cloak, and the man remained in the hall. With a nod, she ordered, "Go down to the kitchens, and Cook will give you something to drink while you wait." The servant kept his head lowered but obeyed.

Ashleigh steeled herself for the role she was about to play. She'd done it before with Violet, behaving like a spoiled heiress. But she didn't know if she could manage it with her father. Any man desperate enough to kidnap a child could never be trusted.

But no matter what her father did, she was going to get Logan out. She and Cameron had made their plans carefully, and if all went well, they would bring their son home tonight.

Her boy had to be terrified. She was eager to see him, and she reminded herself that she had to be strong for his sake. She would endure all of Cecil's rage if it meant getting Logan out. Then, too, she was reassured that her mother was safe with Mrs. Harding.

Ashleigh walked into the drawing room and stood by the window for a moment. As she'd expected, it took only moments for her father to enter the room. His complexion was bright red, as if he were struggling to hold back his fury.

"Where have you been?" he demanded.

"With my husband in Scotland," she replied. "But then, you knew that already, didn't you?" She kept her voice light, as if she hadn't been gone for months. In her mind, she imagined what Persephone might say, and she added, "I don't know why you sent men to bring me back. A letter would have sufficed." With a wave of her hand, she said, "But that doesn't matter. You asked me to come, and I am here. What is it you want from me?"

Her father's rage was boiling at the surface. "You tried to run away from home with a Scot. Your actions have caused a scandal that has ruined our family's name. How dare you?"

In spite of herself, she couldn't stop herself from flinching at his tone. Already, she wanted to sink against the wall to somehow escape the vitriol. Even as she told herself she had to be brave, she found herself falling back into the familiar habit of remaining silent. She sat down, enduring the storm of his words.

Her father didn't seem to notice she'd stopped speaking. "That Scot is not your husband," Cecil snapped. "The marriage was never legal."

Keep him talking, she told herself. Even now, her footman would be searching for the boy. The more Cecil raged, the more time they had.

"You're only angry because the marriage wasn't arranged by you, isn't that right?" She kept her voice even and cool, as if she were utterly bored. "And as it turns out, Cameron is quite wealthy. He might only be a Highland chief, but he *does* own a castle. I believe I made a better choice than that viscount you picked out."

Her father moved toward her, his hands clenched into fists. It was all she could do not to run from the chair, but Ashleigh forced herself to remain seated.

"Your disobedience is at an end, Ashleigh," he warned. "You're not leaving this house. And your marriage will be over soon."

Her skin grew icy, for she knew what he planned to do. The old Ashleigh would have shrunk back, holding her tongue to avoid making him angrier. But if she did, he would leave the drawing room. She had to provoke him, for only then could she be assured that he would stay in the room with her.

"And why would my marriage be over? You cannot have it annulled." Before he could speak, she added, "I suppose you think you can hire more men to kill Cameron, don't you? Did that work well the last time?"

His temper was already flaring. "Your husband was the murderer, not my men."

"Only because they didn't succeed."

Cecil stepped in closer, raising his hand as if to strike her. Before he could, Ashleigh stood from her chair, facing him. Her sudden motion caught him off guard. Then she said, "You have something that belongs to my husband. I am here to take it back."

His smile turned knowing, and he lowered his hand. "I thought you might come for the boy."

She shrugged. "You've made several poor decisions lately. First, the attack on me. Then taking my stepson. I would advise you not to make such a mistake again." She met his gaze evenly. "I can be reasonable. I hardly know the brat," she lied. "But Cameron will not be reasonable. He is a Scot, after all."

It took everything within her to maintain her calm. But she pushed back her fear and added, "I will go and see him now." With any luck, the footman had already helped Logan escape through the servants' quarters. If not, she would do everything in her power to help.

"In the meantime, I brought you something. It's an invitation." She reached into her reticule and pulled out the sealed parchment, offering it to her father.

Cecil appeared confused, just as she'd hoped. "What is this for?"

"It's an invitation to a ball celebrating my marriage to Cameron. It would be wise if you'd attend."

Just as she'd expected, his face turned crimson again. "I would never offer my support to MacNeill. You were supposed to wed Viscount Falkland." He tossed it aside, unopened.

Ashleigh ignored his ire and said, "The ball is being hosted by the Earl of Dunmeath. Everyone in London will be there. Including Prinny. Perhaps even the Queen."

"You're lying," he said. "No one in London wants anything to do with *Mac*Neill." He emphasized the surname as if it were an insult.

"It is your choice, of course. But if you are not there, don't be surprised if you never receive an invitation again. You know how servants gossip. It wouldn't take much for my servants to spread it around what your men did to me." She raised her chin and traced the reddish scar on her throat. "Such a shame, that you went mad after your daughter and wife left you. No one will believe that you've come to your senses."

Without waiting for his reply, she started walking toward the stairs, fully expecting her father to follow. Cecil started after her, but when she reached the first step, she paused and turned to face him.

"You should know that my husband has powerful friends, both in the courts and with the Crown. If you persist with this violent behavior, how many of your friends will remain?"

She continued walking upstairs, and from behind her, he remarked. "Go and see the brat if you wish. But you won't be leaving this house."

She ignored him and continued up the stairs, thankful that he hadn't followed. *Please let Logan be gone already,* she prayed.

CAMERON HAD USED a great deal of white powder to change his hair color, and he'd shaved once again. With the help of some cosmetics, he'd added lines to his face to give the illusion of age. It had been quite easy to blend in with Rothburn's servants. He'd ventured among them at first, needing a reason to go upstairs. When he'd learned that one of the maids was going to the third floor with coal, he'd volunteered to help.

After he'd assisted the maid, it had been easy to slip away from her and find the nursery. What he hadn't expected was to find it guarded by two other footmen, both of whom appeared strong and alert. With the empty coal hod in hand, he nodded to them and went into an adjoining bedchamber. Unfortunately, there was not a connecting door to the room. But he heard his son crying, nonetheless.

He went to the wall and called out to his son, keeping his voice as low as he could. "Logan. It's your da."

The boy didn't seem to hear him, so he knocked on the wall to catch the child's attention. As he'd hoped, he heard the sniffling diminish. He knocked again, and said, "Logan, are you there?"

"Yes," he heard a boy's voice reply.

"This is your da. I've come to rescue you. But you canna tell anyone. Is anyone in the room with you now?"

"No," Logan answered. Then he asked, "Da, how did you get in the wall?"

He smiled at the boy's question. "Never mind that. Is there a key in your door or is it still locked"

"I don't know," the boy responded.

"Go and try to open the door."

Cameron waited while Logan struggled with the knob. A moment later, he returned and said, "It's stuck."

He realized that the latch might be too complicated for a lad who wasn't even four yet. He eyed the fireplace poker, wondering if he could use it to pry open the door if he could get rid of the footmen. Possibly.

He was about to try it when suddenly, he heard Ashleigh's voice in the hallway. She was arguing with the men, and he realized this was his best opportunity to help them both.

Cameron wasted no time in opening the door and walking into the hallway. He slipped back into the role of her footman. "My lady, is there a problem?"

"Yes. These men are refusing to let me visit my stepson." Her expression turned furious, and she added, "I have permission from my father. Now open this door at once."

"Is there a reason why my lady cannot go inside?" he asked the footmen.

"His lordship gave orders that no one was to go inside."

"And what if Lady Kilmartin . . . paid you to give her a few moments with the child?" he asked, pulling out a handful of coins. The footmen exchanged a glance, and Cameron added, "You could wait at the stair landing."

The bribery worked, and he gave both men a generous amount in exchange for the room key. Cameron unlocked the door, and Ashleigh hurried inside. The moment Logan saw her, he ran to her, bawling and burying his face in her skirts.

Cameron secured the door and then moved forward. He checked to see that the boy was unharmed. His clothing was torn, but it did appear that someone had tried to clean him up. Logan inched away from him, clinging to Ashleigh, and he realized the boy didn't recognize him.

"It's me, Logan. Your da," he said. With a smile, he added, "I'm in disguise."

Logan peered at him, confused. "Da?"

He opened his arms, and Logan came near, reaching up to his powdered hair. A slight smile came over his face. "You were hiding."

"I was, aye." He embraced his son, and said, "Are you ready to go home now?"

Logan nodded. "The bad man took me away."

"You were very brave," Ashleigh said. "But we're here now. We found you, and nothing will happen to you again." She kept her voice low and murmured to Cameron, "There's a servants' staircase at the back of the hall. Take Logan down the stairs and you should be able to go outside. I'll remain here a little longer and then join you."

He didn't like that idea at all, for it put her in danger. "I'm not leaving you, Ashleigh."

"Get Logan to safety first. I'll be all right." She held her head up, but he could see the fear behind her demeanor.

"Why don't *you* take him down the servants' entrance?" he suggested. "I'll stay here until I know you're safe."

"They won't let me leave with him," she said. She held Logan close and said, "My sweet boy, we're going to take you home. But you must listen carefully. When you reach the kitchens downstairs, you must slip out the door and run as fast as you can. Be careful and go quickly. Your da will run after you."

He fully understood her idea, and it was a sound one. If they believed Logan was attempting to escape and he was chasing after the boy, they would allow it. Then he could hire a hackney and get them both away. But he still didn't like the thought of leaving her alone.

"Take him to safety," she said, embracing him hard. "And be careful."

He kissed her and then lifted Logan into his arms. To his wife, he added, "When he runs, Ashleigh, you must do the same. Go out the front door, and no one will stop you. Take a hackney and meet me at Mrs. Harding's," he said, handing her more coins.

Ashleigh went to the door first. "I'll go to the landing and distract them."

He waited a moment and when she'd gone, he whispered, "You must be completely silent, Logan. Not a word." He touched his finger to the boy's lips, and he nodded.

He opened the nursery door and saw that Ashleigh was already at the end of the hallway. The two footmen were looking down the stairs while she spoke to them as a distraction. Cameron ran soundlessly with Logan to the far end of the hall without looking back. He found the stairs she'd spoken of, and as soon as he disappeared down the steps, he slowed his pace and lowered Logan to stand.

"We're going to pretend again," he told the boy. "I'll tell them you were hungry, and while they're looking for food, you run out the door. Can you do that?"

The boy nodded his head, and Cameron said, "Good." He glanced up at the stairs, hoping Ashleigh was all right. With any luck, the distraction would allow her to slip out the front entrance.

He walked into the kitchen and almost immediately, the cooks and kitchen maids stared at him. "The boy was crying and said he was hungry. I thought we could get him some bread or something." Discreetly, he twisted the doorknob, cracking it slightly.

The cook was already shaking her head. "He's not supposed to be down here. His lordship will have our heads! Take him upstairs at once."

He saw one of the footmen move toward Logan, and he shoved the boy behind him, hoping he would see the door. "Here now, no need for that. I'll get him fed and take him back upstairs. No one will know."

From behind him, he heard Logan starting to run.

"Catch him!" one of the cooks ordered. Cameron feigned ignorance and blocked the path of a male servant.

"What do you mean?" Then he turned and pretended he hadn't noticed the open door. "Oh, no. I'm so sorry. I'll go fetch the lad. Wait here." He tore outside, searching for his son.

It took only seconds to catch up to Logan, and when he had the boy in his arms, he praised him, "Good lad. We did it."

Cameron picked up his running pace, turned the corner, and hailed a hackney cab. Within moments, they were safely inside.

He ordered the driver to circle the block and go back in front of the Rothburn townhouse, in the hopes that he could help Ashleigh with her own escape.

But when they drove by the front of the house, he saw his wife surrounded by men. Her escape hadn't worked at all, and he saw her return inside the house.

"I want Mother," Logan said.

Cameron held his son's hands. "So do I. And I'm going back to fetch her. I'm going to let Granny take care of you while I go after your mother."

Logan crawled into his lap, and Cameron held his son, feeling both grateful to have him back and afraid for Ashleigh's sake.

But he made a silent vow that after he got her out, the marquess would never lay a hand on her again.

ASHLEIGH WASN'T SURPRISED that her father's men had caught her once more. But from what she'd overheard, it did seem that Cameron had managed to help Logan escape—and for that, she was grateful. There was no doubt that her husband would return for her. But the greatest problem was forcing her father to abandon his quest to control their lives.

Her earlier idea, that Cecil would care about his public reputation, had turned out to be wrong. She'd mistakenly believed that he valued what others thought of him. He was far more concerned about power.

The men had locked her in her old bedchamber. It was strange being here once again, seeing her old wardrobe of gowns and the jewels that her father had chosen for her. It was as if Cecil had wanted to take her back to her childhood, when he had been master of her life.

But she held faith in Cameron. He would find a way to get her out; she was certain of it. She simply had to do everything possible to get herself out in the meantime. Her husband would figure out the rest.

She knocked on her bedroom door and called out to the footman. "Will you please speak to my father on my behalf? I would like to have supper with him this evening to discuss my situation."

"I do not know if he will agree," the footman answered through the door.

"Go and ask," she said, "and come back to tell me."

She walked to the window to stare out at the street below. Afternoon had waned into evening, though it was still light outside. She believed Cameron had brought Logan safely to Mrs. Harding's school, but she didn't know when or how he would be back. He'd proven himself to be a master of disguise, so it wouldn't surprise her if he attempted to return as a servant once again.

A hackney pulled up to the house as she watched. To her shock, she saw her mother disembarking from the cab, along with another gentleman.

No. She wouldn't.

But clearly, Ashleigh had underestimated her mother's intentions. Georgina walked slowly up the stairs, as if gathering her courage with every step. Why had she come here? She'd been perfectly safe at Mrs. Harding's.

Her heart sank at the thought of what was to come. Cecil would not take kindly to Georgina's return. Ashleigh knocked on the door to her room, hoping that one of the footmen would return. "Please, let me out. My mother has come. I need to help her."

But there was no reply. Ashleigh continued rattling the door handle and calling out, to no avail. She glanced around the room, desperate to find something—anything—to help her escape. Her gaze centered upon the fireplace poker. At first, she used it to strike the door while calling out, causing as much noise and damage as she could. When no one responded, she began hitting the door handle over and over with the heavy metal poker. To her surprise, the handle loosened, until she managed to wedge the poker against it and pry it back.

She poured her anger and fear into it, using her body weight against the handle, until at last, the door handle fell off. Satisfaction filled her as she shoved the poker into the opening and managed to get the door open.

When she wrenched it open, plaster and wood broke free from the doorframe, but she cared naught for the damage she'd caused. With the fire poker in hand, she strode toward the stairs, suddenly realizing why no one was guarding her doorway. They were all downstairs in the foyer, more servants than she'd ever seen in one place. Most seemed uncertain of what to do, as if their loyalties had begun to divide.

As she'd expected, her father was raging at Georgina. With the fireplace poker in hand, Ashleigh charged into the dining room, only to have her hand caught by one of the men. She turned and saw Cameron. He was still wearing his earlier disguise, but none of the servants seemed to mind his presence, if they'd even noticed him. The very sight of her husband filled her with relief.

In a low voice, he whispered, "Don't deny Georgina this opportunity to face him. After today, with any luck, she'll never have to see him again."

Ashleigh lowered the poker and went to stand at the doorway. Her mother wore a green gown with a modest black shawl. Her hair was intricately styled, and she stared back at her husband while he cursed and told her what a terrible wife she'd been and how he was going to punish her.

Her father's face was nearly purple, and she noticed that some of his words were slurring. He was rubbing his shoulder as he yelled at Georgina.

"You won't leave this housh—house again." His words continued to slur, and Ashleigh wondered if he'd been drinking. "If you even try, I'll have you restrained and locked away. Anyone who tries to h-help you will be dis-dismisshed."

But her mother's face held serenity. "Cecil, it's over. I came to tell you that I will not be returning home again. I shall live on one of our other estates, or I will live with Ashleigh."

"I won't permit it," he snapped. "You have no choish—choice." The left side of his face appeared to sag, and once again, he rubbed his left shoulder.

"Oh, but you're wrong." Georgina glanced behind her, and only then did Ashleigh notice the gentleman standing behind her. "I've brought with me an official from the Consistory Court. You may not remember, because it was so long ago, but I was only sixteen when we married. My father did not give permission for our union. You obtained a special license, and we were wedded without his consent. Therefore, our marriage was invalid."

"That's pre-preposteroush." He stared at her with disdain. "Your family was honored that I would stoop to marry sh-shomeone like you. I gave you your title, and a far better life than you would have had."

But Ashleigh noticed a trace of uncertainty on her father's face for the first time. Cameron rested his hand on her spine in silent reassurance.

"You are going to let me go, Cecil. We will live our lives apart, and you may tell the *ton* whatever you wish. Tell them I am ill and need country air. But believe me when I say I will *never* live with you as your wife again."

Unexpected tears filled Ashleigh's eyes, and she squeezed her husband's hand, so very proud of her mother for facing him. But her father paled and walked over to a small table on the opposite side of the room. He opened up the drawer and pulled out a small revolver. Then he pointed it at Georgina. "I disagree."

Ashleigh couldn't stand aside and watch him threaten her mother again. In that instant, it was as if she became a different person. She didn't care about the risk to herself or anyone except her mother. All her life, she'd stood aside whenever anyone had bullied a victim. But no more.

She wrenched her hand free from Cameron and lifted the fireplace poker, charging directly at her father. A cry burst forth from her as she swung it.

And then, the gun fired.

Chapter Sixteen

C AMERON WATCHED IN horror as his wife fell to the ground, the poker clattering to the carpet. Georgina screamed, and the marquess had fallen backwards as well, the smoking revolver still in his hand.

It took only seconds to reach Ashleigh's side. Miraculously, she was unhurt, but there was a bullet lodged in the wall behind her. Cameron clung to her, so grateful the marquess had missed his shot. "Are you all right?"

"Yes," she managed, holding him tight. Georgina hurried forward as well, and Cameron used the opportunity to ensure that the marquess could not take a second shot. He gave his wife into her mother's care and went to Cecil, kicking the revolver away from his hand. The man had remained where he'd fallen, frozen in place, half his face sagging, and he seemed unable to move. He was breathing, however.

The butler ventured forward and asked, "Should I call a doctor?"

Cameron nodded. "Yes. See to the marquess, but I will take the revolver so he cannot harm anyone else." He picked up the weapon and removed the bullets into his waistcoat before taking the gun.

Two of the footmen came forward and tried to lift Cecil into a chair. The marquess was unable to maintain his balance and slumped against one side. Part of his mouth was moving, but no words came out, only a single, "Aaaah" sound.

Ashleigh stood by her mother, shocked at what was happening. "Is he . . . having a fit?"

"I don't know," Georgina said. "But it appears that he is unable to harm any of us, which is a good thing." She stared at Cecil for a long moment, even while the marquess was struggling to speak. "I was always so afraid of your rages. It seems only fitting that your own anger has done this to you." She leaned in close and said, "I am glad of it. You deserve this fate and more."

Then she turned to the man she'd brought with her. "It seems I no longer have need of your services, sir. You may go."

The gentleman glanced at the marquess, shook his head in disbelief, and picked up his hat before he left.

Georgina walked with them back toward the front door. Ashleigh asked, "Was that all true—that your marriage was invalid?"

Her mother smiled. "Let us just say that none of it matters anymore. I don't think Cecil will be a threat to any of us."

They continued walking outside, and Cameron signaled for a hackney. While they were waiting, Georgina laughed. "I cannot believe it worked! Mrs. Harding is absolutely brilliant."

Ashleigh sent her a questioning look, and her mother continued. "It was she who gave me the idea. Her partner helped me hire that barrister to pretend to be from the Consistory Court. He wasn't at all, but Cecil believed he was. And that was enough to cause that fit." She started laughing. "I am free at last."

"Do you think he'll recover?" Ashleigh asked.

"I doubt it," Cameron answered. "Most men who have suffered fits as bad as that one tend not to be themselves again. He couldn't even speak."

Georgina hugged herself and then turned to them. "Ashleigh, thank you for what you tried to do for me."

"I wanted to stand up for you," she admitted. "But in my

haste, I tripped over my skirts and fell. I suppose my clumsiness saved my life."

Cameron took her hand, his thumb stroking her palm. "I am very glad of it." He glanced back at the marchioness and asked, "Will you be returning to Scotland?"

She shrugged. "In time. If Cecil remains an invalid, then I must visit all the estates first and ensure that they are in good order. I hope to be back at Kilmartin by autumn, before the snow. I want to spend Christmas with my grandson."

Ashleigh smiled at her mother. "We will be delighted to see you there."

The hackney arrived, but Georgina admitted, "I am staying here, to ensure that the doctor arrives and to look after the staff members. Mrs. Harding will send my belongings to me." She embraced Ashleigh before waving farewell.

Cameron helped her into the hackney, but then spoke with the driver for a moment. When he returned inside, he secured the door and pulled Ashleigh into his lap.

She laughed and asked, "What are you doing, Cameron?" Her arms came around his neck, and he leaned in to kiss her.

"You frightened me today," he told her. "I thought I would lose you. Don't ever put yourself in that kind of danger again. For my sake, please."

She kissed him back, savoring the now-familiar shape of his mouth, tasting his tongue against hers. "I didn't want to stand aside and do nothing."

"You were brave," he admitted, "but I couldn't bear to watch him threaten you. I can't lose you, Ashleigh. I love you."

The words washed over her, and she answered them, "I love you, too, Cameron. So very much." As the hackney continued through the London streets, she noticed that it was traveling in the wrong direction. "Aren't we going home?"

He shot her a wicked smile. "Oh, yes. But we're taking the long way. Logan is waiting for us at home, and I need to ensure that you're all right first." He moved her from his lap to the opposite seat and knelt before her. "I thought we might find a way to occupy ourselves." He raised her skirts to her thighs and tilted her back so her feet rested against the opposite seat.

He pushed aside her petticoats and found the slit in her pantalettes. To her shock, he bent forward, and she felt his hot breath against her intimate flesh.

"I need to taste you," he said, lowering her undergarments until she was utterly naked beneath her skirts. And when his tongue laved at her, she whimpered as the scalding heat of desire roared within. She gripped his hair, falling apart as he licked and teased her.

"Cameron . . . someone might see," she warned.

"No one can see me below the window. Just lie back against the seat and let me pleasure you."

With his tongue, he found her hooded flesh and began to suckle it. Her breathing was coming in soft pants, and he slid a finger inside her, gently stroking. The erotic motion drove her wild, and she gripped the seat, unable to do anything except surrender. She gasped as he drove her over the edge, and she bucked against his mouth while the release erupted within her. He drew back, a smug expression on his face when she sagged against the seat.

"Oh no, you don't," she warned. "I'm not finished with you, yet."

"What do you plan to do to me?" he teased.

She helped him unfasten his trousers and reached down to find his hard length. She freed him from his smallclothes and answered his question by lowering her head to his lap, taking him deep into her mouth.

Now it was his turn to groan. His hands grasped at her hair, and she tasted the salty musk of his skin, suckling the head of him and drawing him in deep.

"Ashleigh, you're killing me," he gritted out. "I can't last when you do that."

"You'll have to endure it a bit longer," she promised, dragging her tongue down his entire length. Then before he could say a word, she lifted her skirts to her waist and knelt on his seat with both legs straddling him. She guided his erection inside and held him there.

The rattling motion of the hackney caught her unawares, causing her to bump against him. The motion was wickedly sweet, and she moved against him while he thrust in counterpoint. Over and over, she took him deep, and he found her hooded flesh again, rubbing her as she moved against him. The raw arousal drove her harder, and she hardly cared if all of London saw them making love in a coach. All she wanted was her husband, and he lifted her hard, their bodies moving skin to skin until the rise of her orgasm pushed her over. She shattered against him, keening as she struggled to hold back a scream. He continued plunging inside, angling her back slightly, and the new position evoked yet another release.

At last, he finished inside her, and held her close, resting his face in the soft part of her neck. She could feel his body joined with hers, and she admitted, "You were the best thing that ever happened to me, Cameron. I love you more than I could have ever dreamed."

He kept her in his arms and teased, "Beard and all?"

"I like you better without it, but yes." She rubbed the prickly side of his face.

"You are everything to me, Ashleigh," he said. "And I won't be parted from you again. I swear it."

And when he kissed her again, she murmured, "Let's go home to our son."

Epilogue

"CONGRATULATIONS TO YOU both!" Lord Dunmeath proclaimed after he'd announced the celebration of marriage. He raised his glass and invited all his guests to do the same. "To the Chief and Lady of Kilmartin!"

Cameron raised his glass, as did Ashleigh, and after he drank the toast, he took her hand and kissed it. At the back of the ballroom, near the hall, he noticed Lady Persephone's sulking expression. In truth, he hadn't wanted to invite her, but Ashleigh had made him promise. His new wife wanted a chance to gloat.

The musicians started up again, and he danced with his wife, savoring the feel of her in his arms. She appeared radiant, and then said softly. "Look at my mother. She's smiling."

And so she was. Georgina was speaking with a group of matrons, clearly enjoying herself. During the past week, the doctor had declared that Lord Rothburn was unlikely to recover from his fit of apoplexy. The left side of his body was paralyzed, and he could no longer walk or speak. Georgina had arranged for servants to provide care for him, but her earlier prediction had come true—she was free from Cecil's abuse. And so was Ashleigh.

"Mrs. Harding has found a companion as well," Cameron remarked. Ashleigh was startled to see the matron with a dancing partner, but she was happy for the headmistress.

Cameron led her to a quiet corner of the ballroom, and then into the hallway toward the other entrance. "Where are you taking me?" she asked.

He touched a finger to his lips and murmured against her ear. "We're lurking in the shadows."

"Why?"

"To eavesdrop. I saw one of your enemies walking back here."

He brought her behind another doorway, and it was then that she overheard Persephone speaking. "I think she's lying. There is no chance that delicious Highland chief was Cameron Neill. That man had a disgusting beard and was always skulking about."

Ashleigh clamped her hand over her mouth, shaking with laughter.

"No, that must be a cousin or other relative," Persephone continued. "He is not the same man at all, of *that* I can assure you."

"You're wrong," came another female voice. "It was always him. You were just too mean to see him for what he was."

"At least I *can* see. Unlike some who must wear spectacles to see anything more than a foot away," she huffed. Then she continued, "Now if he had seen me, *I* would be the new Lady of Kilmartin Castle." She paused and added, "But then, I can't imagine the castle would be very large. It *is* in the Highlands of Scotland, after all. And who would want to live there?"

"I would," Ashleigh said clearly, to Cameron's surprise. She pulled him out of the hallway and moved forward. "Scotland is absolutely breathtaking." She turned and looked at Persephone. "But I, for one, am glad you never looked past appearances. I might never have found the husband of my dreams." She squeezed his palm. "But one day, if you do see beyond your own selfishness, perhaps you'll find the perfect husband. Or if you cannot, I can highly recommend Mrs. Harding's School for Young Ladies."

"The School for Spinsters?" Persephone scoffed. "I would never."

"It worked for Violet Edwards," Ashleigh said. "And for me, in a manner of speaking."

Cameron saw the look of disgust on Persephone's face, but the girl beside her appeared intrigued. He thought he remembered seeing the girl at a ball earlier this year.

"I am happy for you both," the girl told them.

"Thank you, Emma." Ashleigh smiled warmly at her.

Cameron took his wife back to the ballroom floor and began dancing with her a second time. Ashleigh beamed up at him as he turned her in a circle. "You know, it's not fashionable for a husband to dance with his wife this many times."

"Isn't it?" he asked, leaning closer to her face. "Is it against the rules?"

"The rules of the *ton,* perhaps."

"But not against your rules?"

She shook her head slowly. "When I'm with you, Cameron, I want to break all the rules."

He moved his palm against her spine, wishing he could take her away this very moment. His beloved wife had given him so much more than he'd ever imagined was possible.

And he intended to savor every moment for the rest of their lives.

Did you miss the first book in the School for Spinsters series about Violet Edwards and Lord Scarsdale? Enjoy *A Match Made in London,* wherever e-books are sold. If you enjoyed *Match Me, I'm Falling* and would like to receive an email whenever Michelle Willingham releases a new book, visit her website at www.michellewillingham.com/contact to sign up for her newsletter.

About the Author

Michelle Willingham has published nearly fifty romance novels, novellas, and short stories. Currently, she lives in Virginia with her children and is working on more historical romance books in a variety of settings such as: Regency England, Victorian England, Viking-era Ireland, medieval Scotland, and medieval Ireland. When she's not writing, Michelle enjoys baking cookies, playing the piano, and chasing after her cats. Visit her website at: www.michellewillingham.com.